A GHOSTLY TEXAS TALE

Annabelle

CHANA KEEFER
4-TIME #1 BESTSELLING AUTHOR

Annabelle

A GHOSTLY TEXAS TALE

Old Barn Press
Santa Clarita, CA 91350
www.chanakeefer.com
Copyright © 2016 Old Barn Press
All rights reserved.

All Scripture quotations unless indicated otherwise are taken from the New International Version of the Holy Bible. Scripture taken from the HOLY BIBLE, NEW INTERNATIONAL VERSION®. Copyright © 1973, 1978, 1984 Biblica. Used by permission of Zondervan. All rights reserved.

Cover art | Scott Seeto

Cover design & interior layout | Yvonne Parks | www.pearcreative.ca

ISBN: 978-0-9892197-7-8

DEDICATION

For my parents, Lynn & Glenda, who taught me love stays,
especially when times are hard.

ACKNOWLEDGEMENTS

This little novel has been a long time in the making. In the near decade since the seed of *Annabelle*, born in a dream that wakened me with sobs of empathy, my family has maintained it's their favorite of all my stories. While other novels may be louder, more glitzy, perhaps more dazzling from a spiritual perspective, *Annabelle* warms and melts the heart. Thank you to my hubby Mark and our kids, Micah, McKenna, Sky & Madeline for loving this story and for encouraging me to keep polishing it over these crazy-busy years.

Huge thanks to Dana Pratola for those notes on an early draft and for the continuing encouragement. Thank you Brenda Hunten for your sharp eyes and editing skills. Blessings on you, Amy Marten, for encouragement, friendship and insight into this crazy author-thang! Thank you Scott Seeto for lending your incredible artistic skills to the cover art. One word... WOW. And Yvonne Parks of PearCreative.ca, what would I do without you?

To my prayer gals, Amy, Angela, Chikk, Monique & Judith, you are just the BEST. To Real Life Church, and RLC's Prayer Team, thank you for being a home filled with love for us for so many years. To our crazy-fun

Friday Pizza/Movie family, we love celebrating life with you!

To the many authors I've never met in person who provide constant encouragement and assistance in the ever-changing publishing world, THANK YOU! Many blessings on your own awesome endeavors.

Starbucks, The Tea Pot Café, Undergrounds & It's a Grind, many thanks for the office space, yummy sustenance and many smiles.

My wonderful, ever-present Lord & Savior, You are my life, provider, counselor, heart's aim and eternal home. All that is good and lasting comes from You. I put it all in Your hands & ask You to reach broken hearts with this precious story. We are all broken and in need of Your TLC

PROLOGUE

*"We were strollin' along on moonlight bay.
All the Christmas bells were ringin' along the way..."*

Annabelle giggled to herself. She knew those weren't the real words to the song, but she had always liked it better that way. Besides, what could be prettier than hearing Christmas bells as you walked by the seashore? At least Annabelle thought it must be pretty. She'd never actually been to the seashore, but she could imagine. She spent most of her time imagining these days. When she squinted her eyes tight and imagined very hard, the old house was shiny and full of life again. On a really good day, she could even imagine Daddy was working downstairs and humming that very tune to himself, or perhaps listening to it on his Gramophone. If Annabelle imagined even harder, she could hear Mama giggling as Daddy swirled her to the music, causing Mama's taffeta skirts to make that delicious swishing sound.

And the parties! How Annabelle loved the parties. Life smelled so good with lovely things cooking in the kitchen, with spoonfuls of sweeties for good little girls who waited with begging cornflower blue eyes until Cookie couldn't resist giving a taste. And if Cookie was in a bad mood, Annabelle would hide around the corner until Cookie turned her back and steal a taste anyway.

Then the pretty ladies would arrive in their lovely dresses and the

1

handsome men would dance with them in the parlor. Mama was always the prettiest with her bright, golden hair glowing in the candlelight and that little dimple by her mouth that was such fun to watch when she smiled. All the men looked at Mama. Someday, Annabelle thought, she would be the prettiest lady at the party in the prettiest dress just like Mama.

Somehow, remembering the fun times always made her sad, but she did it anyway. It was much better than opening her eyes to the dusty, messy old house around her.

Why did all the fun stop? Annabelle could never be sure. One day Mama and Daddy weren't smiling at each other. The happy light went out in Mama's eyes and she didn't get out of bed. Everyone whispered outside Mama's bedroom door. One dreadful night, Annabelle woke to the sound of weeping and the next day the house was filled with flowers; not the happy flowers in their garden but fancy flowers dying in big baskets. Soon the house was filled with the stink of those sad flowers.

Annabelle put her fingers in her ears and shut her eyes tight. With determination wrinkling her brow, she danced around the room in her lacy white dress with the little pink bows that swirled around her ankles just past the ruffled pantaloons. Daddy gave her this dress for her fifth birthday. That had been a happy day with lots of lovely smells and happy sounds. Daddy had even danced with her to the music of his

Gramophone...

"We were strollin' along on moonlight bay..."

CHAPTER 1

IN WITH THE OLD

The Walden family piled out of the fast-food-wrapper strewn SUV onto the overgrown turf and stared through the iron gate in silence. It was the first silence Kate had experienced all day and if the pit of despair hadn't been growing in her stomach, she would have enjoyed it.

After three days trapped in the metal confines of their temporary rolling home, despite the adventure of untamed acreage sprawling before them, the rivalry of Kate & Jansen's offspring soon continued.

"Come on, Liam! Move it!" yelled fourteen-year-old Rollins.

"I would, but your big, fat shoes are in the way!" retorted six-year-old Liam.

Kate, usually quick to intervene, tuned out the escalating sibling squabble.

Good Lord. What had they gotten themselves into? As if the trip across country hadn't been exhausting enough, the thought of months of backbreaking labor to make this "historically significant gem" livable, turned her knees to Jell-O.

A comforting arm slipped around her shoulders and Jansen's calm voice spoke in her ear. "If you want, you and the girls can spend the night at the hotel in town. The boys and I can camp on the lawn."

Though Jansen's words were only for his wife's ears, the kids didn't miss a beat.

"No! I wanna camp too!" four-year-old Lilly's baby voice cut through before Kate could answer.

A chorus of "Cool!" "I'll get the tents!" and "Can we roast marshmallows?" erupted around her. Although the idea of a hot shower and crawling between clean sheets sounded like heaven, Kate lacked the strength to fight the public outcry. Besides, just a couple hours of daylight remained to explore this three-story monstrosity. No time like the present.

Kate shrugged her consent and received the momentary popularity of "Alright!" and "Awesome!" from all the kids except nine-year-old Phoenix. While Jansen gave Kate's shoulder a squeeze and trotted off with the other three of their four like a mustang let out to pasture, Phoenix silently took hold of Kate's hand and gazed at the old house.

With a sigh, Kate gripped one of the gate's iron bars and leaned her forehead against its cold, unyielding edge. The idea of starting fresh and restoring a piece of history had sounded romantic when considered from the kitchen table of their snug southern California suburban home. Now, it just felt foolish and difficult. But one second's contemplation was all she could allow since adventurous Lilly was already sneaking away from Jansen, who was lost in the rapture of exploring his new project.

Kate grimaced at the thick red rust on her palm and imagined her forehead must have suffered the same fate. Apparently, being dirty was something she was just going to have to get used to. Kate wiped her hand on her jeans and, with Phoenix in tow, ran after her quickly disappearing four-year-old.

At the top of the house, a tattered lace curtain fluttered, though no breeze found its way through the cracked window. A happy giggle broke the silence of dust motes glittering in the late afternoon sunlight as they fluttered down to rejoin others of their kind in the undisturbed layer of grime on the peeling lavender windowsill.

Kate floated through a comforting fog of unconsciousness. Her nose was cold. When she yawned, frigid, smoke-flavored air filled her throat. What she wouldn't give for a hot shower! She felt dirty. The scent of campfire smoke hovered, making the very air feel dirty.

She turned her head to view Jansen's profile in the dim gray light. As usual, he slept as deeply as a child, a soft snore escaping his lips. He could sleep anywhere.

With a shock of panic, Kate sat up. Thank God! Lilly was still there, tangled, dark blonde locks fanned onto the floor of the tent where she sprawled, having kicked free of her sleeping bag. Kate slipped carefully from the warmth of her own bedding to maneuver Lilly's fleece-covered form back into her bag. It was a ritual Kate performed anytime she woke. Methodically, she checked the beds of her children. There was Phoenix, her thick copper ringlets tamed into a ponytail as she slept in a tight fetal position as close to Jansen's reclining form as her sleeping bag would allow. How Kate missed the tangled, erratic mess of Phoenix's toddler sleep habits when she might find those red curls at the foot of the bed, hanging off the bed or, as on one briefly alarming night, under a pile of clothing on the closet floor. With a sigh, Kate engaged the tent's zipper in a brief tug-of-war, then slipped out.

Kate peeked in the boy's tent. Rollins gripped his twisted sleeping bag as if strangling the life out of it, his Jansenesque profile scowling. Though his long legs poked out, Kate fought the urge to cover Rollins. She'd sooner wake a snoozing grizzly bear.

Six-year-old Liam reclined regally on his back, his favorite stuffed Superman tucked safely in the crook of his arm, dark lashes fanned on the still-baby-smooth cheeks. If only she could freeze them all at the age of six; carefree, happy and still under the impression the world was a friendly place.

Kate re-zipped the boys' tent and stood to stretch her aching back and rub her gritty eyes. Sleep had been elusive. Every nighttime bird's call, rustle of a bush or restlessly tossing child had robbed her of much-needed sleep. Once again she sighed at the thought of a hot shower. Jansen had tussled with the old water heater last night and had promised warm water would flow by morning. One could hope.

The gently waking world—fresh eastern breeze, faint pink tinge on the distant horizon and tiny birds chattering in the boughs of an ancient pecan tree—was severely underappreciated by Kate's bleak outlook as she turned her auburn head and red-rimmed hazel eyes to face this daunting adversary.

Was it just her imagination, or did the old house look like it was smiling? With its cracked windows and sagging balcony, the grin was a bit snaggle-toothed. Jansen was the experienced architect, but Kate could easily imagine long columns of building expenses before this eyesore of an historical monument would be livable, much less the old-world showplace her husband envisioned.

She crunched across the gravel of the weedy circular drive. Those stones had proved a poor foundation for her air mattress, but she had been adamant about not placing their tents in the overgrown yard. Snakes and vermin were not welcome bedfellows.

She had to admit the house appeared more inviting in dawn's early light than it had the night before, when evening shadows had seemed to shroud unnamed pests and eerie secrets. Kate had hardly noticed the deep crown moldings or carved banister Jansen had pointed out, so great was her fear one of the kids would step on a rotten board and plunge to their death. But now, with soft sunlight filtering through dusty stained glass that cast watercolor puddles at her feet, she had to admit the wood appeared surprisingly solid and smooth.

First things first. Kate strode through the dining area to the kitchen and turned the ceramic handle with half an "H" visible in its white roundness. Brown water flowed into the dirty sink but finally ran clear. However, its temperature remained decidedly icy. She grabbed the flashlight Jansen had deposited at the top of the basement stairs and descended into its musty depths only to discover the pilot light in the water heater was off. No need to wake Jansen. She was at least handy enough to deal with this. She struck a match and slowly turned the handle connected to the gas line. The tiny orange flame glimmered as she shut the rusty door.

She drew the folds of her hooded sweatshirt close against the morning chill and retraced her steps to the front entrance. As Jansen had noted, the steps leading up to the porch were still sound. He had rambled on about cypress wood and craftsmanship as Kate had chased Lilly up the stairs.

The chandelier suspended above the entry hall was immense and draped with the largest cobwebs Kate had ever seen. Hopefully, it wasn't waiting for an opportune moment to crash onto her head. Kate could imagine carriages pulling onto the drive and richly-gowned revelers entering this glimmering hall, now dingy, dusty and encrusted with broken glass, flaking paint, and the discarded leavings of who-knows-what.

Not for the last time, Kate thought with longing of the energy efficient, suburban home they'd left behind. Well, not so picturesque, with no yard to speak of and surrounded by too many people, but it had been snug, clean and close to groceries, school and her favorite Starbucks. Sure this place showed signs of former glory, but how long would her family have to sleep on the lawn before rotting boards were replaced and the rodent population evicted?

With the thought of mice, Kate quickened her pace as she circled through the adjoining downstairs sitting room and study with a tiny powder room containing an ancient pull cord commode and a sink. How would their family ever survive with only one and a half baths? She continued her tour through the breakfast room which looked out on overgrown acres at the back of the house, the kitchen with its ancient stove and worn flooring and a pantry/china hutch alcove leading to the rectangular dining area with yet another ornate light fixture hanging from the middle of the fourteen-foot ceiling. Cracks snaked forebodingly from dusty gilt edges toward each corner of the room. Careful to avoid walking beneath the threatening antique, Kate completed her downstairs circuit and contemplated the curving banister leading to the second floor.

It was a shame rocks had been thrown through some of the windows. Glittering shards of red, green and blue glimmered on the window seat and across the landing like enticing slivers of hard candy. Kate made a mental note to locate a broom and dustpan before Lilly arrived for a taste.

The wide stairs split and curved both ways past unfaded, picture-shaped outlines in the peeling, olive green wallpaper with large gold, diamond patterns scattered across its surface.

Despite the dust, cobwebs and animal leavings, Kate had to pause and appreciate the charm of the roomy, recessed seat and large leaded window that faced her as she topped the stairs. What a perfect, secluded nook for enjoying a good book or watching guests arrive below.

Her appreciation was cut short by a violent sneeze. Was it possible the air was even dustier than the night before? On her left, she noticed a smoke-like wisp rolling from under the small door they had passed through the previous night. Curious, Kate turned the knob and pulled back the door that popped and protested on its unused hinges. Another sneeze, and she started up the narrow, creaking stairs, trying not to breathe. Perhaps the wind was blowing across the floor and stirring things up?

At the top of the short flight, Kate coughed in the thick dust and struggled with the stubborn window. With a final slap of frustration against the unyielding wood, she turned toward the small window across the room that looked out the front of the house. With the sleeve of her sweatshirt pressed against her nose, she raced across the room, tripping on a small rag rug stretched across her path. Expecting another struggle, Kate was shocked when she lifted the latch and, with just a slight push, the rectangular wood frames swung out.

The pleasant surprise caught her off guard and, as the fresh spice of dew-kissed grasses washed over her, Kate felt the runaway train of her life squeal to a stop.

With wide eyes she drank in the pristine scene of gnarled trees lining the long drive toward the unpaved road. At the iron-gated driveway entrance, the trees marched away in opposite directions, following the line of the un-hewn stone wall that lined the front of the property. Across the road, a purely functional iron fence marked the homestead of their closest neighbor. Dark cattle dotted the green expanse between cattle guard and quaint picture of farmhouse, outlying barns, fenced corrals and a tall, wooden windmill turning lazily in the morning breeze like a snoozing night watchman.

Maybe Jansen was right. Maybe this was exactly what their family needed—a fresh start in a rural setting. Rollins could grow into a man far from the city's less than desirable influences and Phoenix could…. A knife twisted in Kate's heart whenever she remembered the way her cheerful, fearless daughter had lost the light in her hazel eyes, those eyes that seemed to have aged fifteen years in one horrible night.

With a decisive slam, Kate shut off that line of thinking. It did no good to dwell on the past. She needed to be strong for her daughter now. Besides, the angry poison made it hard to think or breathe.

Curious, Kate shut and reopened the window that appeared in perfect working order. So what was up with the dust?

She turned to view the low-beamed room as stirred debris swirled like fog and cleared, coaxed to freedom out the open window. The room was small compared to the grand rooms below. The ceiling followed the roof's angle away from the dormer window. Tattered, flowered wallpaper hung in shreds from the slanted wall and dingy lilac paint peeled away from windowsill, moldings and baseboards. One lone piece of furniture, a curved, dingy white, child's armoire, stood in the corner.

Kate crossed to the armoire and tugged on the wooden handle. She jumped and gasped with fright when something popped toward her and she spied a face staring back. With a sob of relief, she recognized her own reflection in the blurry mirror attached inside the door. At her feet lay a tiny, child-sized broom with faded red handle and frayed bristles.

She studied the wooden floor that sported random stripes in the thick dust. Someone had made a poor attempt at tidying up. But who? The hairs on the back of Kate's neck prickled and her eyes widened with horror. "Lilly," she breathed as a picture of her adventurous four-year-old wandering the booby trap of a house in the dead of night made her heart race.

Kate clenched her teeth and shut her eyes, wrapping her arms tight against her chest as if to prevent it bursting open. Tremors began in her legs and worked their way up until she felt as if a giant dog latched on to her neck with powerful jaws and shook her, threatening to snap those jaws tight and shut off her windpipe. Kate was drowning under wave after wave of despair as she crumpled, sobbing, to her knees. The air she tried to suck into her lungs grew heavier, a monstrous chain forged of mistakes, failure, mind-numbing fear, and absolute, bone-crushing weariness. With a whimper, Kate rocked back and forth, a small ship tossed on a hurricane-wracked ocean of grief. When the storm finally passed, Kate unclenched a trembling hand to push her hair away from her face as she fought to breathe. How long did the episode last this time? She couldn't tell. But she did know they were occurring more often and with less provocation.

"You're losin' it, Kate," she said, as she stood and faced her own traumatized reflection in the blurry armoire mirror. "And talkin' to yourself? Another sure sign."

With a tired sigh, Kate placed the little broom back inside the armoire and shut the door, hearing a gentle click as the latch slid into place.

Realizing the broom incident had drained her already depleted energy, Kate silently pled for hot water for a shower! She turned to exit the room, stirring the thick dust with her sneakers and noticed her own prints leading through the broom stripes to the window and to where she stood. It took her a moment to realize what was odd about the scene.

There were no other footprints.

CHAPTER 2

GETTIN' ACQUAINTED

Kate's shoulders slumped with disappointment as icy cold water flowed from the kitchen faucet. One more trip into the basement's dank depths accomplished even less than before as each match she struck puffed out like a birthday candle. Kate tried again, only to see the tiny flame disappear with a soft "poof." The match supply was running low along with her patience and flashlight batteries. Obviously, warm water for bathing would have to wait.

By the time Jansen and the kids woke, Kate was as refreshed as possible by a frigid kitchen sponge bath, a touch of lipstick and clean, but suitcase-rumpled clothing. Since everyone was crabby and starved, she quickly did what she could to make her kids a bit less like grimy urchins—smoothed Lilly's gnarled curls, found Liam's AWOL sneaker, encouraged Rollins to cover his bed head with a hat—before Jansen drove them into town for breakfast.

"Town" consisted of one main road that widened unexpectedly into a small square lined with a few drowsy businesses. A patch of curb-lined green grass and a gazebo flanked by two trees graced the center of the square. It was the kids' turn to stare in shocked silence as they stumbled, one by one, onto the cracked pavement before Erma's Cafe.

"Everything's old," Liam announced. Kate flushed in embarrassment as two leather-skinned, overall-clad men lounging against the bumper of an ancient pickup guffawed in response. She herded her gawking brood through the café's screen door.

Erma's inhabitants turned to stare as large and small Waldens tumbled through the door to slide between the gray, Formica-topped tables and scarred, red vinyl seats. All hopes of a good first impression disappeared as Lilly began bouncing on the seat's squeaky springs and Liam declared, "This place stinks!"

But inside, Kate agreed. The air was heavy with bacon grease and old coffee while an old-timer sat at the bar adding a wreath of thick cigarette smoke to the stale air. Of course, loudmouth Liam had to point out, "Cigarettes kill people, don't they Mommy?"

As Rollins dove to put a hand over his little brother's mouth, his elbow knocked Phoenix in the head. She started crying. Jansen broke up the fight between the boys as Kate tried to comfort Phoenix with one hand while pulling Lilly up off the floor under the table with the other.

At this auspicious moment the waitress, Judy, according to her nametag, arrived on the scene with ice water, menus and a loud, "What can I get y'all?"

Liam's disappointment over no bagel and Phoenix's horror at the soggy canned fruit cocktail she received in lieu of fresh fruit were soon forgotten as the kids reveled in eggs, bacon, and plate-sized pancakes swimming in syrup—Erma's specialty.

Judy returned to refill juices and deliver more syrup for the ravenous brood. "New in town?" she inquired.

As Jansen opened his mouth to reply, Liam proclaimed in his ever-loud kid voice, "We're gonna live in this really cool place that looks haunted! It has windows like a church and huge trees that look like they're gonna crash down on it!" As his words bounced off the walls of Erma's Café, other voices stopped and Kate felt every head turn their way.

Judy's sky-blue-shadowed eyelids widened. "Ya mean the ol' Pedigo place?"

"That's the one. Mom was a Pedigo," Jansen answered.

"Clara's boy, right? Ya got her eyes. My mama and Clara played there when they were kids." Judy stared at Jansen. "Goodness! That place has been empty for more 'n thirty years. Well, empty of the livin' anyways." Judy opened and shut her mouth. "So, anyone save room for pie?"

"We're ready for the ticket," Kate interjected.

With a nervous cackle, Judy slapped their ticket down on the table. "Right. Pie for breakfast. The ol' girl's losin' it. Bye now!"

"Guess she's ready for us to leave," Kate commented as Judy rushed toward the high counter area that separated customers from the kitchen and began a whispered conversation with the cook, complete with jerks-of-the-head in the Walden family's direction.

As they shuffled out Erma's door into bright June sunshine, Rollins mumbled, "Don't guess I should ask for an Abercrombie or Hot Topic." He looked around the sleepy square in disgust and shoved his hands deep into the pockets of his hooded sweatshirt.

"What have we here?" A deep voice drawled behind them. "Jance Walden come back from the land a' plenty."

Jansen laughed and strode to wrap the stranger in a violent bear hug. After exclamations of, "Why, you sunofa!" and "How ya been?" Jansen introduced them to the tall, sharp-eyed man called Cal.

"So you're the Cal Jansen's been talking about," Kate reached to shake Cal's work-roughened hand.

"The fillies 'round here weren't good enough for ya, so ya went and rustled a movie star." Cal's eyes sized up Kate. Somehow she didn't feel complimented.

"Ya gotta watch this guy, Kate. Broke every heart from here to the county line by the time he graduated high school," Jansen joked as he added a punch to Cal's shoulder.

As the men continued their friendly cut-downs, Kate struggled to contain their impatient brood, chasing Lilly into the street, and shushing Liam as he yelled, "Phoenix, don't touch that dog! He probably has lepersee!" just as nine-year-old Phoenix reached toward a scrawny stray edging toward her with pathetic eyes, tail tucked into its bony behind.

"Look, Mommy, he's bleeding!" Phoenix pleaded as the mutt rolled on one side exposing a long gash on his back leg. All eyes turned toward the cur who whimpered on cue then thumped his tail in response to Phoenix's "Awww!"

Kate gritted her teeth and kept her arms crossed on her chest as Jansen followed Cal to the local veterinarian. In the back of the SUV the mangy dog, wrapped in Rollins' sweatshirt, reclined with his head on Phoenix's lap.

"We'll take care of him, Mom," Rollins said as he ruffled the dog's floppy ears.

"Yeah, right. Like I haven't heard that before," Kate grumbled.

The vet stitched up the wound, discovered the mutt had worms, as if Kate cared to know, and kept the dog for a few more hours to clean him up and begin the "de-worming" process. Phoenix dubbed him "Winston" like the name on the cigarettes they'd seen at breakfast. Oh joy. A canine tribute to nicotine. But, despite the royal pain she expected the dog to be, Kate had to admit Phoenix had regained a hint of her old sparkle.

Fine. She'd put up with the dog.

Her husband, on the other hand, was the one in the doghouse. By late afternoon, Kate's frustration toward Jansen was building to outright fury. After getting them to the vet, he roared away with Cal and left her to deal with the dog, the kids, trying to discover some way to set up house and plan to feed their brood. A steady diet of Erma's grease and pancakes, while tasty, would never do. As she pulled through the gate with a load of overpriced groceries she'd secured at the mom and pop store in town, Lilly was crying from her tumble off the concrete steps in front of the store, Rollins was in a surly mood, complaining about the severe lack of *anything* in this town, and Liam had conked out in the back seat. He'd be a bear to wake up.

Kate was fried. If she ever spoke to Jansen again, she'd give him a huge piece of her mind.

But the sight that met her eyes as they pulled through the gate and onto the circle drive made Kate's jaw drop in amazement. Their moving truck had obviously found them. The monstrous vehicle sat on the far side of the yard as men maneuvered up and down the gangplank like busy ants. But the massive truck, flatbed trailers, and random pickups were not what commanded Kate's attention. To the left, set between two large oaks as if they had been planted precisely for this purpose, stood a doublewide manufactured home. Speechless, Kate emerged from the car.

"This must be the little woman!" A beefy hand reached for hers for a firm shake and Kate found herself surrounded by a noisy, friendly crowd.

"Surprise!"

"Welcome to the neighborhood!"

"What beautiful children!"

"I'll bet you're just plumb tuckered out!"

Jansen stepped forward to make introductions but names and faces blurred as Kate, overwhelmed by the warmest of greetings from total strangers, blinked back tears. Jansen leaned close as the cheerful crowd resumed their tasks. "You didn't think I'd make us sleep in tents or live without proper electricity, did ya? Cal's been working on the connections. In fact, I hired him a month ago to set things up so all we had to do was roll in the manufactured home and hook 'er up. Surprise." Jansen smiled and searched Kate's eyes. "I know it's kinda small but …"

Kate shushed Jansen with a hearty kiss. "It's perfect, Sweetie."

Cal walked by with a large box. "I do all the work and he gets the kisses. Don't tell me life's fair."

As if produced out of thin air, in no time, a long table was set up and overflowed with a country feast. Kate found herself seated with a heaping plate of homemade goodies before her.

Out of habit, Kate counted to four, taking note of the whereabouts of her children. Lilly, seated on her Daddy's lap, snuck fingerfuls of icing from a chocolate layer cake as a middle-aged woman doctored her scraped knee. Liam divulged God-only-knew-what family secrets to a grandfatherly farmer and gestured broadly with a fried chicken leg while Rollins, who had been sullen all day, joined the workers unpacking the moving truck. He actually laughed as they tried several angles to get the family's oversized sofa through the narrow front door of the manufactured home. Phoenix sat close to her mother's side and shyly smiled at a tall, fresh-faced woman who reached a hand to introduce herself.

"I'm Allison McKinley. Call me Allie. What's your name, Sweetheart?"

After quick introductions, Allie said she lived about a half mile up the road. "You'll have to come sometime and visit our zoo." She went on to describe their furry family ranging from a blind Border Collie to a pet wallaby and a silver fox. "I'm the bleedin' heart of the county. If there's an animal that needs rescuing, folks know I can never turn 'em away!"

Phoenix's eyes shone at the discovery of this kindred spirit and she launched into an animated description of Winston, her own rescue of the day. Kate hadn't seen Phoenix string together this many sentences in the past six months combined.

Later, after a hot shower and careful maneuvering between still-packed boxes, Kate slipped gratefully between the clean sheets of her own bed and nuzzled Jansen's still-damp hair at the base of his neck. "Thank you, Babe."

Jansen rolled over to embrace her. "Anything for my little woman."

After several nights of sharing hotel rooms and tents with the kids, Kate savored the moments of uninterrupted smooching. Yes, she and Jansen fell asleep mid-smooch, but at least they fell asleep smiling.

CHAPTER 3

BUTTERFLIES
& HIDDEN THINGS

Kate was surprised the next morning to discover she was the last to wake. Happy sounds emanated from the kitchen where the kids dug into leftovers from the night before. Yea! She didn't have to fix breakfast. With the unaccustomed reprieve, she jumped at the opportunity to primp. For once she felt rested and optimistic. In her suitcase, she located the white tank top with crochet edging Jansen loved and paired it with her favorite jeans. There now. With her hair falling in shiny auburn waves and a touch of make-up, she felt clean, presentable and downright cute. Time to go hug and kiss the man who had made a good night's sleep possible.

Cal's huge white pickup sat at the front of the house. As she once again passed under the chandelier, Kate heard voices rising from the basement and called a cheery, "Hi Babe!"

When he topped the stairs from the basement, the ashen look on Jansen's face made Kate stop cold. "What's wrong?"

Jansen didn't answer. Cal mumbled something about getting some stuff out of his truck and strode toward the front door.

"What?" Kate prompted.

"By all rights, you and this house should have been blown to kingdom come yesterday."

As Jansen explained the large leak in the gas line connected to the hot water heater, Kate went pale. With horror, she remembered the fiasco of striking match after match in her attempts to light the thing.

"Couldn't you smell the gas?"

"How could I smell gas over the rest of the stench in the basement?" Kate responded with a bit more volume than she had intended.

"The handle wasn't even shut off properly," Jansen continued. "I still can't figure out why the air was clear when we went down this morning. You coulda died, Kate."

"So this is my fault! As I recall, you lit the thing and left it on overnight."

Part of her wanted to stop arguing and give Jansen the hug and kiss she'd prepared. But when he rubbed his eyes and said, "Just… please… promise you'll leave these things to me from now on," in a painfully patient tone of voice, Kate lost it.

"Don't talk to me like I'm Lilly," she hissed. "I was trying to help and I don't recall you noticing the leaking line. You could've blown us all up that first night!"

Immediately she regretted her outburst when Jansen flinched as if punched in the gut.

How she wanted him to respond, to fight back and justify her anger, but he just clenched his jaw and turned away with a pained grimace. For some reason, the defeated expression, the one she'd seen too often in the past year, scared Kate more than if he had struck her.

At that moment, Cal returned with a large toolbox and a wide grin. "Aw Jance, don't be too hard on the little lady." He addressed himself to Kate. "Darlin', a gal as pretty as you can blow up my house anytime!"

But the jovial smile froze as Kate turned toward Cal with murder in her eyes.

"The name's Kate." She took a step closer. "Not 'little woman' and not," she punctuated the word with a pointer finger to his chest, "Darlin'!" She gave Jansen a scathing look. "Guess I'd better kick off my shoes and get in the kitchen where I belong." Face hot with anger, Kate wheeled to exit the room.

"Does she always smell like vanilla when she's angry?" Cal's teasing voice followed her as Kate opened the front door then slammed it so hard some broken glass in the dining room window crashed onto the porch.

"Sorry about that," Jansen replied, his voice trailing through the many broken windows of the old house. "Things are kinda strained right now."

"She's a racehorse, Jance. The good ones always have plenty a' ginger."

A flush of rage caused Kate to clench her fists. "You smug, smart-aleck, son-of-a ..." she grumbled a few less-savory titles, "I'll show you ginger!"

She looked toward the manufactured home and her shoulders slumped in defeat. She'd be yelling at the kids in no time if she showed up like this. Instead, Kate stomped and huffed toward the overgrown backyard.

As she rounded the house, Kate saw Jansen slap Cal on the back and laugh. She tromped faster, not wanting to be seen. "Probably discussing whether I'd respond better to spurs or a riding crop," she muttered.

She would have practically jogged in her angry rampage, but vines like grasping fingers were turning her stroll into an obstacle course. What was this? A walk in her new backyard or a jungle safari? "Ow!" Kate yelped as a thorn found its way through her thick jeans and she bent to detach herself. Her ankle was bleeding, but it was nothing serious.

Suddenly the silence engulfed her. Her ears strained for any sound—the drone of a bee, chirp of a bird—but nothing. It was as if the world continued to turn without her, but she had stepped out of time.

Kate examined her surroundings. Flowers bloomed in brilliant profusion, crying out to be noticed. The air felt heavy, as if it hadn't been stirred in decades, like entering the fancy sitting room at Grandma's house that was only opened on special occasions. Behind her, the vines and branches formed a deep green veil, obscuring the house and anything else but this drowsy, living canopy. The only sounds were her breath and racing heartbeat. Life, reduced to its most basic functions.

She looked around with wide eyes, aware those trees had been growing, inch by patient inch, before she was born and, more than likely, they would carry on when she was long gone. They were steady, reliable, and calming.

A flit of color caught her eye. The largest butterfly she'd ever seen, vibrant in hues of rich purple and gold, hovered just out of reach above flame-tipped leaves to her right. In silence, they studied each other. Finally, the purple brilliance landed on a flower close to Kate's hand. Cautiously, Kate placed her finger next to the flower. To her astonishment, the butterfly walked onto it then sat, slowly opening and closing its wings.

As if satisfied with its assessment, the butterfly rose and flew into a beam of sunlight then turned back as if beckoning Kate to follow. Mesmerized, Kate obeyed. The butterfly's path kept her feet on a trail where the undergrowth was less thick, leading her around a flowering bush and across a thin band of smooth stones that Kate guessed might once have been a decorative stream.

Her eyes were so focused on the stones below and the bushes that blocked her progress that, when the path ended, it caught her off-guard.

Before her loomed what appeared to be an impenetrable wall of tangled vines that rose to disappear into the branches above. Intrigued, Kate explored to find the dimensions of this obstacle, discovering, after a scratch on her face and a close call with an enormous spider web, the obstruction was about twenty-five feet long.

Further investigation revealed the vines formed a large rectangle. Okay, now she had to know what was in there. She grasped a handful of vines and pulled with all her might. While intertwined, dense and thick, the long cords were brittle and broke easily. Kate began to clear a small patch. After a couple minutes, she felt something cold and hard. It was wrought iron, similar to the entry gate. Manhandling another bunch of vines, Kate put her face close to the iron, but her own shadow shut off the light. All she could see was a deep, green haziness that only heightened her curiosity.

"What in the world?" she mumbled.

Kate walked to her right, finding the middle of the short side of the rectangle. Perhaps if she created another hole, the added light would aid her investigation. She pulled and tugged, ignoring a broken nail and the trickle of sweat working its way down her back. The vines grew even more thick on this side so Kate was close to giving up until she could return with the proper tools when, with a gasp, she found herself staring at a gate's latch. When the latch proved stubborn with rust she gave the bolt a sharp kick with her foot as she'd seen in Rollins' karate class. The gate released and she forced it open just enough to slip through.

Her foot crunched onto something that sounded like eggshells. She waited for her eyes to adjust to the dimness as a small patch of light fell on glimmering tile under her shoes. The thought of going to fetch a flashlight crossed Kate's mind, but she blew it off. For once, she would be the carefree child pushing the limits.

As she stepped forward, the hush grew deeper and heavier, like entering a cave or… tomb. With a chill of fear, she wondered if this was indeed some sort of family crypt. What a morbid thought on a bright summer morning.

Annoyed by her childish imagination, Kate held her arms in front of her though the dim glow reached no further than her elbows. Nothing. She groped overhead but felt nothing, even when she stretched on tiptoe. The footing felt firm enough, so she inched forward, her fingers groping in the darkness. She took a longer stride forward, meeting no resistance. So far, so good. As she gathered her courage for another forward plunge, a glimmer of brilliant color drew her eyes to the hole where she had first broken through the vines. The butterfly she'd seen before landed on a leaf, its wings opening and closing

A soft coolness, like a breath, moved along the exposed skin on Kate's arms and face. As the chill ran down her body, she heard a whispered, "Stop." Kate leapt in fright and stumbled, landing on her backside as bits of flooring scattered.

Kate froze as the sound of echoes, like sonar, probed a hard surface several feet below. For one eternal second, she wavered between terror and curiosity. To run out or to discover? "Oh come on." Kate grumbled. "Probably more to fear from sitting on some unseen critter than from imagined voices." Thus Kate gritted her teeth and patted the ground, gingerly exploring the surface of leaves and branches on cracked tile until, a mere six inches from her shoes, it fell away into thin air.

Her gasp sounded muffled against the heavy air. Hands shaking, Kate retreated, inch by careful inch, to the promise of sunlight where she had entered. With a determined gulp of air she hoped would fill her with courage, Kate gripped a mass of the vines and pulled. Whether due to fear-infused super-strength or just super-dead, dry vines, Kate landed once more on her backside, this time with a mass of dusty vines on top of her. She blinked in sudden, blinding light and hopped up, shoving away woven vines that looked for one terrifying moment like a nest of intertwined snakes. Heart pounding, Kate kicked away the pile and turned.

"Oh my God," she breathed. Rays of piercing light illuminated what appeared to be an unearthed Roman bath, complete with graceful columns and stone benches. But Kate's eyes were fixed on the yawning void inches from where she had fallen earlier. She crept closer on trembling knees and peered down to still-shadowed depths, the deepest portion of a vast bathing pool, the bottom of which was covered with mounds of debris. But with her imagination on red alert, the mounds resembled a lumpy graveyard waiting for a bony hand to... One of the mounds shook. A growl reverberated in the dimness. Kate shrieked and scurried back out into the blessed sunshine.

CHAPTER 4

DISCOVERIES

Kate's attempt to slip into the kitchen and grab the flashlight unnoticed was foiled when Jansen peeked from under the kitchen sink.

"What happened to you? You're white as a sheet!" Jansen came closer to inspect her dirty, scratched appearance, pulling a web and twigs from her hair.

"I, uh, found something… out back." Kate stammered. "It's, um, aaak!" She swatted away a spider on her arm. "Just, come see."

"Well," Jansen wiped his hands on an already-grimy hand towel. "Gotta let this glue dry anyway."

Soon, armed with hatchets and flashlights, Jansen and Cal followed Kate toward her vine-covered mystery. With just a couple well-aimed strokes, the men widened the opening around the gated entrance. As sunlight flooded the enclosure, Jansen gave a low whistle accompanied by Cal's, "I'll be damned!"

Kate stepped forward, emboldened by the men's presence but Cal put out an arm to block her path. "Best to let the dust settle a minute." Both men aimed their flashlights into the gloom.

"Ya know," Jansen mused, "Mom mentioned once how they baptized a whole slew of folks way back when a travelin' preacher came through. I assumed they used a nearby creek or pond but I'll bet they used this."

Cal broke off a vine and tossed it toward the empty pool's edge. Kate yelped and jumped toward Jansen when a snake slithered across the opening and disappeared into the grass.

"Just a gopher snake," Cal informed as he yanked another handful of vines away. "Good thing he's been around to keep the rats down."

Jansen took a step inside the enclosure and crouched down, shining his flashlight on Kate's clear footprints. "You came in?"

Kate nodded, inwardly cringing at the thought of snakes and rats in the darkness.

The beam of Jansen's flashlight traced Kate's scuffling prints until it shone on the cleared debris at pool's edge where her bum had landed.

"Did you fall?" Jansen asked.

"Kinda."

"Lucky you didn't fall in this thing and break your neck," Jansen muttered.

Cal gave Jansen's back a good-natured smack. "Aw, probably a nest of snakes down there. They woulda made for a soft landing."

Kate refused to shudder at those words. Instead, she crossed her arms and addressed Jansen. "I need to get back to the kids. Are you going to work on this now?"

Jansen aimed his light higher, letting out a quiet whistle as vine-covered columns and a tiled ceiling came into view. "Don't think I can resist. Whaddaya think, Cal?"

"I'm in an Indiana Jones mood if you are."

"Sounds good," Kate turned away. "I'll tell Rollins to grab some work gloves and join you."

Considering the fact Cal probably assumed Kate had a death wish since she'd almost blown up the house, Kate held her tongue about the whisper that prevented her plunge into the empty pool. Better not get the rumor started the new filly at the old Pedigo place heard voices in the dark.

Just a couple hours later, Kate gaped in awe at what the men's labors had accomplished. Dappled sunlight filtered into the pool house through vines that now draped decoratively here and there, a vast improvement over its former Bat Cave-like façade. The bottom of the pool now bore tidy piles of who-knew-what that were ready for removal. Now that the pool area had been opened up, it still felt like a mausoleum, but it was at least a ventilated mausoleum. Rollins was sweeping rubbish into piles between the pillars while Cal & Jansen inspected cracks in the tiled wall.

"You missed it, Kate," Cal said. "Rollins got acquainted with a nest of coons, didn't ya?"

Rollins' eyes were wide, almost childlike, as he put a hand to his chest. "God! I thought that mama was gonna eat me! Had no idea raccoons were so mean!"

"That explains the growl I heard earlier." Kate took a cautious step closer to the edge of the pool where she had almost toppled a few short hours before.

"You heard something growling down here?" Rollins gaped up at Kate. "Geez, Mom. Thanks for the heads-up."

"Aw, that woulda spoiled all the fun," Cal drawled. "Never seen a city slicker jump so high."

Rollins pointed the push broom toward Cal. "Yeah, and thanks for all the help. You, up there splittin' a gut laughin' while I was about to be shredded."

Kate's heart warmed to hear Rollins play along. From the look of things, Cal was going to be around a lot. Well, if he could help bring Rollins out of his months-long funk, she'd be happy to put up with the cowboy's macho attitude.

So, raccoons, huh? But there was no explanation for the whisper she'd heard. The memory caused the hairs on her arms to once more stand at attention. She peered down into the still-shadowed depths to view the deep end of the pool, a good ten feet below. Not a pleasant thought to fall into that sight-unseen. Her eyes trailed up toward the shallow end where gaps in the tile revealed concrete beneath the sloped floor. There was some sort of design she couldn't make out so Kate walked around the long edge for a better vantage point. Just then, the setting sun won its fight to pierce the heavy canopy of trailing limbs in the yard, its rays falling directly on the center of the shallow end. There, partially hidden by a pile of leaves, was an intricate tile design, a large P encircled by a geometric circle of gold and Navy blue tiles that glimmered in the golden light like gems scattered on a field of battle.

"Oh my!" Kate exclaimed. "What a work of art."

"Yep," Jansen replied. "Old Jed was pretty proud of his name. Too bad such beauty has been buried and forgotten for so long. A little neglect and something priceless turns into junk."

Cal stood up and gazed around. "Man, if these walls could speak. Doesn't make sense that something like this was just overgrown and forgotten.

"It's totally creepy," Rollins grumbled. "Saw some cool lizards though."

"For now, we'll clear out these piles and padlock the gate," Jansen stated as he wiped an arm across his forehead. "Until it's fixed, this thing is a hazard."

For safety, Jansen put a new padlock on the gate to the pool and the kids were told it was off-limits until repaired. Of course, that action simply heightened the mystery.

Two months later

Kate breezed in the back door to the manufactured home feeling refreshed after her morning walk with Allie, but her outlook was still apprehensive. Even after several social occasions and a couple months of feverish activity on the old house, she still missed her home and friends in California. Now, Jansen would be gone for two weeks to oversee construction on a subdivision back in California, an opportunity he couldn't pass up with the Pedigo Manor bills mounting. In fact, all but Lilly would be abandoning her for their first day at school. Of course, right across the road was widow Hayney's farm that had become a second home for the kids who had a standing invitation to swim in her pond or play in her hay barn, and Allie lived right around the corner. Besides, Cal's ranch was only five miles away, a short distance in this wide country. Jansen had hired his old friend to oversee the renovation so Cal would be coming and going every day.

But none of them would be around in the dreaded quiet hours of night. Ever since the incident in the pool house, Kate had been a bit jumpy. On top of that, widow Hayney had, just yesterday, confided a few of the rumors that circulated about the old Pedigo place. Kate could have laughed them off, most were just the farfetched product of drunken teenagers clambering into the house on a dare, but Ima Hayney's own story had struck a cord of familiarity.

Kate shook herself back to reality. Time to get the morning going or Jansen would miss his flight and the kids would miss the bus.

Liam was up with a bound of excitement. She had no worries about her confident little superhero in regards to school. He'd already made several friends at church and was developing a busy social calendar.

Rollins, on the other hand, had remained a bit of an outcast, partly due to his standoffish attitude and partly, Kate had to admit, due to a sense of distrust toward newcomers that still prevailed in some pockets of their new hometown. He'd developed a following among some of the teen girls since he was the tall, good-looking new kid in town, but most of the young men made fun of his baggy skater clothing and "city" ways.

When Kate said, "Time to get up!" Rollins simply growled and pulled the pillow onto his head.

Kate peeked into the girls' room. As usual, Phoenix wasn't in her own bed but Kate knew right where to find her. Lilly's tangle of curls and one bare foot poked from under her knotted bedclothes. Kate shut the door quietly. Let the little dynamo sleep.

Back in the master bedroom where their king-sized mattress swallowed the limited floor space, Kate located her oldest daughter wrapped in the comforter from her bed and pressed close to Jansen's side.

How would Phoenix handle Jansen's absence for two whole weeks? For that matter, how would she handle school? She'd become a frequent visitor at Allie's place, helping to care for the animals and building a special bond with an orphaned baby raccoon, but most of the time she had simply played in the still-overgrown garden in back of the house. Kate was afraid Phoenix, with her red curls and slightly plump physique, would be a prime target for teasing, but Jansen thought the regular routine and playing with children her own age would bring their oldest daughter out of her shell. Kate hoped, rather than believed, he was right.

It came as somewhat of a shock when the forty-five minutes of chaos ended, the kids roared away on the bus, and Jansen pulled away looking handsome in trim khakis and his brown leather jacket. She envied his return to civilization.

Kate had to convince herself she'd been looking forward to this moment. Finally, she could do something she'd been waiting to do since she first set eyes on Pedigo Manor.

Wiring and pipes were new, rotten boards were replaced, the foundation was leveled and even the sagging balcony was no longer a lopsided grin. The house was still an eyesore, but it was evolving into a well-built eyesore.

So, armed with ammonia, rags, and brushes sufficient to clean the Titanic, Kate rolled up her sleeves, put on Jansen's Yankee's ball cap, toted a small DVD player to occupy Lilly, and set to work. She opened every window in the house before she started but, after two hours, it seemed she'd done nothing more than work up more dust and a healthy appetite. For a while Lilly tried to help, but when it was obvious real work was involved, she opted for the DVD babysitter. Kate scrubbed, accompanied by the sound of Lilly singing along with a mermaid and a rebellious lion cub.

But suddenly, in the middle of scrubbing out the kitchen cabinets, Kate realized it had been several minutes since she'd heard her daughter's lisped accompaniment.

Kate dashed through the house calling her daughter's name. She wasn't in any of the closets, the door to the basement was still locked thank goodness, so maybe she'd escaped the dust and gone outside?

With an effort, Kate suppressed her panic. "Lilly!" she called out the front of the house as her eyes scanned the grounds for any sign of movement. She called again as she moved toward the backyard. Please, God. Not the pool house.

She opened her mouth for another shout, but stopped, straining her ears. Was that a child's voice? She rushed in the direction of the sound, dismayed to find her feet leading toward the tangled backyard jungle. The singing grew louder.

"Wook for the bear thethidees, the thimple bear thethidees..."

Kate sighed with relief. Obviously Lilly wasn't in danger. Her voice was content, happy, and carefree. Kate stopped to soak in the sound. For a moment, the carefree childhood joy lifted her spirits. The sun's rays sparkled on dew-kissed leaves as birds chattered and hopped in the bushes.

Kate took a deep breath as her pounding heart began to slow. These were the moments that made life worth living.

Lilly was talking now, carrying on a conversation with an imaginary friend. Kate moved closer, not wanting to ruin the moment. She peeked through the leaves to spy Lilly, happily chattering away surrounded by tiny beams of light that danced with the movement of a soft breeze through the trees. A few feet away, Winston, their spoiled mutt, lay with all four paws splayed in the air as a brilliant butterfly flitted above him.

"Okay Belle, thing your thong," Lilly requested. Kate giggled at the effect of her daughter's lisp as Lilly reached for another daisy to add to the small mound of bright flowers in front of her. Sunlight glinted off the shiny head as she nodded in time to the imagined music and started twisting two of the flower stems together.

Suddenly, Lilly threw down the flowers in frustration. "It's not wike yours!" she exclaimed and crossed her plump little arms with stubborn anger. "I tan't bwaid!"

Surely that was a mom's cue to come to the rescue on this lazy morning. However, the greeting for Lilly froze in Kate's throat.

Were her eyes playing tricks on her? Could it be the wind… blowing only on the spot where the daisies lay?

"One, two, free… " Lilly counted as the flowers leapt into her hand as if attached to invisible strings. Lilly started carefully laying the stems… one to the middle, one to the middle… in faltering braid formation, just as Winston started kicking his hind leg as if enjoying a satisfying scratch. Lilly began singing again.

> *"We were thaywing awong on moonwite bay*
> *All the Cwithmath bellth were wing-ing… "*

Kate grasped the tree trunk for support as the scene from widow Hayney's kitchen the night before played through her mind… the children's voices wafting through the screen door, the scent of Ima's fresh, crusty biscuits making her mouth water, the slight smell of Pine-sol-scrubbed cabinets in a lovely pale butter shade, her seventy-something friend sitting across the square, cloth-covered table clad in a bright homemade something between a dress and a nightgown. Ima's voice, a soothing blend of Texas and her Kentucky hillbilly roots, had droned on.

"I was so lonely. Clint had been gone for about six months and everywhere I went in this old place, I felt he was gonna be there like always, but he never was. I walked across the road, drawn to that old Pedigo place. Maybe I thought it looked as lonely as I felt," Ima had cackled as Kate spread butter on the biscuit in her hand and watched with satisfaction as it melted into the fluffy layers.

"Anyways," Ima had continued, "I sat on that old porch in that creakin' swing, rockin' back and forth for hours and cryin' for the first time since Clint died. Finally, the sun started to set and I begun ta get chilled. As I stood to go, I heard a child singin'. We raised eight younguns so children singin' is just about my favorite sound in the world—how I've missed it now they're all growed and gone. But I didn't think it was safe for a child to be there with night comin' on so I thought I'd make sure they got home safe an' all.

"The singin' sounded like it 'us comin' from inside the house so I peeked in a few winders and tried a few doors but they was all locked. Whoever it was, they sounded happy enough singin' about moonlight and Christmas bells, but the sun was gone and I was worried so I walked around the house callin, 'Hello! It's Miss Hayney! Time to git home!' The singin' stopped. I figured I'd scared 'em away so I started on home myself.

"I've never been one given to fancies, but I shore felt watched as I stepped onto that drive. Now ya gotta remember I was plumb wore out with grief and I've thought many a time I was well nigh' losin' my mind. I was just in the middle of that circle of grass when I turned 'round an' saw a little girl standin' on that crooked balcony, her little blonde head just barely reachin' the rail. I shouted up to her, 'You come on down from there before you git yourself hurt!'

"Do you know what that little bugger did? She peeked under that crooked rail and blew me a kiss! Next thing I knew, she 'us gone, just faded like a rainbow when the sun goes behind a cloud!

"Lots of folks is scared a' that place, but I'm here ta tell ya it's blessed. I just figger God sent me a kiss from an angel when He knew I needed it most."

Kate had laughed and dismissed Ima's story as the product of fatigue and grief, but now, watching Lilly braid daisies, which she'd never done, as Winston enjoyed an apparent belly scratch from an unseen hand, the tale took on new merit.

"Lilly!" Kate tried to keep the panic out of her voice, "Ready to eat?"

Lilly looked up from her daisies with a smile. "Look what I can do!" Kate's heart thumped with relief as Lilly ran closer, proudly displaying the beginnings of her daisy chain. "Can Belle eat wif us?"

Kate forced a nervous laugh. "So does she have a bright yellow dress and hang out with a beast? That guy'll have to watch his manners."

Lilly rolled her eyes. "Not that Belle. My fwiend." Her brown eyes scanned the clearing until she sighed with disappointment. "You scared her away!"

Kate couldn't help but cast a nervous glance over her shoulder as she guided her chattering daughter into the house.

CHAPTER 5

STORMY WEATHER

Soon enough, Kate's motherly duties left no room for concern over unseen companions. As she was wiping the jelly off Lilly's mouth and hands, the phone rang.

"Miz Walden? This is Principal Horner. There's been a little, heh, heh, incident with your son."

Kate had no choice but to remove the ball cap from her dusty curls, grab Lilly, and rush to her meeting with the principal, a cheery-faced man who inserted a chuckle into every sentence.

"Now, heh, heh, I don't know how things were done in Californiyay, but we can't have this street fightin'. I'll have ta tell ya, any more of this kinda behavior, heh, heh, and we'll suspend your boy."

A throbbing headache was building behind Kate's right eye as she drove home with Lilly chattering in the backseat while Rollins slumped against the passenger door, sullen and silent.

"What happened?" Kate asked when she finally got Rollins home and alone in his room.

He shrugged and kept staring at the floor, arms shoved into the pockets of his loose jeans.

"You were in a fight. You punched a kid in the face. At least tell me why."

"He deserved it," Rollins mumbled.

"Rollins, lots of people deserve it, but that doesn't mean you go around throwing punches!"

"So am I grounded or what?" His face was expressionless and bored.

"I… I'll talk it over with your dad… but yeah, this is serious."

"Fine."

With that, Rollins slouched to his room and shut the door while Kate stood feeling like a million knives had stabbed her heart. Why, oh why did kids have to grow up, gain hormones, and have hurts a mother's kiss would no longer heal?

When Liam and Phoenix arrived on the bus, the drama continued as Phoenix ran to her room in tears. Kate followed and held her sobbing daughter. "What happened?" she asked, but never found out because at that moment Lilly's wailing shriek catapulted Kate into the dining room to tend her four-year-old's bleeding fingers.

"He slammed my fingers in the door!" Lilly wailed.

"It not my fault!" Liam yelled back. "I told her not to follow me!"

"He (sniff) did it (sniff) on (sniff) purpose!" Lilly accused, her little face red and streaked with tears.

Kate was beyond losing it, as she ran cold water over Lilly's bruised, bleeding fingers.

In the madness, Kate hardly noticed the building clouds, or the fact the air felt heavy, weighing down on her shoulders—like her life. As the rain began to patter, Kate took out her frustrations on a pile of dirty dishes, scrubbing with angry clunks and slams, then channel-surfed, trying to find something besides weather reports, without really seeing what was on the screen. Finally, about 2 a.m., she fell into bed, too tired to cry.

Rocks crashed down from above, striking Kate's head as her hands and knees grew bloody, grappling for footing and handholds. Lilly was clinging to her neck and the other three children hung by ropes from her shoulders and legs. Above her, Jansen slipped and almost fell. Kate steadied him, frightened of losing her grip on Lilly, but knowing, if Jansen tumbled, they were all going down.

Her arms and legs shook with fatigue. Sweat trickled, burning, into her eyes. She was losing her grip. God no! They all depended on her! She had to be strong! Raindrops fell, turning the rock into slick mud. Kate watched, horrified, as her handhold dissolved. The children's screams filled her ears. Just as she was ready to plummet, Kate looked up to see a light on the rocky ledge above. There, bathed in tiny sunbeams that sparkled like diamonds on her blonde curls, stood a little girl. With a happy smile, she blew a kiss.

Kate woke with a start. Pounding rain drove against the window and the wind howled around the house. A trembling Phoenix slipped into her bed.

"Mommy, I'm scared."

"It's just a thunderstorm, Sweetie."

"But there was banging and someone was yelling."

"Go back to sleep," Kate instructed groggily. "It was just thunder."

BAM! BAM! BAM!

Kate sat bolt upright in bed, all mental fuzziness gone.

"See?" Phoenix huddled closer.

There was a blinding flash then a shouting voice that was almost lost in the wind rushing through the trees.

"Kate!"

"See?" Phoenix said again.

Kate got up and peered through the window. There was Cal's truck, headlights illuminating the driving rain.

"What is it, Mommy?" Phoenix's voice quivered.

"It's okay. It's just Mr. Cal. I'll go see what he wants."

Kate rushed toward the door, aware she wore only one of Jansen's overlarge t-shirts and panties. She unlatched the door and peeked around it.

There was Cal, face obscured by a hooded slicker that fell below his knees.

"Grab the kids and come on!" he shouted. "Storm's headed this way!"

"Um… " Kate struggled with whether to let him in out of the rain first or grab a robe.

"Move!" Cal barked the command. "Shoes. Coats. Now!"

"I've got the coats," Rollins' said from behind her, already opening the entryway closet and handing over Kate's long raincoat.

She slipped it on and went to gather the kids.

Soon they were following Cal through driving rain and gusting wind. Cal toted the comatose, Superman-clutching Liam, Lilly was in Kate's arms while Phoenix rode piggyback-style on Rollins. Onward they slogged to the sheltering porch of the old house and down into the musty basement that, in all honesty, frightened Kate more than the storm. Cal returned with a radio, flashlight, and a tarp that he spread on the dank floor where Kate and the three younger kids huddled. Lightning flashed like strobe lights on their frightened faces as Cal's radio crackled with every flash, giving a play-by-play of the storm.

"You ever seen any tornadoes?" Rollins asked as he paced the floor, matching Cal's restless stride.

"A few."

"Ever seen anything really cool?"

"Don't know what ya'd call 'cool' but I once saw a cow impaled by a tree branch."

Phoenix gasped.

"Oo-kay, let's play Twenty Questions," Kate interjected as she shot Cal a warning look. "Rollins, you first."

The game distracted for a few minutes until the kids guessed Rollins was thinking of a cow, then things fell apart when Liam, finally emerging from his sleepy stupor, asked, "Have you been in a house when it was spinning around like in 'The Wizard of Oz?'"

"Nah," Cal turned from the window to squat down to Liam's level.

"Tornadoes don't tend ta take people for a ride."

Kate breathed a sigh of relief as she saw Liam's worried face relax. "Good, I wouldn't like that." He hugged Superman a bit tighter.

"Usually, in a tornado, a house just kinda explodes without warning."

Liam, Phoenix and Lilly sucked in a breath and cowered closer to Kate.

"But we're safe in the basement." Kate injected a forced calmness into her voice even as she shot an angry look Cal's way. "That's why Mr. Cal brought us here."

"Well, ya never can tell. There was a house in Chester County yanked completely out of the ground, basement and all. They found shutters from the windows two counties away, along with the kid who lived there, a boy, just about your size," Cal glanced lazily toward Liam, "most of 'im anyway."

Liam's eyes grew wide with horror.

"Enough!" Kate's mother instincts took over. "This isn't the time or the place…"

Cal let out a burst of laughter. "Sorry, it's just too much fun to see ya riled." His eyes glittered in the dim light. "Believe me, kids, ya better fear this little lady here more than any windstorm. I do believe she'd tear a body limb from limb to protect you."

Kate felt her face flush even as she had to smile in acknowledgement. "Yeah, and don't you forget it," she warned, her words interrupted by a loud tapping on the small basement window that turned to a clatter.

"Is it raining rocks?" Phoenix asked with wide eyes.

"No stupid, that's hail. It's ice," Rollins informed with exaggerated disdain.

"But how can ice fall from the sky when it's not cold?" Liam asked, unfazed by Rollins' ridicule.

Rollins had no answer so Cal chimed in, "What your big brother would like ta say is that hail is the product of a high pressure air mass and a low pressure air mass comin' together. As the churning clouds rise higher and higher, the moisture gets colder...."

Kate's eyebrows rose as she grew more and more impressed with Cal's mastery of the subject. From hail, Cal went on to an overview of air currents and the direction they generally moved, "kinda like the currents in the ocean, they move along like a highway in the sky."

He described jet streams and even explained why the area of the United States called "Tornado Alley" saw the lion's share of such storms every year. The children, with glowing eyes and mouths agape, watched Cal's hands act out air currents pushing higher.

"The warm air is forced up by the cold and, as they try to mix, the air swirls and picks up speed until they become one of the deadliest forces known to man."

"Impressive! I didn't realize you needed to understand meteorology to tend cattle," Kate interjected.

The excitement in Cal's face died and an almost audible door slammed shut in his eyes. "This is Tornado Alley. A dumb cowpoke don't even have ta know how ta read ta learn this stuff," he drawled in exaggerated hick and moved back to the window.

"I didn't mean," Kate stammered. "It's just that…"

Cal cut her off. "Looks like the worst is past." He reached a hand to ruffle

Liam's hair. "Maybe you'll live after all, kid."

Soon, even the rain stopped and they were slogging back across the muddy drive, shrugging kids out of soggy coats and ushering them back to bed. Lilly, carried by Cal, was asleep before her curls hit the pillow.

"Hey Mom, come 'ere," Rollins called.

Kate followed the sound of her son's voice and gasped when she beheld the scene in his room. An enormous branch poked through the window and glass was scattered across Rollins' bed.

"Dude! I'm glad I wasn't in bed when that happened!" Rollins exclaimed.

And while Kate was still trying to process what a close call her son had had, Cal was already outside with the tarp she and the kids had been sitting on in the basement. With a bit of "heaving and hoeing" between Cal and Rollins, they pulled the branch out of the way and then tacked the tarp on the outside of the house while Kate cleaned up most of the glass and set up a bed for Rollins on the couch.

"That'll hold 'til morning," Cal said, observing their handiwork. "I'll be back then to finish the job."

"What do we owe you?" Kate asked as she followed Cal to the front door.

"I'm a friend helpin' out a friend," Cal replied. "Ya don't charge for that."

"Well… can I at least offer you some coffee? It's decaf… and it's instant but…"

"Ya don't owe me." Cal turned with hands upraised as if in surrender. "Relax, Kate."

And there was that teasing smirk on his face that seemed to be present every time he looked at her, the condescending grin that made her feel he could see inside her; could see the little sister too squirrelly to hang out with big brother, and the academic geek left out of the "cool" crowd.

"At least let me thank you." Kate was suddenly conscious of her mussed curls and make-up-free face. It was bad enough she had to be standing there in a belted raincoat with bare feet while Cal looked like he'd stepped off the range in his boots and cool-in-any-decade long, canvas coat. "I don't know what we would have done… and Rollins… the window."

"My pleasure," Cal said quietly.

Kate looked up in surprise. The grin was gone. His expression was sincere.

"Well," Kate ran a hand through her hair and stared at the linoleum while Cal took his hat off the peg by the door. "Thank you again."

"Ma'am," he said, and tipped his hat, the grin back in place.

It was 5:00 a.m. when Kate reached to flip off the bedroom light, and caught sight of her reflection in the closet mirror. The auburn curls were mussed and her face was a bit pale. As Jansen always told her, she could pass for a teenager without makeup. With a sigh, Kate turned out the light and fell in bed, trying not to think about why her appearance should matter in the wee morning hours after a storm.

CHAPTER 6

FISTS & CHAINSAWS

Next morning, evidence of the storm was everywhere. The TV news carried footage of a mobile home community less than five miles away completely wiped out by a strong twister. In their own backyard, Kate stared, horrified, at the huge pecan tree, roots plucked out of the ground like a giant weed, laying on its side a mere two feet from their back door.

Part of the school had lost its roof so the kids wouldn't be returning until the next week. Liam was the only one disappointed by this news. Rollins' mood improved immediately and Phoenix was happy to retreat to her room with a book.

About nine a.m. their power went out. Great, now the kids wouldn't even have public television to distract from bickering. Within twenty minutes, Kate wordlessly handed Rollins the dog's leash and held open the front door.

"Good! It's better than being stuck with a whining baby!" He delivered the parting shot at Liam and slammed the door.

Kate watched from the kitchen window as Rollins threw the leash into the weeds and stalked away. He couldn't have looked more miserable if he was being eaten alive by ants. He hardly said two words to her anymore, and when he did it was to grumble about how there was "nothing to do" or other insults about "Hickville." Granted, they had zero internet or cell coverage so even she felt cut off from civilization. But unplugging from computers was something she and Jansen had agreed needed to happen, for many reasons. Unfortunately, until Rollins filled his time with other interests, home felt like being caged with an angry bear. And when Kate asked about friends at school, Rollins just rolled his eyes.

"Rollins, at least try to find something in common," she had implored.

Rollins had thought a moment then responded, "They hate me. I hate them. There. Happy?"

If only he could find a couple good friends,.

Immediately, Kate felt the bile rise in her throat. Friends.

Her mind raced back a few years to a simple dinner scene with a dirty-faced, messy-haired, twelve-year-old Rollins. He'd sat at the table shoving mashed potatoes into his already overflowing mouth as he rambled on about "Dungeon Masters" and his friend Nick's guidebook that revealed secrets about each level of the game and how they'd already reached level five. Apparently, none of the kids at school had done that, so it was a pretty big deal.

What had been her concerns about him then? That he wasn't bathing enough? That he wanted to wear the same "Dungeon Masters" t-shirt for weeks on end? That he would become a computer geek like Nick? Ah, for those simple times.

Soon after, Alex and his family moved in across the street and it was, "Alex this" and "Alex that" and Rollins was always begging to go to Alex's house and fixing his hair like Alex and listening to different music. Suddenly her son took showers without being reminded and was concerned about the label on his shoes and clothing.

For a short time, Kate had been grateful for the changes in her son. He smelled better and dressed better. That was a good thing, right?

Another scene came to mind. In hindsight, she saw red flags all over it.

Thirteen-year-old Rollins had raced into the kitchen. "Mom, can I have twenty bucks?"

"Why?" Kate had licked the spaghetti sauce from her finger thinking how she had ten minutes to get everyone fed, had to locate Phoenix's missing shin guard for Tae kwon do and had to turn in the fund-raising envelope with cookie order money she had sitting by her purse where she wouldn't forget it.

"Alex is getting a new game for me on-line."

"Honey, we've talked about this. No ordering stuff on-line without my supervision."

"But," Rollins voice went up in pitch and volume, "he's already ordered it!"

"Did you tell him to?"

"We talked about it then he found this really good deal he couldn't pass up."

"He's, what, thirteen? How does Alex do this stuff? With his dad?"

"Um, I guess," Rollins had hedged. "So, can I have the money. I'll do chores or whatever."

Kate had dismissed the desperation in Rollins' face. Everything was a huge deal at that age. "Not now. We'll talk later." She had stepped away to yell up the stairs. "Phoenix, did you find it? We're gonna be late. Liam. Lilly. Let's eat!"

When she had turned back around, Rollins was gone.

Later, when she was turning in the cookie earnings, she had discovered the envelope was twenty dollars short.

That moment had been the end of Kate's blissfully ignorant existence. She had worried about Alex's influence on Rollins. But how do you keep your son away from someone who goes to the same school and lives across the street and has serious enticements for a thirteen-year-old boy, like unlimited computer access and tons of unsupervised time? She had met Alex's parents who were television producers and were always speaking into the phone devices attached to their ear. But she didn't know them well enough for a parenting conference. Besides, they were hardly ever there.

So she had started inviting Alex to their house and having him join them for dinner and inviting him over on the weekends. Then, she had reasoned, the boys were at least supervised. And, she truly hoped they could have a good influence on Alex who, according to Rollins, hardly ever saw his parents.

But she couldn't keep up with them all the time. Lilly and Liam required every ounce of energy, and Phoenix had soccer twice a week. Jansen's construction business had been in the midst of a new subdivision, and there was PTA, and piano, and dance lessons, and, and, and.

So Kate had done all she could and then worried to fill in the gaps while her eager, talkative, eldest son had become secretive, moody, and defiant.

"It's just teenage hormones," Jansen and well-meaning friends had assured her and, honestly, she had wanted to believe it.

Kate snapped out of her unpleasant memories to realize she was gripping the edge of the sink so hard her knuckles were white. The blood was pounding in her ears and her jaw ached from clenching it. God, she wanted to hit something, kick something, grab a kid with expensive clothing and smack the smug grin off his face.

She peeked at the kids. The power was back on, so cartoons babysat the younger two and Phoenix had her nose in a book in her room. Kate snuck out the door.

Though the sky was serene and cloudless, the scars of the storm were everywhere with scattered limbs and trees whose leaves had been ripped away. Kate took a deep breath. The air smelled good—clean and earthy.

With a sigh, she sat on the porch step and dropped her throbbing head into her hands. How she wanted to reach into her mind and tear out the torture of her memories, all the regrets, the horror her family had endured.

A solid "whack!" made her raise her head to the sunlight, eyes searching the bedraggled trees and leaf-strewn lawn as a flock of birds not far away twittered into the air. She walked toward the sound that seemed almost like an ax fall. Soon she could hear grunts of effort with each hit. Finally, she saw Rollins tall, black-clad form through the trees, thick branch in hand as he pummeled the trunk of a large oak. When the branch broke, Rollins threw the pieces far and high then resumed his assault on the tree trunk, kicking and punching with frightening intensity.

Kate watched her son vent his rage, tears running down her cheeks as she shared his furious frustration. She understood only too well the need to beat the hell out of something or go berserk. And she didn't need to read her son's mind to know what cocky, fashionably coifed face he was seeing in his rage. Alex's self-assured, charming grin was always in her mind and was a face she had beaten to a pulp in her own fantasies on many an occasion. But try as she might, she could never beat away the memories. Kate wiped an arm across her eyes and stood, ready to keep Rollins from breaking his hands, but a gentle pressure on her shoulder held her back. She turned in surprise to discover Cal.

"Let me handle this, okay?"

Kate was so stunned to find him there, so embarrassed to be crying in front of him and so grateful for help of any kind with Rollins that she nodded her head in mute agreement and ducked behind the nearest tree. As she watched Cal amble toward her son, she replayed the expression she had seen in his eyes, the look that had brought a lump to her throat and made her want to bury her head against the shoulder of his jacket and weep away her fears.

It was an expression she hungered for and had missed desperately, that concerned, fierce determination that had blazed, making his unshaven, angular jaw and lean, denim-clad form as breathtaking as any knight in shining armor.

"Now wha'd that tree ever do to you?" Cal drawled as if commenting on the weather. He pulled out a pair of work gloves and slapped them against his knee, raising a cloud of dust.

Rollins whipped around. "Just doin' some, uh, karate." He wiped a self-conscious hand across his nose, unknowingly leaving a red streak in its wake.

"I can see that, but I don't think your ma's gonna like what you've done to your hands."

Rollins surveyed the ripped knuckles. "Yeah, whatever."

"Ya won't be sayin' that tomorrow when they hurt like hell. Come on. We'll patch ya up."

"How?" Rollins looked dubious as he followed Cal's ambling stroll.

"Don't worry." Cal looked back at Rollins with a grin. "I've had plenty of practice on horses." He chuckled as Rollins hesitated. "Haven't lost a patient... lately."

As they moved off through the trees, Cal talking about nothing in particular with Rollins a step behind, sweatshirt hood firmly in place, Kate breathed a sigh of relief. This was just what Rollins needed, some time with a man who could give him friendship and guidance, hopefully help him through the no-man's-land between boy and adult.

"It should be his father," she grumbled as she headed back to their temporary home between the oak trees.

Kate spied on them as she worked in the kitchen, noting when Cal washed her son's hands in the water from an outdoor spigot and added some sort of goo from a large jar he pulled out of the cab of his truck. Then came the wrapping of bandages and another set of work gloves. And... a chain saw?

She paced nervously in the kitchen, the protective mother warring with the side of her that wanted her son to grow into a self-sufficient young man. Maybe she should have left him punching a tree. Better than accidental amputation, right?

Jansen had kept telling her to relax, to let their son grow up a bit, but the last time she had decided on non-interference... well. The familiar knot tightened in her stomach as those days of mounting fears about Rollins had kept her pacing the floor by night until, finally, she had perused his email account. The next morning, after a sleepless night, she and Jansen had confronted Rollins with the messages.

"Who's 'Bugle Boy'?" Jansen had asked.

Rollins had looked up with a trapped expression. "What?"

"The one who sends you emails with the 'f' word in every sentence." Kate's hands were shaking and there was an acidic taste in her mouth as she held the stack of papers toward her son.

Rollins had flipped back the long strip of hair that fell strategically over one eye. "Huh?"

She hadn't missed the fact her son's eyes were riveted to those papers as if they were a handful of poisonous snakes.

"Son," Jansen had interjected in a calm voice, "there're links to porn sites here. Who is this person? Is it a kid from school?"

"I… I'm not sure." Rollins had looked around at the walls of his room, down at his feet, anywhere but at their faces. "I started getting them a while back. I usually just ignore 'em."

Kate had resisted the urge to peek at his backside and ask, "Pants on fire?" like she had when he was three.

"Oh, come on, Rollins. Your replies are right here." Kate had wished they weren't in her hand and she could believe her son was an innocent victim. Granted, his responses to "Bugle Boy" had not been so crude but… they existed.

"Did ya see the one where I told him to stop sendin' that stuff? Don't I get credit for that?"

"You shoulda blocked 'Bugle Boy' the first time somethin' like this came through," Jansen had replied.

Rollins had shrugged and slumped in his chair.

Jansen's tone had remained even. "We told you the computer was in your room on trial. Trial's over. It's out. Use the one in the family room."

"But, that's not fair! I can't help what someone sends me! It's not my fault! You can't take my computer."

"*Your* computer? Who pays for it?" Kate had felt her own anger rise as Rollins had accused them of spying on him, of not trusting him.

"Ya think?" Kate said aloud to the hateful memories. Her stomach clenched as she recalled the downward spiral of their relationship with Rollins during those horrible months. It was the first of many intervention attempts that had degenerated into a yelling match focused on Rollins' horrible attitude rather than the real issues. No matter what they did, how they tried to love, what privileges they took away, their son was drowning and there didn't seem to be a damn thing they could do to stop it.

Laundry was interrupted by a knock at the back door so Kate abandoned her mountain of unmatched socks to view something truly frightening. There stood Cal and her fourteen-year-old son with chainsaws in hand.

"Just wanted ta let ya know Rollins is givin' me a hand." Cal set his own chainsaw on the ground as he put on his gloves. "Might be a bit loud."

Kate opened and shut her mouth, nonplussed that he wasn't asking her permission. She felt the panic in her eyes as she cast a glance toward the limb-severing beast in Rollins' hand. "Um, well, he's never… "

"I told you she wouldn't go for it," Rollins grumbled.

Cal grinned. "Aw, relax, mama bear. I been cuttin' wood since I was eight.

I'll show 'im the ropes. He'll be fine."

So Kate's protests were squelched before they were on her tongue. Next thing she knew, she had closed the door after a lame, "Be careful."

She glanced through the window in time to see Cal slap her son on the back with a smug grin. Through the manufactured home's thin door, Cal's words came through loud and clear. "Wha'd I tell ya? Piece a cake."

Kate flushed with humiliation as she realized the cowboy had, once more, played her like a fiddle. But as Rollins' face spread into a conspiratorial grin, her mother's heart was reduced to a grateful puddle at Cal's dusty boots. It was six-year-old Rollie, the happy boy she'd thought was only a memory, peeking out of sullen, teenaged eyes. She'd thought that boy was gone forever.

So as the morning wore on, Kate went about her household duties in a haze of joy even as she stole frequent glimpses of the chainsaw duo, bracing herself for the sight of blood. But noon rolled around without mishap and, as Cal and Rollins munched sandwiches on the porch steps, she slid up the kitchen window, unabashedly listening in on their conversation.

"So… you're not gonna tell Mom I was beat up by a tree?"

"I figger a kid's gotta blow off steam every now and then. No big deal. Might as well accomplish somethin' with it."

"The yard sure looks better. We about done?"

"Just gettin' started, city boy. Anyways, from what I saw between you and that tree, you got a lot of steam to blow. But that's a good thing if I'm gonna hire ya."

"Hire me?"

"There's money to be made cuttin' and haulin' wood. When winter comes, folks'll pay good money for firewood and I need help to be prepared."

"Money'd be cool," Rollins mumbled around a mouthful of sandwich.

"Well, nobody's gonna hand it to ya, Slick." Cal aimed a napkin at Rollins' head. "Let's see what you're made of."

Soon they had a large pile of logs cut to Cal's specific dimensions, the perfect size for a fireplace, stacked neatly beside the old house.

But Cal was just getting started. While there was still daylight, chainsaws buzzed and branches fell as they cleared a wide swath around the manufactured home then started on the jungle around Pedigo Manor, trimming monstrous shrubbery and branches that in some places had been bent to the ground. Still they cut and bound and hauled, pausing only for gulps of icy water, as the sun sank lower in the sky. After showering and carefully bandaging his numb hands, Rollins nearly nodded off into his supper and didn't budge until eight the next morning when Cal was at their door ready for another day's work.

By day three, Rollins could hardly move to get out of bed but slowly, as the week progressed, his sore muscles became more accustomed to the backbreaking labor and his blistered hands began to callous. On day five, Cal handed Rollins one hundred dollars and said he was hired for the weekends.

CHAPTER 7

DOING HARD THINGS

"Miz Walden? This is Coach Wills. Wanna talk to ya about your boy."

So began the phone conversation that had perplexed Kate so much she sat with the phone still in her hand and did nothing for a full five minutes, such a surprising event that Lilly asked, "Mommy, are you thick?"

Kate had to face it. She was prejudiced. Oh, not on racial lines, small town folk might have forgiven her that. But Kate, after years of rolling her eyes behind the backs of strutting letter jackets in high school and college, was prejudiced against… football. In her new hometown, that was akin to blasphemy.

She recalled Coach Wills' incredulous pause when she had said, "We'll have to think about it."

"Alright, but I'll need an answer soon." Another pause then Coach Wills said, "Miz Walden, it's true your boy's got ability and I'd like to groom him for coming years, but I see myself as more than just an athletic director. There're some kids that need football, the discipline, the team, the challenge." He had stopped abruptly and cleared his throat. "Well, we've got equipment for 'im if he wants to suit up tomorrow afternoon."

Every other parent she knew would have been bursting with pride to have the Coach Wills personally invite their son to try out for his championship-winning Falcons.

Alas, a long list of "buts" jostled in Kate's head.

He could get hurt.

His schoolwork might suffer.

Jocks were animals whose bodies had outgrown the size of their brains.

Schools should focus on the three R's, not on turning boys into gladiators.

Small-town sports eclipsed scholastic achievement.

And… he could get hurt. The statistics on concussions due to football rattled through Kate's mind. She winced as visions of life flight helicopters and Rollins in a body cast trounced through her head.

A knock interrupted Kate's stupor and she moved, phone still in her hand, to the front door to find Cal standing there, a catalog of light fixtures in his hand. "Hey, Jance said to run these by you. We need two for the master suite and one for the downstairs bathroom." He pointed a finger at the pictures on the page that swam before Kate's unfocused eyes.

"That one's fine," Kate mumbled.

"Which one and for where?" He glanced up to find she wasn't even looking at the book. "I thought you gals went crazy for this decoratin' stuff."

Kate gave an apologetic grin. "Sorry. Bigger decisions on my mind, I guess." She paused a moment. "What can you tell me about Coach Wills?"

"Known 'im for years. Salt of the earth. Why?"

"He wants Rollins on the football team."

"Congratulations!" Cal paused and cocked his head. "So why do you look like somebody died?"

Kate hesitated, memories of Cal's mocking, "mama bear" ringing in her ears. "Nothing. As for the light fixtures, you're more qualified to choose so… "

Cal put out a hand and the closing door thudded against it. "Hey, hey, hey, hold on there. Wha'd I say?"

"Nothing. I just need to… think things through."

"The fixtures? The football thing? Ya gotta help me here." Cal bent down to force himself into Kate's line of sight.

Kate smiled and put up a hand to stifle a snicker.

"What?" He lifted up his baseball cap and shoved it back down on his head in frustration. "I tell you, woman, your moods change faster than the wind. Haven't figured why you're ticked and you're already laughin' at me."

"I'm sorry, you just reminded me of some… one."

Cal put his fists on his hips and stuck his chin in the air. "Handsome devil?"

At that, Kate laughed out loud. When she looked up into Cal's confused face, the hilarity she tried to suppress escaped with a snort and, just like in school when laughter is forbidden, she lost it. Finally, as she wiped away tears of mirth she explained. "I'm sorry, for a second there you reminded me of… of Winston."

"Aw!" Cal threw up his hands and stepped away. "Aw! A dog?"

"No, no it's just, you know, he does something wrong and then ducks his head and looks up with those big eyes."

Cal crossed his arms and looked away with a wounded expression. "Guess it's good to know where I stand."

"But he's really cute when he does it." Kate tried and failed once again to keep a straight face.

Suddenly, chubby arms wrapped around her knees and Lilly's happy face peeked from the vicinity of Kate's hip. "Hi, Mithter Cal!"

"Hey there, Lilly."

"Where's the funny?"

"You're lookin' at 'im, kid."

"Mithter. Cal, you're thiwee," Lilly chuckled then peered up at Kate's face. "Mommy, you're tho pwitty! Like a pwinthess!"

Kate cocked a suspicious eyebrow. "Alright, whaddaya want?"

"I have a wowwipop?"

"Not before lunch."

"Pweeeth!"

"No, Sweetie."

Lilly's shoulders slumped.

"So do you still think mommy's pretty?"

Lilly's eyes sparkled. "No."

"You!" Kate reached down and tickled Lilly's belly causing a peal of shrieks and giggles. "And no you can't climb the cabinet and get it yourself!" Lilly ran from her in a whirl of chubby limbs, laughter and curls and Kate found herself gazing after her daughter, savoring the after-scent of baby shampoo.

"You're a good mom."

Kate looked up and rolled her eyes. "You know better than that. Rollins complains about me all the time, right? I can't do anything right in his eyes."

"But you don't give up."

"Don't you believe it."

"Well, not like my mom anyway. She skipped out." Cal shrugged. "I probably drove her to it." He grinned, but this time the humor didn't quite make it to his eyes.

"I bet she gave up on herself, not you. Mom's tend to be their own worst critics, ya know." There was an awkward pause and Kate wondered if she had somehow offended him.

"So what was troublin' you just now?"

"You'll make fun of me."

"Then hurry up and spill it so's I can restore some manhood here."

"Alright. It's the football thing."

"Have a seat," Cal indicated the porch step. "The doctor is in."

Kate sat and stared at her hands clasped around her knees.

"Uh, oh. She's back."

"What?"

"Uptight. Serious. Thinkin' too hard. All the fun beat out of 'er."

"Gimme a break. Not everybody can be 'free-as-the-wind-Cowboy-ridin'-the-range'."

"Yeah, somebody's got to get beat up with responsibilities. Isn't that what it means to be grown up?"

"Who are you, Peter Pan?"

Cal tilted back the bill of his hat and lifted his face to the sun. "Nah. I just never got it why people think bein' responsible means forgettin' how to have fun. Let me ask you, when's the last time you laughed like you did just now?"

"Oh come on. I'm not that bad, am I?"

Cal fixed his too-blue eyes on her. "How long?"

Kate looked away and thought a minute. How long, indeed. It certainly hadn't been lately so it had to be "Before." Before hell broke loose in their lives, that is.

Kate sighed and wrinkled her nose. "Okay, ya got me. A long time."

"Tell me about football. Seems perfect for Rollins. In fact, now don't get mad, but I told Coach he ought to give 'im a try."

"Ah, you're to blame."

"Hold on there. It's every boy's dream, ain't it, ta be a football star?"

Again Kate wrinkled her nose, but this time it was as if at a bad smell. "Why? To spend the rest of your life lookin' back at the good ol' days? To squeak by in education because you're a hero on the field, then graduate with the writing skills of a third grader?"

Cal gave a low whistle. "Somebody's bitter."

Kate's mouth gaped. "I am not!"

"What was it? Dumped by the team captain?"

"No!"

"Didn't make the cheerleading squad?"

Kate rolled her eyes. "I'll have you know my big brother played football, even went to college on a scholarship."

"And where'd that leave you?"

"Whaddaya mean?"

"Brother's a local hero, apple of Daddy's eye. Mustabeen a hard act to follow."

Kate felt her gut twist. She had loved her big brother. Admired him as her hero. She felt her jaw clench. "I never saw it that way."

"Really? I'm jealous of 'im and I've never set eyes on your brother."

"Point is, football chewed him up and spit him out. It killed him when he didn't make All-American, when he wasn't able to go pro. What was he left with but bad knees and stories of 'the glory days'?"

"Ah!" A self-satisfied smile spread over Cal's face.

"What."

"Just gettin' a clearer picture. And what did you get a scholarship for?"

"How do you know I got a scholarship?"

"There's too much fight in ya to be outdone."

"I wasn't trying to 'outdo' anybody. We were raised to do our best."

Cal put his hands up as if in surrender. "Sure, sure. So tell me about your scholarship."

"We were talking about football."

"No. We were talkin' about your attitude toward football."

"You trying to psychoanalyze me?"

"I never said you were psycho."

Kate narrowed her eyes. "Point is, I didn't like what football did to my brother."

"Does he regret it?"

"What? Not making pro? Of course."

"No. Does he regret the journey? The memories, the friends, all that."

Kate had been ready to answer, but the reply lodged in her throat.

Cal persisted. "Has he ever said, 'Little sis, I wish I'd never played'?"

"Well, um, not exactly."

"Then this isn't about him. It's about you."

"No, it's not."

"Yep. He eclipsed you and it ticked you off."

"He did not. I was a Rhodes scholar and I had a scholarship in volleyball."

"But that didn't light the same kinda fire in Daddy, did it?"

"You're way off base."

"Just callin' a spade a spade."

"Well, you're barking up the wrong tree this time. Anyway, I've got things to do." Kate rose.

Cal stood. "So what're ya gonna tell Coach Wills?"

"That's my business." Kate tried to keep her expression light, but she felt her mouth twist into a hard line. "Oh wait. There's no such thing in this town."

"Don't you believe it. We've all got secrets. But," he held back up the catalog, "I still need a verdict."

So Kate flipped through the light fixtures and made her selections although her mind was preoccupied with irritation toward Cal. Finally, she shut the door a bit too hard and descended on dirty dishes in the kitchen sink with undue vengeance. How dare he say she was jealous of her brother? How dare he smugly sit there analyzing her life? The stupid cowboy knew nothing. Nothing! Obnoxious. Nosey. Judgmental.

The knife she had been wielding to cut Lilly's apple slipped and sliced a deep cut in her finger. Lilly ran in as Kate was just sticking the gushing appendage under the faucet's stream, causing the water to run red. With one look, Lilly ran, shrieking, "Mithter. Cal! Mithter. Cal!"

"Lilly! Come back here. I'm okay!"

But Lilly was already out the door so Kate grabbed a paper towel, wrapped it around her hand and raced to catch up. Lilly had already reached Cal's truck and hopped about shouting, "Mommy cut off her thinger!"

"Lilly, I'm fine. Stop that."

"But you did!"

"See," Kate bent and unwrapped the paper, "I still have ten."

"Eeeeew!" Lilly exclaimed.

Cal peered at the bloody mass of paper towel. "Let me take a look."

"It's fine. I just didn't have time for a Band-Aid."

"That's gonna take more than a Band-Aid. Come 'ere." Cal walked toward his pickup and began rummaging in the toolbox. "Might be able ta save ya a trip to the emergency room."

Kate felt her eyes widen and she tucked her hand behind her back.

Cal looked up and grinned. "Have a problem with needles and cat gut?" He chuckled. "Aw, get over here city gal. No stitches. I promise."

"Mommy, I'll hold your hand," Lilly offered.

Kate swallowed hard and tried to be calm for her daughter's sake, but her hand trembled as Cal inspected it. He poured some liquid from a brown bottle over the wound.

"I use it ta get grease off my driveway."

"What?" Kate yanked her hand away.

Cal grinned. "Peroxide."

"Oh."

"What were ya doin'? Choppin' logs?"

"Apple."

"Shoulda known not to chop angry. Nearly severed a toe with an ax that way once."

"I wasn't angry."

"Uh huh. And that was kindness spittin' from your eyes a little while ago."

Kate kept her voice low as she shot a wary glance toward Lilly who had squatted down to pet Winston. "I dislike it when people jump to conclusions."

"I've usually found the more riled people get, the closer I am to the mark."

Kate forgot the angry comment on her tongue when the sticky goo Cal dabbed on her finger dug in with a stab of pain. "Ow!"

"Sorry, that'll sting a bit."

"Thanks for the warning," Kate said through clenched teeth as she bit back another yelp.

"Too used to workin' on animals. They don't require a bedside manner."

"What is that stuff?" Kate cast a wary eye toward the smelly substance that resembled an overgrown jar of rubber cement.

"Liquid bandage. Now," Cal pulled out what appeared to be a tiny Scotch tape dispenser, "these strips will hold it closed like stitches, but you should still go easy on it awhile."

Kate studied the glint of rusty waves with strands of silver as Cal's head bent over her hand, admiring the confidence of his movements as he unwound the first-aid tape and ripped the end with his teeth.

"I should probably apologize for earlier," Kate began.

"Naw. As usual I stuck my big foot in my mouth and my big nose in somebody else's business." Cal smoothed the tape and released her hand. "I'll re-bandage it tomorrow."

"That won't be necessary."

"Ya can't bandage that on your own. Jance is out of town and Rollins won't be in 'til late tomorrow, what with football practice an' all."

Kate felt a wave of anger, but bit back her sharp retort when she caught the teasing glint in Cal's eye. "What about that big foot and nose?"

"Doesn't bother me. I'm used to it," Cal drawled. "Just tossin' in my opinion. Think it'd be good for the kid."

"And when did it become your business?"

"My friends are always my business. If I didn't care, I'd keep my mouth shut."

And Cal just looked at her. No anger. No blame. Just still waters reflecting her storm-tossed emotions.

"Um, thanks for doctoring… my finger," Kate mumbled and, with Lilly in tow, she set a quick pace toward the manufactured home.

But she wasn't fast enough to miss Cal's parting tease. "Rollins is pretty good with that chainsaw now. Might oughta let him slice the apples."

CHAPTER 8

VALLEY OF THE SHADOW

"Don't see what it would hurt. No one says he's signing up for life. So coach really called and asked for him?" Jansen couldn't hide the pride in his words, even through the phone. "Wow. That's somethin'."

"But Jansen, I keep thinking about Aidan. His knees and neck will give him trouble the rest of his life all because of a stupid game."

"Honey, this is high school. Might be just what he needs to make some friends, ya know, fit in."

Kate hung up the phone and paced the floor grumbling. "Just like a guy! Probably sit in the stands and slap his buddies on the back while Rollins breaks his."

She stopped and a slow smile spread over her face.

"Rollins," she breathed.

After all, this decision was his as well, right?

Never was football presented in such a negative light. Kate emphasized the grueling practices, even in the rain, and the smelly locker room and the coaches with their whistles barking orders like Marine drill sergeants.

"And you know your Uncle Aidan still has trouble with his back because of that accident in college."

Rollins shrugged. "Yeah. What's for dinner?"

So Kate ended the day satisfied Rollins wasn't interested in football. That was that.

"Uh, Mom? I'm stayin' for football. Can you pick me up around six?"

"But I thought we… you… had decided not to."

"Yeah, well, can't hurt to give it a shot. So can you pick me up?"

Kate spluttered her agreement and hung up the phone, stunned. What could have happened to change his mind?

She looked through the kitchen window toward Cal who whistled as he toted an armload of crown molding up the steps of the old house. Hmmm. Perhaps her finger needed a new bandage after all.

Soon Kate stood once again by Cal's truck as he redressed her wound. "So, Rollins is staying for football practice," Kate commented.

"Can't hurt to give it a shot," Cal mumbled around the first-aid tape in his teeth.

"You talked him into it, didn't you?"

Cal didn't miss a beat as he smoothed the tape around her finger. "Yep."

"But Rollins had already decided he didn't want to."

"Can't know 'til he tries."

"You deliberately went around me."

Cal ignored the accusation. "Wha'd Jance say about it?"

"Don't drag him into this." Kate felt her face flush with anger as she yanked her hand away.

"He's the boy's father, Kate."

"You still had no right... "

"And, as his father, he realizes Rollins needs some sense knocked into 'im and it's not gonna happen around a protective mama bear."

"Don't call me that."

"Rollins needs this. If he doesn't get to fight on the field he's gonna explode off it."

"And how many sons have you raised?"

Finally. A flash of anger in the laid-back manner as Cal slapped his work gloves on his thigh. "Woman, you do beat all!"

"Now, I understand you're Jansen's friend and you're working here but... "

"But the hired hand ain't allowed an opinion."

Kate's mouth hung open a second. "That's not what... "

"Look here," Cal took a step closer. "I'm involved, whether you like it or not. I don't know what you got up your craw. That's your business. And I don't know what's eatin' Rollins, but just maybe I've got a clearer view and some common sense about what a boy needs to be a man."

Kate looked up into Cal's too-near face, her fists clenched around the desire to slap it. His words had stirred up a well of poison that made her want to spit and cry and curse and break something, starting with that chauvinistic expression.

But, damn, the tears. Why did she have to cry when she was angry? She hated women who used tears to control the opposite sex. Plus, it was too embarrassing, too… female.

She wheeled and just barely controlled the desire to run to the house where she let the screen door slam and added the unsatisfying thud of the thin front door. Her gut was in knots and her head pounded with the phrases, "clearer view" and "common sense."

"Up my craw," Kate grumbled as she slammed the clothes into the washer and slapped sheets into place on the beds.

When Liam and Phoenix got off the bus after school, Kate fought the urge to hop in the car and spy on football practice. However, when her neighbor, Ima, showed up as if on cue and offered to stay with the "younguns," Kate headed out a bit early, relieved to discover other parents, mostly dads, leaning against the bleachers to watch the final drills.

When the team disbursed, Coach Wills called, "Walden!" and Rollins trotted over to him, helmet in hand. The conversation was short but, to Kate, it seemed Rollins walked away from it minus his customary slouch.

Then, rather than joining the rest of the team trotting toward the locker room, Rollins picked up his duffle bag on the sidelines and headed toward Kate. She knew communal showers were one aspect of team camaraderie her son would avoid.

On the drive home, Rollins actually offered information without prompting. "I won the forty-yard dash."

"That's great. So did you like it?"

A lift of the eyebrows, a shrug, then he stared out the window.

How Kate wished he would talk more, if nothing else, to keep her safe from remembering why her son didn't like to shower away from home.

When they pulled up in front of the house, Rollins grabbed his bag and bolted. Kate gripped the steering wheel and took a deep breath. She had to shove down the past and act normal for Ima and the kids.

Kate choked on the memories and emotions throughout the rest of the evening. She had to admit Rollins was a bit more pleasant than usual, even going so far as to compliment their dinner of canned chili.

But when all had settled in for the night, even Rollins who took an extended shower and went to bed early, loneliness descended on Kate like a choking fog. The walls of the manufactured home leaned in until she felt her lungs would collapse with their weight. She burst out the front door in a claustrophobic panic and stood drinking in gulps of moist evening air, the night noises of wind in branches, frogs, and crickets singing an incongruent lullaby.

As if on cue, the moon's glow appeared over the roof of the old house and grew, bit by bit, into a bright three quarter sphere. Was it an optical trick that made some of the glow melt into a small shape on the third floor balcony? Kate snorted. She didn't have time for imaginary fears. Reality was scary enough.

She had never believed in ghosts, had always considered fascination with the paranormal a waste of time. So what if the rumors were true and there was some tortured soul wandering the halls of Pedigo Manor in the dead of night? Great. They would have a lot in common with her.

Her feet crunched on the gravel as she drew closer to the silent, shadowed structure. Nothing would entice her to go inside. It wasn't fear of ghosts. She just couldn't stand the thought of being shut in with the beast of her past. Best to remain outside where she could see something larger, something unaffected by her personal hell. Thus Kate skirted the porch and headed toward the side yard where Rollins and Cal had cleared a path. As soon as she knew none of the kids would see her even if they looked out a window, the bitter memories pried open their vaults and a rush of dread swept her body.

It was a year and a half ago. They might never have found out if Jansen's friend on the police force hadn't been investigating sexual predators on the internet.

Jansen had called Kate into his office after the kids were in bed, his face ashen.

"I've gotta show you somethin'. There's no easy way."

With that, he had pushed a button on his computer and the poorly lit image of a young man came to life on the screen. The kid was tall with dark hair. His back was to the camera as he stood to pee into a toilet.

"That's gross. Do we have to watch this?" Kate said as she rose to leave.

"Wait." Something in Janson's voice had sent a chill through Kate's body.

The young man had turned toward the shower to undress.

Kate's world had ground to a halt as bile rose in her throat.

It was Rollins.

But the beast in the closet wasn't finished. With a shudder, she re-lived what remained of that night, the one she thought at the time was as horrible as things could get.

Rollins' expression when they had shown him the video was burned on her mind. The color had drained from his face and he had jumped to his feet to fumble for the button to freeze the image.

"What is this? Why is this on there?"

And when Kate and Jansen remained silent, he had stared at them, the horror in his eyes shattering Kate's world. "You can't think I knew about this!"

The rest of that night and into the next day had been a journey through hell.

Rollins had denied any knowledge of the video. Tears had flowed as he begged them to believe him.

As to who was responsible? They hadn't thought hard for that one. The bathroom in the video was Alex's.

Kate clutched her arms around her chest like a straight jacket and rocked back and forth in the moonlit garden as the events of the following afternoon poured over her, gasoline to the fire of her pain.

Kate had opened the front door to Alex's dad, a once-stunning man, now a bit soft around the edges, but always attired in nothing but the finest.

"I suppose you heard what happened," he had said without preamble.

"Yes. We were up most of the night with Rollins."

"What do you plan to do about it?" He had leaned toward her a bit.

"We're not sure…"

"Because I thought it only fair you know we're considering pressing charges."

"*You're* considering pressing charges."

"Your son is completely out of control."

"*My* son… "

"Assault, death threats…"

"What are you talking about?"

"Your son attacked Alex."

Fear exploded in Kate's stomach. "Is he okay?"

Had that been a glint of triumph in the man's eyes? "See for yourself." He had shoved a legal-sized envelope into her hand.

Kate had pulled out the photographs and stared in horror at Alex's bloodied, bruised, and swollen face.

Alex's dad had moved a bit closer and his voice in Kate's ear had been calm, and confident. "I'm sure we don't want this situation to escalate into something ugly, especially for your boy. A mark on his record of 'assault with deadly intent' would hardly put him on the path to success." His voice lowered further, taking on a curdling sweetness. "As far as the internet thing, you just try to push that and my lawyers will come at you with guns blazing. The video will be presented as evidence. It'll be in the papers. Everyone will talk. Do you really want to do that to Rollins?"

Kate had looked up into what, for her, had become the eyes of the devil himself.

"Keep the photos," he had added as a parting shot. "I've got more."

Kate was alone in the darkness beside the hulking, moonlit form of Pedigo Manor. Give her ghosts anytime. They were nothing compared to the monsters in her head.

She didn't have to be a good example for the kids, didn't even have to maintain sanity for Jansen. A sob broke from her throat and she sank to her knees in the grass, hidden from the light of the moon by the old house's shadow.

This anger... no... she couldn't call it that. This was a beast devouring her insides. She was trapped, drowning, suffocating, and burning alive all at once as she relived that horrible night.

~~

Rollins' face had drained of color as he had stared at the photos of Alex.

"But, I only hit him once!" Rollins had insisted. "He wasn't even bleeding!"

"You admit you hit him," Jansen had stated. "Was anyone else around?"

"No. I went to his house. I didn't wanna bring this up at school."

Jansen had shut his eyes. "No witnesses. Not good."

"But I didn't do that to him. You believe me, don't you?" Rollins' frightened eyes had mirrored Kate's panic.

"Whether we do or not," she had struggled to keep her voice quiet, "we can't prove anything. The evidence is on their side."

"His dad's in the movie business. Maybe it's special effects, ya know, make-up," Rollins had studied the photos again.

Jansen had raked a hand through his hair as the lines in his face deepened. "I'll discuss it with Tom," he referred to his police officer friend. "Maybe he'll have some ideas. For now, stay away from Alex; his house, his parents, his email. They'd only use it against you."

There had been a knock on their back door, so quiet they almost missed it. Kate had dreaded to answer, afraid it might be Alex's father. She had pushed aside the curtain that covered the panes of glass in the door.

There had been Alex, his face even worse than the pictures had shown. This was no special effect and no act. The boy had indeed been beat up. And he was terrified.

Kate snapped back to the present to discover her arms clutched her shoulders and her fingernails dug into her skin.

She opened her eyes to the night sky, to the menacing old house whose shadow hovered over her. Or was it extending a protective wing?

All Kate knew was that the poison refused to be dammed any longer. She hardly noticed, in the midst of her sobs, when Winston edged close and curled up by her side. There, flanked by an orphan dog and a derelict house, Kate wept like there was no tomorrow.

Kate woke in a fetal position, the scent of earth in her nose and dry leaf bits in her hair. She was sore and confused but… peaceful.

She sat up and Winston whimpered in his sleep. Perhaps he was the reason she didn't feel cold even though a chill wind blew through the treetops. Fragments of a dream still flitted on the edge of her consciousness, nothing concrete except for a hand stroking the hair from her face while a gentle voice said, "There, there."

She wrapped her arms around her knees and tried to make sense of the fact she had just lost her grip, had leapt right off that brink of no return… and had survived the fall.

Perhaps this was the comfort of insanity? She nudged the memories and they leapt up, live coals longing to flare into a wildfire. Nope. She was still sane enough to keep the beast alive. But this peace, no matter how temporary, was too good. The hell of yesteryear would have to wait its turn.

She glanced up toward the moon that bathed her in a soft glow. A good chunk of time must have passed for the light to have shifted so far.

The moment. How long had it been since she had lived in the moment? Usually she was tormented by the past, dreading the future, and enduring the present.

Although nothing was "fixed" and tomorrow promised more to make her cringe, Kate chose to sit on the ground with a sleeping dog at her side, bathed in silvery moonlight and caressed by a soft, clean breeze… and… breathe.

CHAPTER 9

ROOTS OF PREJUDICE

Kate pushed a cart through the narrow aisles of Colt's Grocery, manhandling the wayward beast that managed to keep at least two wheels off the floor at all times while she tried to keep tabs on Lilly and check the shelf dates of every grocery item. Colt's could afford to be lax and overpriced since it was fifteen miles to their nearest competition.

"Find everything ya need, Miz Walden?" Ella Colt chatted as she rang up the groceries.

"Mmmhmm." Kate tried to match Ella's friendly smile as she pried a dusty candy bar out of Lilly's fingers.

"Been hearin' a lot about your boy these days. Here ya go, Sweetheart." Ella plopped a round tub of nickel candy on the counter. "A treat for bein' such a good girl."

"Only one," Kate admonished as Lilly went fishing through the bright wrappers with greedy eyes.

"Hear he knocked ol' Dwight Adams right on his can in football practice."

"Really?" Kate tried to look duly impressed.

"Ever seen that Adams kid? Has ta be over two hundred fifty pounds if he's an ounce. And mean! Hoo! That boy'd stare down a rattlesnake!"

"Doesn't sound like a very good choice for an enemy."

"Enemy! Are you kiddin'? Dwight's followin' your boy around like a lap dog and tellin' everybody the story. Coach Wills is mighty glad, too."

"Really."

"Fast and mean. Aw, it's like Christmas for Coach. Now if that boy can catch a ball, won't that be somethin'!"

"That'd sure be somethin'." Kate tried to smile as she coaxed the extra handful of candy from Lilly's clutches.

Obviously, there wasn't a problem with Rollins' "street-fighting" tendencies if they were helping to move a pigskin ball downfield.

That afternoon, Kate drove to the football field and sat in the car, windows down to let in the unseasonably hot breeze, as the team ran drills and practiced formations. She was beginning to look forward to this daily respite when Ima would show up and shoo her out the door to fetch Rollins from practice.

It would seem that Kate, with a star football player for a brother, would know more about the game, but her understanding was shallow. Compared to the old sages who were permanent fixtures on the sidelines discussing the action with more finesse than professional sports announcers, Kate was ignorance personified. She could only guess it was a language learned from playing the game.

She had played a little—in the yard when Aidan needed someone to knock down to catch a pass from dad. She had even learned to throw a mean spiral. But she was a girl. So she became captain of the volleyball team and won the English and Science awards. Dad said he was proud and had even attended a few of her games.

But he'd never missed one of Aidan's.

Suddenly the car was too stuffy. Kate threw open the door and made her way to the sidelines, keeping a buffer between her and the middle-aged commentators.

Rollins was with the group running passing drills.

"That Quinn's got an arm on 'im, don't 'e," Kate overheard.

Low whistles of appreciation sounded as the young man called Quinn threw a tight arc that threaded between two defenders to land in the outstretched fingers of his receiver.

She saw Rollins, tall and skinny compared to the other players, one toe back like at the start of a race. A short blast of a whistle and Rollins took off, leveled one defender, dodged the other, then reached his hands out for the ball that fell into his fingers. Even to Kate's amateur viewpoint, Rollins had gone a good ten yards farther than the other runner.

"That's what I'm talkin' 'bout!" one of the sideline announcers yelled. "Beautiful, Rolls!"

Kate turned toward the familiar voice and spied Cal, squatting close to the fifty-yard line, excitement etched on the angular features under his customary baseball cap.

She felt a pang of sadness. That should be Jansen shouting for their son. But at least he had changed his weekly flights to be home on Fridays in time for the games. She should be grateful something lured him home these days. But even when he was there, Saturdays and most of Sunday, his attention was on the old Pedigo Manor.

Didn't do much for a girl's ego.

Why had he moved them here then taken on the job in California? Sure there was the expense of renovation and his need for employment. Kate got that. But was there another reason? Something or *someone* that also drew him back to California?

Ugh! Usually the kids clamored too loud for her to hear these ugly thoughts.

"So ya made it," Cal was there beside her. "Rollins is lookin' good, huh?"

"Yeah."

"How's the finger? Bandage holdin' up?"

"Fine."

"Heard from Jance lately?"

"Sure. He'll be home Friday," Kate answered a bit too quickly.

"That boy's gonna work himself into an early grave if he's not careful."

"Thanks for the encouragement."

"Aw, I'd probably work that hard too, if I had what he has."

Kate stared at the field where Coach Wills addressed the tight circle of boys. Had that been a compliment?

"Look," Cal went on in a quieter voice, "I was out of line the other day. Think I'm developin' a taste for shoe leather."

An awkward pause hung between them.

"So?" Cal prompted.

In unspoken agreement, Kate mirrored Cal's stealth, eyes on the field, expression unperturbed. "Give me a minute to get over the shock. Was that humility?"

"Yes, eatin' crow here, big piece a humble pie. Ya gonna help me out?"

"Okay, I agree. You were out of line."

"Aw, you're heartless."

"I thought you macho types like it when women agree with you. Or would you ask me to stoop to false repentance?"

There was the hint of a smile in his voice. "Touché'. Naw, I'd never ask ya to be less than you are."

"Does this mean you'll keep your boot out of your mouth in the future?"

"Prob'ly not."

"So what's the point?"

Cal chuckled. "Sure make me feel better."

"Well, forget it." Kate quipped with mock sternness.

"Good ta know where I stand."

Practice was over. Rollins was trotting toward them.

"Ya know, I'll be happy to bring 'im home after practices," Cal offered.

"Nice time of day ta take a break."

"Thanks for the offer, um, I'll think it over."

Rollins was silent on the way home and Kate wondered if he would talk if Cal was driving him. That guy had certainly gotten her to talk.

"What're you smiling about?" Rollins' question caught her off guard.

"Hmmm? Oh, I was just thinking about some of those passes you caught. Pretty impressive." Kate smoothed past the lie. "You have homework?"

CHAPTER 10

DEMONS OF THE PAST

Kate watched the younger kids board the bus. She felt a special tug on her heart as Phoenix's bright curls disappeared inside the yellow transport. Her daughter was quieter than ever these days. She was making excellent grades but her teacher said Phoenix sat alone during recess or even remained inside claiming a stomachache. Lately, she'd been wetting the bed, which was most unpleasant since she slept next to Kate when Jansen was away.

Rollins had arranged transportation in a buddy's pick-up so he got to sleep a bit longer. She was worried about him too. Sure, he didn't argue with Liam anymore, but he hardly engaged in conversation with any of them these days. Well, he would have to converse with her this morning. His report card demanded it. Maybe he was too tired, doing too much. Maybe he needed to quit cutting wood on the weekends. She'd discuss that possibility with Cal since Jansen wouldn't even be home this weekend. The planning for the new subdivision was at a crucial juncture and walkthroughs for investors were scheduled for the weekend. Was Jansen more upset about missing Rollins' ballgame or about missing family time? Perhaps missing her? Kate couldn't tell.

She moved through the house trying to set things right after the morning rush. A tornado ripping through could hardly do more damage than her frantic kids finding matching socks, scattered homework, and lost shoes. Rollins' room was worse than ever. He used to be a neat freak, but lately he'd taken to wearing the same jeans a week at a time and having to be told to change his shirt. He should be up by now to have time to shower and eat. Also, the talk about his report card couldn't wait. Why in the world would his grades slip from B's to C's and D's in six weeks?

"Rollins! Time to get a move on," Kate called as she opened the door on the cave-like dimness of his room. She wrinkled her nose at the musty smell.

Wait a minute. This was more than the odor of dirty socks and sweaty football jerseys. Memories washed over her like a tidal wave. This was how the family room smelled in the morning when her father had fallen asleep, again, in his lazy boy recliner, beer cans strewn on the floor and end table beside him. This was how Uncle Horace had smelled when she was a kid at that family reunion and Horace had wanted her to play a "tickle" game. She flicked on the glaring overhead light and whipped open the blinds. Rollins moaned and turned, pulling the pillow over his head.

Usually his equipment bag remained untouched by Kate. She'd made it clear the pads and cleats were his business as long as all the sweaty items made it into the wash. This morning, however, something red and shiny peeked through the gaping zipper. She yanked open the bag and empty beer cans clattered onto the floor. Rollins sat up with a start only to grab his head and lay down again. Beneath the empty cans and shoulder pads sat an untouched six-pack.

Kate's heart and lungs clamped shut. She hardly cared if she took the next breath. She knew only too well what had caused the changes in Rollins. She'd lived it all before.

Her dad's business had failed and he had spent more and more time away from home. When he was home, he spent the time drinking beer in his chair, TV remote in hand. Her parents' marriage had dissolved, her mom had started working as a waitress and Kate was the primary caregiver to her little sister, Rosalynn. Somehow, Kate blamed it all on the beer that had sucked the life out of her father and had ruined her life in the process.

She pulled the pillow away from Rollins' tousled head and studied the still-smooth cheek with peach fuzz barely visible on the upper lip. Dark circles rimmed his eyes.

How could she have been so blind? Had she not wanted to see it? For a moment Kate watched her son, recalling how she would gaze in wonder when Rollins was a chubby-cheeked newborn, tiny fist clenched on the corner of his blanket, rosebud lips puckering over toothless gums; the perfect picture of peace. With a sigh, Kate bent closer. No doubt. The sickly stale breath said it all.

Wordlessly she sank to the floor still hugging the pillow, shaking in the effort to control the emotional overload. She couldn't fall apart. She had to strike hard and fast. He was only fourteen. Maybe discipline and a tighter leash would straighten him out. She'd call his coach and teachers, find out who he was hanging with, perhaps track down his supplier.

Tires crunched on the drive. Probably Cal, arriving early to start work renovating the old bathroom today. Maybe he'd know something. After all, Rollins spent more time with him than anyone these days.

As she crossed the drive, Cal emerged from the truck, customary jeans, t-shirt and a paint-speckled, open flannel shirt hung from his lean frame.

Kate hardly knew where to start. How do you ask casually, "Hi. Has my son told you who gives him beer?" She folded her arms tightly across her chest. Maybe her hands would stop shaking if she hid them. "Um, Hi, uh... I just found... I mean, Rollins has..."

Cal's expression morphed from casual to alert to concern as Kate felt her composure crumble. Something in his eyes reminded her of Jansen in a fully attentive, caring moment. If only he was here.

"What about Rollins?"

"I think he's been drinking, a lot, for a few weeks actually." As Kate fumbled for words, her eyes fell on a red something in the floorboard of the pick-up. It was then Cal's turn to watch Kate's mood alter at the speed of light. By the time her eyes shot up to his, the near-tearful helplessness was replaced by the narrowed eyes of a snake ready to strike.

"So Cal, teachin' him to handle more than just a chainsaw?"

"What're you talkin' about?"

"I, *we*, trusted you. I can't believe you'd give him beer. He's only fourteen!"

Cal held up his hands as if at gunpoint. "Look, I don't have any idea what you're so worked up about."

"I'm sure you don't." Kate's words dripped with sarcasm. Now that she had an outlet, she was gonna let him have it with both barrels. "Let's teach him to haul wood and spit and drink like a good ol' boy. That's what the poor kid needs. That'll help him fit in around here."

"Now hold on there!"

"No, *you* hold on!" Kate stepped closer, eyes blazing. "Maybe you're an old pal of Jansen's, but that doesn't mean I have to put up with you giving beer to our underage son!"

Kate was just warming up. Her next words, if she hadn't been interrupted, would have barred Cal from their property and their lives.

"Mom, stop!"

They turned to view a barefoot, rumpled Rollins coming down the steps of the manufactured home.

"Cal didn't do it. Some of the guys last night... they gave it to me. I'm sorry." His eyes, besides bloodshot, were embarrassed, pleading.

Kate didn't believe that explanation. It certainly didn't account for his entire downward spiral, but it did pull her up short enough to realize she had been accusing Cal without any evidence beyond one beer can in the floorboard of a grown man's pick-up.

With a heavy sigh, she rubbed a hand over her eyes. "I'm sorry, Cal. I just... " What else could she say beyond pleading temporary insanity? "Obviously, I have some things to discuss with my son." Kate turned away, Rollins following at her heels.

Cal removed his hat and slumped against the side of the truck to run a hand through his thick, rusty waves desperately in need of a trim. He didn't envy that boy one bit. No-sir-ee. Man! The little spitfire had been ready to rip him to shreds!

Although... Cal had to smile as he hoisted a heavy pack of ceramic tile to his shoulder and recalled the rage in those hazel eyes, and the morning sun glinting off Kate's red-tinged curls. "What a way to go," he muttered.

Kate called the school, called Rollins' buddy to inform he wouldn't have a passenger, and settled down for the hateful heart-to-heart. Her son was the picture of penitence. He took the news of being grounded for a month pretty well, but balked at missing out on football. That was hard. Word would circulate around the school and in no time the whole town would know he was in the doghouse. At least he'd be back on the field by homecoming.

Just as Kate finished the emergency meeting with Rollins' Coach, encouraged by his no-nonsense response to Rollins' drinking and low grades, she was summoned to the office of the elementary principal to encounter a tearful Phoenix. Gentle questioning produced nothing more from her daughter than a desperate, "Can I please go home?"

As she was set to escort her sniffling daughter to the van, a grim-faced teacher sporting tight, swim cap style grey curls on her head led a red-faced, dirt-smeared Liam and another boy holding a paper towel to his nose into the office. Kate could only gape wordlessly at the scene. What now?

Persuading Liam to stop talking was impossible. Obviously, the fight had something to do with Phoenix.

"He said she's a loon and I told him he'd better take it back and he wouldn't and I said he better and he said if she wasn't a loon then she's a liar and he wouldn't take that back neither… "

Liam's play-by-play continued as the other boy swore he had been attacked for no reason and started dripping blood on the principal's carpet. Obviously, their accounts disagreed. Unfortunately for Liam, others on the playground had sided with his opponent.

Kate wanted to scream as she endured yet another smiling, chuckling reprimand from the head principal. "Given the behavior of your older boy, I gotta say ah'm not surprised that the youngster is followin' in his brothuh's footsteps, heh, heh."

That night, as the kids ate cold cereal for dinner, Kate was at a loss. How could she reprimand Liam for defending his sister?

Later, she sat in the floor of the bathroom in an exhausted stupor, barely able to rouse herself to answer the phone. It was Jansen, voice full of excitement, calling to report he'd been asked to undertake yet another subdivision in the burgeoning housing market of southern California.

Kate's lack of enthusiasm baffled him. "I thought you'd be excited. This means good, steady income. We need this, Kate."

"What we need is a father and husband at home," Kate spoke through tears. "I'm losin' it. Or don't you wanna hear about my red-letter day?"

Twenty minutes later, Jansen hung up the phone and buried his face in his hands. Once again, his best wasn't enough for his family. What was he supposed to do? Become bankrupt so he could "be there" for them?

Kate had sounded desperate, accusing, as if he'd planned to abandon her at the worst possible moment. Maybe he was a poor husband and father. Well, he'd do what he could. Tomorrow's meeting was unavoidable, but maybe he could catch an afternoon flight to at least be there for the weekend.

The next morning Kate hardly knew what to do with herself when Ima Hayney came over to take charge of Lilly, said she'd be there for the kids that night, and ordered Kate out of the house. "Go have some fun, Hon. Don't worry about a thing."

Obviously, Allie had been in on the plan. Already she had arranged a movie for that afternoon and a shopping spree at the new outlet mall in the city. Kate didn't want to splurge, but the fluttery black blouse with sheer sleeves was on sale and Allie claimed to have the "perfect" skirt to pair with it. After a visit to the salon, Allie suggested a night on the town. "I'm not gonna waste this much gorgeous on my horses and dogs!"

That evening, Kate found herself entering the smoky, noisy atmosphere of Rustlers, the hot spot for steak-eatin' line dancers, clad in Allie's swingy black skirt, slightly large western boots and the new blouse. There were no wallflowers allowed with Allie who pulled Kate out onto the floor for a quick tutorial in line dancing basics. It took some effort, but soon Kate was actually having fun scootin' to the music as she stubbornly shoved away thoughts of the problems awaiting her at home.

"Here ya are, Sweetie," the buxom twenty-something waitress set a red beer can in front of Kate. "Compliments of the gentleman over there."

The "No, thank you" died on Kate's lips as she recognized Cal under the indicated black hat.

"Sorry sir, this doesn't quite suit my taste," Kate said as she placed the can on Cal's table. "Listen, I'm sorry about yesterday. Um, no hard feelings?"

"Well now, I don't think a simple apology's gonna do the trick." Cal pushed back his hat and smiled. "Around here, ya gotta pay the piper with a dance."

Kate glanced toward the dance floor where the band's energetic tune about "jambalaya" had encouraged most of the participants into some sort of fast-stepping western swing dance. "I'm definitely not up to that!"

"Can't know 'til ya try." Cal took Kate's arm and steered her to the center of the floor. "Just start with a stroll," he began the quick 1,2,3 steps and pulled Kate closer to his side.

That was easy enough. Once she had the timing, Kate was willing to add a careful turn and a spin. Cal slowly increased the momentum until their steps were double-time and the full skirt flared and wrapped around Kate's knees with gusto.

"Not bad for a tenderfoot," Cal remarked as the band switched gears to bemoan "All the gold… in Ca-li-for-nia…"

"So my apology's accepted?" Kate offered a handshake as she prepared to return to her table.

"Ya don't think I'm gonna let 'cha quit now I've got the prettiest gal on my arm and they're playin' my favorite song?"

Kate laughed at the flattery. "Surely you can do better than a washed up mom of four."

But Cal insisted so, for the first time in more than eighteen years, Kate found herself slow-dancing with someone other than her own husband… and it had been at least five since she'd danced with Jansen.

She enjoyed the carefree conversation about nothing in particular and the way Cal held her at a very displayable distance as if to give everyone in the room the best possible view.

In fact, she began to feel a bit uncomfortable. Kate didn't want to notice the nice, clean aftershave scent that hovered around Cal or the smooth feel of the muscled arm beneath her hand. How could she decline further dances without seeming rude? The problem was solved for her when a small group of noisy partiers called Cal. Kate lost track of the names after Jim, Grady and a pretty, vivacious blonde named Lydia who gave Kate an openly curious, calculating stare.

"You remember Jance Walden…" the introductions rolled as Kate was established as the California transplant who had married their old pal.

"He used to hunt with my big brother. I had such a crush on him!" Lydia gushed before stealing Cal's hat to playfully place it atop her platinum mane. "Ten minutes I been here and not one dance!"

Soon, Kate was back at her own table, anxious to get home but Allie, apparently, was just getting started. After turning down a couple dance requests from strangers, Kate, unaccustomed to the very non-California second-hand smoke, stepped outside.

Moments like this reminded Kate why she was glad she wasn't single. Flirting and flattery had never been her strong suit. Luckily, she didn't have but a couple years on-the-dating-market before Jansen. Somehow she had never felt single after setting eyes on the tall, shy, polite boy with the charming, soft southern drawl.

Their dates hadn't been typical. Whereas most boys asked her to dinner and a movie, with Jansen she took hikes and climbed on rocks at the beach and explored old missions and historical structures and talked about his passion for architecture, and about his desire to build things to be enjoyed for generations to come.

He had a way of seeing beyond the surface of things. Kate would look at an old farmhouse and see… an old farmhouse. But Jansen would turn the same scene into a study of how folks used to live before air conditioning, Wal-Mart, and fast food.

She loved his knowledge and the way he clung to old-fashioned values of family, God, and country. He spoke unashamedly of wanting children. His father had been deeply devoted to his wife and kids—campouts in Colorado and touch football on the lawn—but he died when Jansen was still in high school. His family then moved to California to be close to his mom's clan, but Jansen had carried the open spaces of Texas in his heart, vowing to raise his kids there someday. She'd never met anyone with such focus and drive. Jansen knew exactly where he was going and just how to get there while other guys seemed stuck in a shallow, junior high mentality of selfish fun and games.

But Kate had been able to make Jansen laugh. She'd encouraged him to take breaks from his studies, to watch the occasional cartoon, to take jogs on the beach and enjoy a freshly baked chocolate chip cookie. He'd said they were the perfect match, that they balanced each other's strengths and weaknesses.

So what had happened to her? Right now, she felt lost and hardly knew how to laugh anymore. As the raucous talk and loud music floated out the swinging double doors of Rustlers, Kate leaned her head back and shut her tired eyes.

"So, ya callin' it a night?" The question startled her as she turned to see Cal shrugging into a light jacket.

"Afraid I'm not the life of the party. But you're not ready to abandon your fan club are ya?"

"Can't handle the late nights like I used to. Never liked the idea of noddin' off while handlin' power tools. But I can give ya a lift if Allie's not ready. Besides, I'd like to talk to ya about Rollins."

Kate nodded at the suggestion, knowing desperation poured from her eyes. Cal reentered Rustlers, told Allie the new plan, and soon Kate and

Cal were breezing through the night in his massive twin-cab pickup, headlights clearing a shallow path on foggy country roads.

CHAPTER 11

MOONLIGHT DRIVES

"Rollins is a good kid," Cal broke the silence. "A hard worker, got a good head on his shoulders. Don't let a few mistakes scare ya. Lord knows I gave my ma enough grief."

"Maybe I'm just overreacting." Kate stared out the window as memories of helplessly watching her father's descent into alcoholism brought a familiar ache to her heart.

Perhaps it was the tranquil moonlit countryside or the perspective a short holiday from household duties had provided, but Kate found herself rambling about her family, about the way she'd blamed beer for destroying her parents' marriage.

"I hated those beer cans. I never even wanted to drink socially. Certainly never wanted it in our home when raising kids." She shuddered as if from an icy wind. "All of that just… hit me broadside when I found the cans in Rollins' bag. Guess I was afraid he'd inherited Dad's weakness."

"Be glad your dad didn't choose somethin' worse like mine."

"Like what?" Kate glanced at the hard line of Cal's profile.

"Women. Became an addiction for him. Mom just waited for us to get out on our own before she left him. Can ya believe the ol' cuss was actually surprised when he came home and she was gone?"

Kate was silent as she considered the pain Cal had endured. He was right. Her father could have chosen worse.

"Guess we start out thinkin' our folks are heroes, then they fall hard off that pedestal, and we grow up and realize they're just human."

"The cowboy's a poet?" She didn't look at Cal as she said it. She didn't trust herself to do even that much. How long had it been since she and Jansen had talked like this? She couldn't remember. There'd just been too many responsibilities, too much pain that didn't want to see the light of day.

Something about the night sky with the moon playing hide-and-seek behind the high, fleeting pillars of fog and the darkness, pressing in like a cozy, insulating blanket on the abandoned road, felt so familiar…

Jansen had driven a pickup in college. He'd never acted self-conscious about his country boy image or complained when rich friends had money to blow on expensive dinners in their status symbol sports cars when he had to pinch pennies and do his eating in the school cafeteria. When his internship at a top architecture firm in L.A. turned into a modest wage for a part-time position, he and Kate had celebrated with dinner at a posh restaurant in Malibu where he'd always sworn he'd take her someday. A year later, they had returned to the same restaurant. Afterwards, Jansen had proposed during a moonlight stroll on the beach.

They had driven the Pacific Coast Highway for hours, dreaming and planning their future, the ocean breeze filling them with such joy and anticipation as the moon had flirted behind dense wisps of marine fog. "Stop!" Kate had shouted to Jansen when she saw the white stretch of lonely beach. "Pull in there!" He had obeyed, laughing at her enthusiasm. "Come on, get out. We are going to dance in the moonlight."

"You're nuts, you know," Jansen had teased, but he had complied nonetheless. He had even let her teach him how to waltz. And, oh! How Jansen had laughed when that ice cold wave had rushed up the sand and drenched Kate to the knees! Kate almost sobbed aloud at the thought. How she loved Jansen's laugh, deep and rich. Very rarely did he laugh like that therefore it always felt like a gift when Kate was the one responsible. Kate leaned her chin on her hand, seeing in her mind's eye the lovely drive home, wrapped in Jansen's dinner jacket as she stole delighted peeks at the diamond ring on her finger and she pressed close to his side. How grateful Kate had been that her fiancee, husband-to-be, did not drive a fancy sports car with bucket seats. How long had it been since she'd ridden through the night snuggled close to Jansen's side?

"Maybe it's the bucket seats." Kate hadn't meant to speak aloud, but too late.

"Pardon?" Cal shot her a quizzical look.

"Jansen drove a pickup when we were dating. I, um, guess I've missed it." She trailed off, glad the darkness hid her blush of embarrassment. Time to turn the tables. "So, you've never married?"

"Escaped the noose every time."

"Why?"

"Guess I never met anybody I disliked enough ta make 'em put up with me."

They talked a bit more about life in a small town versus the city. Inevitably, that conversation brought them to the struggles Kate's kids were having in their new home.

"I still can't believe that Liam of all people, made another boy's nose bleed!" Kate's astonishment overflowed. "He's never had one moment's trouble in school before!"

"Wish I'd been there to see that," Cal chuckled. "So whose nose was it?"

"Oh gosh, what was that kid's name? Oh yeah, Liam called him 'Jack.'"

Cal laughed out loud, "Hoo, that mustabeen good! Jackson Garfield Wilson got taken down a peg, eh?"

"You know him?"

"Aw, his family's been pushin' folks around since my granddaddy was in knickers. Jack's just the new generation of old-guard. Not too many of 'em left these days with so much new blood, but they still wanna call the shots—claim ties to a couple Presidents, have the family tree to prove it—run Wilson's Dry Goods, the Masonic Lodge, own the bank, bought the stained glass for First Presbyterian. Big muckety mucks 'round here." He chuckled again. "Really hate I missed that! Explains why the other kids wouldn't speak up."

"They're scared of this family? At six years old, they're already intimidated?"

"Don't take long ta see some kids get in trouble and some don't. By the way, the boy Rollins decked is a Wilson cousin—smart mouth and bad attitude. Probably got exactly what he deserved too."

Kate's mood was improving. Maybe her boys weren't turning into playground bullies after all. But there were still other concerns.

"But, the bad grades and the drinking…."

"Well, I'm no shrink, but I can sure tell when a fella's got anger eatin' 'im alive. A bit of that's normal, bein' fourteen an' all, but Rollins seems ta have more than 'is fair share. Maybe he's just tryin' ta take the edge off."

Once again, Cal surprised her with his insight. Kate grew silent as they turned in the gate and stopped in front of the manufactured home.

She didn't want the drive to end. The night was so quiet and reentering the house meant stepping back into the fray. Her hand reached for the door handle, but remained there, unwilling to leave the peaceful moment behind. "How can I love my family with all my heart and yet, right now, I just want to keep driving forever? Does that make me a horrible person?"

Cal gripped the steering wheel with both hands and shot a sideways glance toward Kate. Every impulse at that moment was pushing him to do something to comfort her; a hand on the shoulder, a hug… but he also knew those impulses wanted to provide more than just comfort.

He was no fool. He knew a vulnerable woman when he saw one. Truth be told, he'd always been a bit jealous of Jansen. His old friend had been half an inch taller, made better grades, and danged if he couldn't even out-swim him! But somehow Cal had never resented anything Jansen had… until now.

"Well," Kate took a deep breath as if to jump into icy water. "Thanks for the ride. Sorry to unload our troubles on you." She gave a determined yank on the handle but the door didn't budge so she began fumbling with buttons in the dark. Somehow, it was a perfect picture of her life. She was trapped, doing her very best, but accomplishing nothing. The bitterness welled into a stifled sob that lodged painfully in her throat.

"Sorry. I still forget. Gotta fix that door," Cal mumbled as he pushed a button and reached across to give the door a shove. "Wait a minute. Some gentleman I am. Sit tight."

He opened his own door and jogged around to let Kate out. They said awkward goodbyes without so much as a handshake and in no time Kate was in the house.

As he drove out the gate, Cal wiped a hand across his cheek as if to erase the feel of Kate's hair brushing that very spot when he'd reached for the door. God, she smelled good!

One thing he knew for sure. If his old pal Jansen could read his mind at the moment, that'd be the end of their friendship.

They had been too distracted to notice, but someone had watched the whole thing from the third-floor balcony of Pedigo Manor. Although she wasn't the least bit cold, the little girl in the bright white dress shuddered.

CHAPTER 12

OLD & OLDER

Wearily, Amy smoothed her black hair back into a tight ponytail as she made her rounds at the Sunset Assisted Living Facility. Who were they kidding with that name? This was a place where folks came to prepare to die, not to live. Just half an hour remained until Amy could drive home and smell something, anything, besides the lingering aroma of disinfectant and oldness. Sometimes she feared that particular potpourri clung to her even when she had a much-deserved day off and wore civilian clothing, not the simple purple scrubs she'd chosen because they complimented her mocha-toned skin and were supposed to brighten the depressing atmosphere of her work.

What Amy wouldn't give to go home to the smell of Mama's homemade fried chicken. But Mama was no longer living with them as she had been for the three years she'd fought cancer. Though it had been almost a year since they'd lost that fight, the grief was fresh.

In the dining area, Mr. Cisneros was wandering from table to table mumbling about running low on wine. Apparently, he was still reliving his years of owning a successful Italian restaurant.

When Amy approached, the bandy-legged, stoop-shouldered man looked startled and rattled off a list of the day's specials.

"Sure, Mr. Cisneros. I'll try the veal just as soon as you're back in bed." Amy put a hand on his elbow to guide him down hall C to his room.

She heard a commotion in room 432 and peeked inside. Poor Mrs. Cartwright. She must be having nightmares again. Amy stepped inside and checked the bedding. All clear. That unpleasant task could be avoided for the moment.

Most of the residents of this place seemed to have simmered over the years until only their worst traits remained—selfish, paranoid, angry, hopeless—but not Mrs. Cartwright. A stroke had stolen her powers of speech, but she could communicate volumes through her eyes. Once Amy had come into work on the verge of tears after a sleepless night and a fight with her husband. Mrs. Cartwright had patted her hand as Amy cleared the breakfast dishes, her expression one of understanding and empathy. Mrs. Cartwright had then pointed toward the worn Bible on her bedside table.

When she had a free moment, Amy took to reading passages aloud to Mrs. Cartwright. All she had to look for was a portion that was underlined, highlighted, and in parentheses; sure indicators this was one of Mrs. Cartwright's favorites. Apparently, there were lots of those contained in the well-worn pages of that black leather book. Amy would read and Mrs. Cartwright would smile. Sometimes a tear would slip down her pale cheek. Those moments came to be the most precious of Amy's workdays.

Tonight, Mrs. Cartwright yanked at her covers with unexpected strength as Amy tried to arrange them around the bony shoulders. When Amy put a straw to the dry lips for a sip of water, the thin, blue-veined hand shot out to grip her wrist and Mrs. Cartwright's eyes flew open, the pleading urgency of her expression more disturbing than the tensile strength of her grip.

Slowly, the pale eyes registered recognition and her hand relaxed as she took in the scant, lamp-lit surroundings with resignation. Pity overwhelmed Amy as she reached a hand to cup the sagging cheek. The soft smile of gratitude that lit Mrs. Cartwright's wrinkle-wreathed features brought a lump to Amy's throat. How could this old woman, with apparently nothing left to live for, still expend the energy to be kind?

"Go back to sleep," Amy whispered. "Everything's okay." She loved that Mrs. Cartwright had perfect hearing. In fact, Mrs. Cartwright seemed to be the only person in Amy's life who could hear her loud and clear.

Amy straightened the bedclothes and stroked the smooth, white brow until Mrs. Cartwright slept.

The old house was a flurry of activity. Jansen had hired a crew of extra workers to speed the renovation process. In just ten days Pedigo Manor, as history dubbed it, would host a camera crew from American Heritage, an historical architecture magazine with nationwide distribution. This was a huge boost for Jansen's morale and another golden opportunity for business prospects because, as he explained to Kate, his name would be associated with historic renovation, his first love in architecture.

"Kate, this could be the answer! If I get some opportunities for restoration, that paves the way to being my own boss!" His eyes had flashed with a boyish enthusiasm Kate hadn't seen in years. "No more bein' at the beck and call of cookie-cutter housing developments, Babe. Business can be based here!"

That all sounded well and good, but in the short term it meant even less of Jansen's attention for Kate and the kids as he juggled calls from California and spent every waking minute working his fingers to the bone transforming Pedigo Manor into a magazine-worthy showplace.

It also equaled greater strain on their budget as hourly wages and exclusive material costs turned into long columns of debt. One night, worry drove Kate from her bed to pace the floor. Two a.m. and still the light burned through the window across the drive where Jansen painstakingly restored the long, carved banister.

It felt like, the better the old house looked, the more of a shambles their family became. For a while after the discovery of beer in Rollins' room, things had improved. He'd aced a test and had actually taken to speaking to his family again. Now, however, the surliness was back like a dreaded intruder and complaints from teachers were mounting. Kate had searched his room but found no trace of alcohol, yet Rollins seemed wrapped in an impenetrable fog. Once again her oldest son was grounded, but he hardly seemed to care.

And she was worried sick about Phoenix. Just that evening, as Kate had brushed her daughter's heavy red locks, she'd been shocked as clumps of the shiny tresses had fallen to the floor. Also, the child's once creamy, freckled skin now bore dry, red patches and the naturally athletic, scrawny frame continued to add new padding as Phoenix shunned her former active lifestyle of climbing, riding bikes and running like a wild young colt. These days, Phoenix preferred to spend her time on her bed with a book and hoarded cookies.

Just that afternoon, Kate had endured a conference with Phoenix's teacher who was convinced the child was simply not "forced" to interact with others. Kate had been too weary to argue with ignorance and too cautious to divulge Phoenix's painful history.

But how long could she protect her daughter from small town gossip? Was she the only one who overheard Phoenix talking to herself? Apparently the conversations were good ones because those were the only times Phoenix laughed. When she brought up the subject with Jansen, he said Phoenix was just a child with an active imagination and they shouldn't worry.

Was her daughter losing her grip on reality? Sometimes Kate felt her own mind wouldn't be far behind as the stress and sleepless nights took their toll.

Kate opened the blinds on the bedroom window and stared toward the light shining from Pedigo Manor. The old house had become "the other woman" in her husband's life—more interesting, more challenging, and more entertaining. Maybe Jansen would work his wife into his schedule if she covered herself in peeling paint.

With renewed energy, Kate threw on her long coat and fleece-lined boots for a chilly, determined march across the drive. If this was the only time Jansen could talk without interruption, so be it.

As she gained the porch, the scene through the dining room window told the whole story. At the drop cloth-covered dining table, Jansen slept, his pillow, a hefty stack of bills, pencil still in his hand. It was the first time Kate had actually seen him sleep in weeks since he retired and rose while she slept. Not having the heart to wake him, she grabbed another drop cloth to wrap around his shoulders then stepped back out to the stillness of the porch with the widescreen view of steely, bright stars in the midnight velvet sky. How long had it been since she'd stopped to catch her breath? Besides, if she returned to bed, if she was able to sleep, she would only wake to the same exhausting pace; another day of watching her life careen out of control. Why hurry?

The porch swing beckoned, aglow in its new coat of white paint. Two minutes. Surely she could take just two minutes to enjoy a little peace. She settled into the curved wooden slats and leaned her weary head against the glimmering new chains that attached to strong springs hidden in the shadows above. What a great idea to add a slight bounce to a porch swing. Those springs made the smooth, swaying movement more soothing than ever.

Somewhere in the distance an owl hooted and a dog barked. As if on cue, Winston trotted up the steps and hopped up to sit beside her. If anyone in Kate's life was neglected, it was Winston, yet here he came, nestling up to her side without offering a single reprimand. She didn't have the heart to dump him out of her lap when she couldn't even remember the last time she'd given him so much as a passing pat on the head. As she reached to lay a hand on his soft, furry side, Winston gave a deep sigh of contentment and stretched his neck to lay his floppy-eared head on her lap. Back and forth she rocked, absorbing Winston's frame of mind, enjoying the quiet moment. Just another minute, then she really must get back to bed.

She felt a warm, wet kiss on her cheek and opened her eyes to discover golden sunshine, flitting butterflies among purple flowers, and wide blue eyes staring into her own. "Hello!" the little girl said. "I like your dog."

Dog? Kate looked beside her to the snoozing Winston. She was too relaxed to care how the family dog got into her dream. And it was a dream; a warm, colorful, happy dream.

Soft scents of roses, lilacs, and an early-morning sweet spring breeze flowed over her in soothing waves. "I'm supposed to tell you, to warn you, about some bad stuff." The little girl hesitated and tilted her head. "But this is the kind of day for only happy talk, right?"

Kate nodded, mesmerized by the flitting of a snow white butterfly close by her hand. The little girl spoke again. "You're a pretty lady."

"So are you." Kate enjoyed the flush of pleasure on the little girl's face at that remark.

"Do you really think so?" Kate's young companion plopped into the porch swing beside her. On the other side, Winston flopped over on his back in his sleep. "I want to be pretty. I want to make people smile when they look at me, just like mama does, but sometimes I get all messy and mama tells me 'pretty is as pretty does.' But sometimes pretty can be boring. Don't you think so?"

Kate simply nodded. In the back of her lazy mind, she knew she was supposed to be sad for some reason. It was nice to not remember why.

"I used to think pretty people were nice and ugly people were bad, but then I met an old man who had only one leg and didn't have any teeth at all. Have you ever met anyone with only one leg?" The monologue continued unabated. "He was the nicest, goodest person I ever met. You know what? The more I talked to him, the prettier he got! Then I met a very beautiful lady who called me 'little girl' and stuck her nose in the air and kicked my little white birthday dog. She was very ugly!"

"So your mother was right."

The expressive blue eyes filled with tears. "How did you know?

"How did I know what?"

"That my mother… was."

"You mean she died? I'm sorry."

"They put her in the ground right over there." The girl pointed toward a fenced area to the right of the house. "She was in her favorite dress that was the color of those flowers." The little girl pointed her dimpled hand toward flourishing lilac bushes that flowed over the wooden porch rail. "She was so pretty."

The child's somber mood was replaced by excitement. "Would you like to see my room?"

Kate took the outstretched hand and followed her hostess into the house. She stared in wonder at the magnificence of the "dream" Pedigo Manor. Rich oriental rugs adorned every room. Gleaming, candle chandeliers were cobweb free. Ornate furniture reflected the warmth of sunlight that flowed through heavy draperies drawn back to afford gorgeous glimpses of rose gardens, trimmed trees, and even a bright peacock with plumage unfurled.

Rich colors of burgundy, navy and gold, a recurring theme throughout the décor, peeked back at Kate in tapestries, upholstery, and even the delicate china she spied on the huge dining table. Above the stained glass windows that commanded her view beneath the entryway chandelier, a gigantic coat of arms in those colors filled the entire expanse of wall that reached to the high ceiling.

Kate followed the exuberant child who practically danced with excitement. "I'm so glad you came! It's been so long since we've had guests, especially someone as nice as you! Do you like to play hopscotch or hide-and-seek? I always win at that game—but first we will have tea. That's the proper thing to do."

Kate gazed at walls painted a soft yellow with creamy, white crown moldings. The upstairs was clean and welcoming, every window thrown open to capture sweet, fragrant breezes through white ruffled, fluttering curtains. She paused. As her little friend skipped away to the left, Kate sighed with contentment. This was everything a home should be, tasteful and comfortable with gilt-framed family portraits gracing the walls. From where she stood, bits of every room reflected in a dressing table mirror here or a freestanding full-length mirror there. The effect was perfect not too ornate—a harmonious blend of simplicity and opulence.

A portrait to her right captured her attention. A stately gentleman with mutton chop sideburns and a thick mane of flowing gray hair stared down at her with a serious expression. As she stepped closer, captivated by the twinkling eyes, (what artistry it must require to make eyes appear so alive) she realized her hostess had rejoined her.

"Wasn't grandfather handsome?" the childish voice asked.

As Kate opened her mouth to agree, the light began to fade.

"But we haven't had tea!" The little girl sounded tearful even as her voice receded like a fading melody.

Just as darkness closed in, the gentleman in the portrait gave Kate a broad wink.

OF DREAMS & NIGHTMARES

"Kate."

Someone was shaking her shoulder. Kate frowned. She didn't want to open her eyes, she wanted to stay in the pretty dream. It was warmer there.

Something wet, slimy, and prickly brushed her cheek. She pried open one eye to behold Winston's gaping muzzle and lolling tongue puffing doggy breath into her face. Above him, a rumpled Jansen looked down on her, amusement bringing out the familiar crinkly lines at the corners of his blue eyes.

Kate yawned and stretched as if waking from a full, refreshing night's sleep, still encased in a happy fog. With her palm, she shoved the dog's grinning muzzle away from her nose. Now she could take in the sight of this handsome man before her, wood shavings peppering his dark curls, short jacket over his favorite sweatshirt, long, denim covered legs. He looked… good. Very good.

She reached a hand toward him and he squatted down, eyes still smiling into hers. How she'd missed that look, the adoring one that always made the blood rush to her face. Kate felt the heat in her cheeks as naughty thoughts of sneaking into the old house and wrapping the two of them in one of those drop cloths flitted through her mind.

"You crazy woman." Jansen cupped her cheek with his hand. "How did you end up on the porch?"

"I'm crazy?" Kate flicked a wood shaving out of his hair. "You were drooling into a pile of bills."

"Slept better than I have in months. Go figure."

A gray light above the trees signaled dawn. With a rush, life's demands flooded over Kate. The kids! The bus! "What time is it?"

"Almost seven."

"Ohmigosh!" Kate vaulted from the porch swing, immediately in full combat mode, but Jansen's gentle yet firm grip caught her arm.

"Without so much as a 'good morning'?" There it was again, that spark of excitement, that joy that had defined their relationship from the start. With a sigh he pulled her close to his chest, arms warm and reassuring, their strength filling her with peace. Layers of worry and stress began to melt away.

Suddenly they both heard it. A wailing that struck dread to their hearts. "Phoenix!" Kate and Jansen rushed down the steps toward the manufactured home, each reliving the waking nightmare of those horrible moments six months before.

It had been the dead of night. Kate had woken out of deep sleep to a scream, the kind of scream no parent should ever hear. As if yanked to their feet, she and Jansen had burst out their bedroom door just in time to see Alex—Rollins' ex-friend they had allowed to spend the night because he had convinced them he was terrified of his father—make a mad dash away from Phoenix's room.

Now, the all-too-familiar panic propelled Kate up the manufactured home's concrete steps in one bound. It was stupid to sleep on the porch. How could she have been so irresponsible?

In the house, a panicked Phoenix stood outside Rollins' room. "MOM! MOM!" She yelled over and over as Liam and Lilly gathered in bleary-eyed confusion.

"I didn't know where you were! I went to ask Rollins, but he wouldn't wake up!" Their daughter's tearful explanation continued as Kate and Jansen rushed to Rollins' bedside. All sound stopped for Kate as she looked down on her son's pale face.

"Dear God! Is he breathing?" Kate whispered. Everything came into sharp focus. There was a pulse, but it was weak. "He's not breathing," she heard herself say again, pressing her face to his nose and mouth. Jansen was calling 911. That wasn't fast enough. He needed to breathe now! She yanked Rollins up to lean over her arm and slapped his back. She climbed behind him and pulled her fist hard against his chest. There was a slight gurgling sound. Something was happening.

"Jansen, get in here!" He was describing the situation but dropped the phone and took Kate's place behind Rollins whose body still slumped as dead weight. He brought his fist up under Rollins' sternum with a sharp jab. The gurgle became a rush of vomit and Rollins coughed and retched again. He was breathing! Kate grabbed the boy, forcing his eyes to look into hers. He seemed desperately sick and weak, on the verge of retching again, but he was conscious.

"Mom?" Rollins mumbled. That one word held fear, apology, and desperation, stirring thoughts of a much smaller, less complicated Rollins crying out for her after a nightmare. Blindly, Kate gave orders for towels and wet cloths. She cleaned him up and had the soiled sheets stripped from the bed by the time paramedics arrived to pepper them with questions. Jansen and Kate provided what answers they could but Rollins appeared unable, or unwilling, to fill in the blanks.

Kate stumbled blindly through that day of doctor's examinations and questions. If she'd thought things couldn't get worse, she was wrong. She felt suspicion from all sides as if everyone wanted to believe the worst.

Rollins' protective armor was firmly in place. Even after combined barbiturates and alcohol were revealed in blood tests, she could get no information from him.

"These cases just keep gettin' younger and younger." The detached doctor with clipboard in hand skimmed the information before him as if reading the morning paper, without so much as a glance at her son who shivered on the paper-covered examination table.

"He needs a blanket," Kate commented. "Now," she added with sufficient force to compel the surprised doctor to call a nurse.

She looked at Rollins' pale face. He was just a little boy in a tall body. How did he get in this mess? She didn't have to think long and hard to know when the trouble began. Their entire family had been reeling for six months now. Their safe world had been invaded and shattered by one erroneous judgment call. They had all been duped. All were scarred. Obviously, moving half a continent away hadn't been far enough.

Oh, how the Walden family infused the sleepy little town with excitement in the coming days. Now the gossip line was rife with stories about "that oldest Walden kid." The most popular rumor, according to Liam, was that Rollins had tried to "suiticide."

"Are they making fun of his clothes again?" Liam's wide blue eyes looked up into hers.

Had Rollins tried to end his life? That thought plunged knives of fear into Kate's heart.

Later that week, they sat before a fresh-faced, HMO-appointed "therapist" who seemed to have learned one phrase in school. "And how does that make you feel, Rollins?"

Kate started to tell the story, but Rollins interrupted. "Let's go."

Kate remembered the look on Rollins' face when he had chickenpox at the age of eight. Now he bore that same "ready to crawl out of his skin" expression.

She knew exactly how he felt. "Let's give this a chance, okay?"

"Why? This is stupid. He's stupid!" Rollins sneered at the gaping therapist who scribbled on paper and tried to look unruffled.

She could understand Rollins' frustration. They were well-acquainted with the damage an over-eager therapist could inflict. Six months ago, when the wounds from Alex were new, they'd gone to the plush office of a highly recommended "family counselor." The pain had been too fresh and Phoenix hadn't been ready. The counselor had pushed too hard. Kate had held her shaking, tearful daughter all the way home. That night, about eight months ago, was the first time Phoenix had wet the bed since she was a baby.

As for Rollins, his therapy session that same day had ended with a broken chair and a hole in the therapist's wall. From the nature of the questioning Rollins was willing to share with his parents, that particular therapist should be glad the damages hadn't included his own broken neck.

At the moment, this optimistic, young psychiatrist with barely enough peach fuzz for a thin mustache had more chance of breaking into Fort Knox than probing the hurting areas of Rollins' psyche. "We'll call you," Kate lied as she followed her son's long stride out of the office door.

CHAPTER 14

OLD FRIENDS

Except for the basic schedule, their family was on lock-down. Kate took the kids to school and brought them home in the afternoon where everyone was put to work. Somehow, as they poured themselves into the old house, scraping away years of neglect and bringing it back to life, their family was going through a type of metamorphosis as well.

One busy Saturday, as Kate juggled paint and fabric samples, she had to pause in wonder at the sight of Rollins giving Liam a lesson in painting baseboards. He guided Liam's small hand to make graceful strokes between strips of tape. "Nah, ya gotta put it on thicker. There ya go. It's all in the wrist."

In the backyard, Lilly's dolls were arranged in perfect, tea party formation on a blanket next to the new tire swing Jansen had hung from a monstrous, freshly trimmed oak. Through the open window, Lilly's happy, young voice floated in on an unseasonably warm December breeze. "One for Belle, one for Wisabef, and one for me." Winston lay near, inching closer to the carefully placed Vanilla Wafers on their tiny, flower-sprigged china plates.

Kate had begun expressing her preferences in color choices and furnishings, even taking to flea markets and antique shops, scouring the countryside to prepare Pedigo Manor for its debut. When Rollins wasn't in school, he was part of the construction crew, constantly under his father's watchful eye, where he scraped and sanded and caulked and painted his heart out. Even when workers came to start repiping and re-tiling the pool area, Rollins was the one who made trip after trip with the debris-filled wheelbarrow.

Slowly the old Pedigo Manor was taking shape.

Kate stood her ground when a local decorator pushed for bright, flowered wallpaper in the dining and sitting rooms. Despite the backbreaking labor to prepare the walls for simple, creamy yellow paint and white moldings, Jansen agreed the effect was much more charming.

Only four days remained until the magazine photoshoot and interview. The house was almost finished except for the small bedroom at the top of the house that led to the balcony. They'd just keep the cameras out of there. Kate needed to focus on filling the bare walls and adding to the, as yet, sparse furnishings. Also the grounds, though cleared and trimmed, were a bit bleak. With a surge of energy, Kate called a local nursery and finagled a deal to mention their business name in the article in return for plants to beautify the home. By mid-afternoon, several large trucks arrived with small trees and winter flowers. The metamorphosis was amazing. The old place now appeared cozy and framed by life. Kate thought creeping, flowered vines wrapping around the posts on the porch, perhaps lilacs, would be a nice touch, but that would have to wait for spring.

The next morning, Kate received a call from a local antique dealer. "I hear ya'll are fixin' up that ol' Pedigo place. Ya might wanna have a look-see at the Briggs Homestead County Museum."

She rushed over that afternoon, fitting in the visit between the grocery store and picking up the kids at school.

Museum? Kate thought with a chuckle as she pushed open the creaking screen door on the very authentic, although rather small, country house. How much history could one fit in such a tiny house?

The wood floors creaked with every step as she maneuvered carefully through the home, arranged in authentic, late-nineteenth century fashion. The small sitting room with tiny pot-bellied stove in one corner housed a plastic-encased Queen Anne settee, matching chair, and spindly-legged end table, all in impeccable condition. Kate could imagine this was the room children in the household were never allowed to enter. Stepping through the kitchen doorway, the furnishings became decidedly rustic and hand hewn. Ah! This was where the family actually lived. There were well-worn traffic patterns in the floors that bore scrapes and stains from countless meals around the plain, bleached wood of a thick, rough table. Rustic, chipped pottery plates and tin cups were arranged as if the dinner bell was about to sound.

"What in the world did they do for cabinet space?" Kate wondered aloud as she took in the freestanding sink and authentic black, wood-burning stove.

"Did most of the preparation out here," a gravelly voice startled Kate. She turned to spy an angular, white-haired man framed in the doorway that led to a small porch. "Granny would pull the vegetables out of the cellar or right out of the ground, get some meat out of the smokehouse, wash and cut it all out here before bringin' it in to cook. That's the way food oughta be, right outa the ground like God intended!"

Kate liked him immediately; from the dapper, silver, carefully combed hair and gruff, no nonsense voice to the teasing smile and firm, knobby-knuckled handshake.

"Jefferson Briggs at your service, little lady!" He gave a smart though stiff bow. "Call me Jeff."

"I'm Kate… Kate Walden." She felt a bit overwhelmed at the unaccustomed courtly manner. "So, this house belongs to your family?"

"Known this place since I was knee-high to a grasshopper!" Jeff answered. "Ya know, back when Hector was a pup!" He grinned and winked.

Kate stared a moment. Why did that seem familiar?

"I, uh," she shook her head to jumpstart her thoughts. "Someone told me to come here because we're fixing up the old Pedigo place."

She expected to add more explanation but Mr. Briggs' eyes opened wide with interest. "So the rumors are true!" He reached to shake her hand in both of his as if greeting an old friend. "Well now! Ah'll be! Pleasure to make your acquaintance! Yes sir, you've come to the right place." He took Kate's arm and wrapped it around his forearm as if escorting her into high society. "Right this way!"

They exited through the back of the house and down the steps that led to a spacious yard with the remains of a well-kept garden and numerous, large fruit trees. Everywhere she looked, Kate saw touches of tender loving care: a wooden swing peeked from a shady tree alcove here, a stone path and flowered border wound through flourishing flowers, a winged cherub fountain spilled onto shiny stones, and a quaint footbridge spanned a tiny stream that could have been crossed with a standing leap.

As they walked, Mr. Briggs kept up a lively conversation asking about her family. He said he remembered Jansen as a small boy who used to come into his variety store to purchase gum in little bags that resembled tobacco pouches. "Used to make him promise he'd never use the real thing—nasty stuff!"

Finally, at the end of a neat stone path, Mr. Briggs brought out a large set of keys. "Been savin' some of these things more than thirty years. Hoped someday the family'd have use for 'em again." With that, he removed the padlock on a large, well-built storage barn Kate knew her kids would love to explore. "I'd have more on display in the house, but I like ta give folks a taste of what a home really felt like. Ya start addin' glass display cases and labels and it just don't feel like a home anymore."

She followed as he stepped onto the concrete pad flooring. "Had to make this place as safe as possible from the weather and varmints—hate ta see antiques ruined by neglect." He led the way around and through an eclectic collection of life's leftovers, and stepped toward a tarp-enshrouded mound.

Shivers of anticipation trailed down Kate's back as Mr. Briggs lifted away the plastic covering. When he stepped aside, she gasped in wonder.

Bedsteads, chairs and tables, stacked and layered with long cloths between, caught the sun's light with a warm, red-brown glow. She watched as Mr. Briggs lifted cloths and pulled out a chair or gilt mirror to point out details in the craftsmanship. Lovely lamps and wall sconces with prismatic twinkling crystals cast little prisms around the dim walls and ceiling. Kate was no antique dealer, but it didn't take an expert to realize she was looking at a fortune in art and furnishings.

"You say you've had these items for thirty years?" She interrupted Mr.

Brigg's rapturous description of the gold leaf detail and flowing lines of a mirror and table ensemble.

"Thirty-one years this April," the white-haired man answered without hesitation.

"But, how did you come by it and…why on earth didn't you sell it?"

"Wasn't mine ta sell," he answered as if that closed the topic.

"But Mr. Briggs… "

"Mr. Briggs was my daddy. It's Jeff. Watch your step." He led her around a draped easel to another tarp-covered mound and lifted the dusty edge to reveal a group of burnished, wooden frames of various sizes stacked in a line on a raised metal structure with wheels at either end. Each frame was separated from the next with long strips of oilcloth and all had corner protectors on the frame tips. Kate couldn't imagine anyone taking better care of their own family's heirlooms.

"I have to ask, Mr… Jeff," Kate searched the kind, wrinkled face, "Why?"

"Aw, just returnin' a good deed. Besides, this is what ol' Jed would want."

"You must have known him well."

"He and my grandpappy were best friends."

"Still, to have taken such care…"

"And," Mr. Briggs' eyes twinkled, "it was all spelled out in his will and added into his son's will that these things went to my family's keeping if ever the house was unoccupied. He knew I loved the old place almost as much as he did."

Kate was speechless as she contemplated the wealth before her, perusing the long stack of family portraits and pastoral scenes, seeing in her mind's eye the perfect spot on the home's walls for each. "I've wondered about the place," Kate mused as she fingered through the treasures. "Why people talk about it like it's haunted or something, what really happened there so long ago, why that old pool house looked like it had been completely forgotten."

"Ya discovered the pool house, huh?" Jeff rubbed his chin. "Last I saw, it was in bad shape. Don't think it's been used for," his brow furrowed with thought, "must be at least seventy years. There was only distant family and they just didn't have the funds or the heart to make the necessary repairs once ol' Jed and his son passed. With no one livin' there, just seemed to be safer to let an old pool be kinda forgotten. We talked about fillin' it with concrete but I hate to see art destroyed. That tile was imported from Spain, ya know."

"Oh my!" Kate didn't know which deserved the exclamation more, the imported tile Jeff mentioned or the gorgeous painting of what looked to be an Italian landscape. "So much history. I'm so glad you've taken such good care of it."

"Well, his granddaughter officially inherited everything but we haven't heard from her for decades. She kinda had a fallin' out with ol' Jed when she married a foreigner." Jeff paused. "Darn shame," he muttered. "But, now that the house is gettin' fixed up, these things can finally go home!"

"But there's no way Jansen and I can afford… I mean, all this is worth a fortune."

"Little lady, I wouldn't take one red cent for what rightfully belongs to the Pedigo family." Jeff's eyes grew moist. "Loved that man. And I owe them more than I could ever repay."

Kate smiled, a warm, genuine smile that felt like it bloomed out from her heart. "How wonderful to have friends like that. I wish I could have known them, Jedediah and his family. But it's good to know at least some of the history. I think my mind's been playing tricks on me, dreams and such to fill in the blanks." Kate rolled her eyes as she ran a hand over the top of a leather settee. "I know, sounds crazy."

With a start, Kate's present duties rushed back to mind and she pulled out her phone to check the time. "Ohmigosh! I'll be late!" Kate jabbered an apology as she raced toward her car, thanking Mr. Briggs and shaking the large hand as he struggled to match her frantic pace. She promised, through the van's open window, to send Jansen over to work out details, then the tires of her car crunched on the gravel and she tore down Cherry Street at a frantic pace.

Mr. Briggs stood on the wooden porch as the dust from the van's tires rose slowly around him. With a spring in his step and vigor he hadn't known since he was a youngster of sixty, he strode back to the storage barn toward another cloth-covered item near the window where the afternoon sun shone strongest. Taking hold of the bottom corner of the cloth, he lifted it away.

"Been waitin' a long time, eh, Jed? Yep, I think they'll do. Think they'll do just fine."

With that, he began working on the canvas before him, a dab here, a careful application of a tiny sponge there, as rich colors became more vivid beneath his expert touch. The afternoon light illumined his hands that moved with surprising grace and steadiness as he labored over the painting, a portrait of a silver-haired gentleman with mutton-chop sideburns.

CHAPTER 15

SET TO REPEAT

Thanksgiving came and would have been ignored in the Walden family if not for Mrs. Hayney who invited them over for an old-fashioned dinner with all the trimmings. Out of guilt, Kate dug through boxes until she found her grandmother's sweet potato recipe, the one the kids loved, with dripping melted marshmallows and butter on top. Even that simple offering would have burned if left to Kate's frazzled attention. Luckily, Lilly had stationed herself before the oven to watch the marshmallows "grow" and reported when they started to smoke.

Only two days remained until the magazine people were coming so, after the short reprieve of stuffing themselves on Mrs. Hayney's turkey and homemade rolls, the younger kids stayed at their kind neighbor's house to watch "Miracle on 34ᵗʰ Street" while Kate, Jansen, Rollins and Cal, who had also dined at Mrs. Hayney's, continued doing paint touch-ups and removing the tape from already dried walls throughout the house. Though there had been much discussion of the aesthetic appeal of bright colors to bring out details of craftsmanship on its exterior, they had decided Pedigo Manor should remain a traditional, creamy white.

Late in the afternoon, Kate was surprised to see a large, heavily laden circa 1960s flatbed truck pulling through the gate. A smiling Mr. Briggs ambled toward Jansen with a twenty-something young man, whom he introduced as his grandson, Jefferson III.

Kate wanted so badly to remain, but the winter light was failing so, hating to exhaust the kindness of Mrs. Hayney, she left the heavy lifting to the men, showered and scraped away her resinous spattering and gathered her younger, hay-coated brood for much-needed baths and bedtime.

By the time she was able to return, the men had gone for another load. Kate stepped through the front door and gasped. Her dream from the night she slept on the porch rolled to the forefront of her mind. There was the gilt-edged mirror and matching half-moon shaped table on her left. The high-backed, velvet entry chairs stood guard on the right and a large, gleaming dining table with matching claw-foot chairs had replaced their smaller, tarp-covered, flea-market find. As Kate's eyes fell on the mauve tapestry settee and delicate, graceful curves of the early French Provincial sitting room ensemble, she collapsed onto the bottom step of the staircase, overwhelmed by the sense of familiarity.

You're supposed to be here.

The thought flowed, unbidden, through Kate's mind, comforting her tired body and spirit. It was odd to think, if not for the ugliness her family had endured, they wouldn't have been ready to uproot from their comfortable, familiar existence in California. Kate's head slumped against the banister. Could there be some vast, divine plan in all of this?

Just as quickly, peace was displaced by rage. Oh yes! Some great, sovereign hand was powerful enough to lead them halfway across the country, but had passively allowed her daughter to… Kate felt sick. Bitter anger suffocated her. Hatred, so strong it crushed her heart, shook her small body. No! That door was locked tight. She'd go insane if those emotions were stirred. But—why? Why Phoenix?

She whimpered in despair. There was no answer, just more questions and the stifling emptiness that ate at her heart, ripping and tearing the core of her being.

"Kate?" She jumped at the sound of her name. There stood Cal, paintbrush and bucket in hand, eyes full of concern. Embarrassed, Kate moved to sit up only to discover a thick goo attached to the side of her head.

"I, uh, just covered up a scratch in the paint there," he stammered.

"So I discovered," she tried and failed to run a hand through her now-coagulated tresses.

"That'll be real stubborn to get out. Come 'ere." Cal led the way to the kitchen to warm, running water and the pasty soap they used daily on paint-coated hands.

Kate struggled with the matted tangle, working in the gritty soap and rinsing with the warm water. After two applications, a smaller but persistent snarl remained and the hair on that side of her head felt like hay sprigs. Cal stepped out of the kitchen but soon returned with a large white bottle. "This'll do the trick."

She tried to see what he was doing, but Cal turned her head away and went to work, kneading in something strangely fragrant, taming the stubborn knots inch by inch. The gentle tugging on her hair was soothing, coaxing the tight knots in her neck and mind to relax with each persuasive stroke until the comb slid smoothly through to the ends.

"Wow! I need that stuff for Phoenix. What is it?"

Cal grinned and handed her the bottle that bore the small silhouette of a horse and the words "Mane and Tail" in plain black letters. "Ha, ha. Always knew you put women and horses in the same box."

"Not by a long shot." His eyes flicked over her with an appreciative glance that made her blush. "Horses are a lot less trouble."

Kate had to laugh. "Guess you're right. So do I rinse this stuff out?"

"Might keep ya from slippin' off your pillow tonight."

Cal turned to locate a towel, trying to keep his eyes on something besides the drops of water running down the nape of her neck. He'd always been a sucker for a long, graceful neck. Perhaps that was why he preferred the aristocratic Arabians, head held high, long mane blowing in the wind. In this case, auburn waves with just a hint of gold.

"I won't end up with purple hair or somethin' will I?" Kate asked as the warm water slid through her slick tresses.

"Aw, if anything, it's leanin' more toward a nice green."

"What!" Kate whipped her hair from under the water, flinging a wet stream across his face.

"Relax!" Cal laughed. "I'm kidding!" He wiped a shirtsleeve across his dripping face.

"Ooh, you... " Kate dug her fingers into the jar of gritty soap and brandished them toward his mocking grin.

"What? You threatenin' me—city gal?" His smug expression dared her.

"City gal, eh?" She shrugged and rubbed her hands together as if in preparation to wash them. With lightning speed she struck, leaving a thick line of goo down both sides of his face, satisfied with the look of shock that replaced his smugness.

Slowly, Cal twisted the towel in his hand into a long, rope.

"Oh no! Don't even think about it." Kate remembered all too well the pain of a well-executed towel pop from poolside fights in her younger days.

Kate noted the excitement of battle in Cal's eyes, the eyebrows raised in triumph as if he'd just stumbled upon buried treasure. She felt a perverse thrill, with just a touch of fear. It had been so long since she'd felt this way. For just a moment the weight of responsibility was forgotten. It felt wonderful.

Their eyes locked in recognition, in unspoken understanding. They weren't kids here. This was dangerous ground.

Cal tossed her the towel and turned toward the still running water, splashing his face, finally sticking his entire head under the faucet.

By the time he emerged dripping from the sink, the towel rested on the cabinet beside him and Kate was gone.

Later, thoughts of depleted finances and troubled children were kept at bay. Kate fell asleep with a smile on her face, recalling the feel of Cal's hands in her hair.

Mrs. Cartwright was restless again. Maybe it was something she ate. She had never been fond of turkey, especially when it tasted like it came from a can. In frustration, she grasped the steel bars beside her but had no strength to pull herself upright. She toyed with the idea of pushing the button for assistance but Amy was not on duty tonight. It was that other one, Mrs. Holtz, who would just stick a bedpan under her or give another pill to relax her. She didn't want to relax. Something was terribly wrong. If only she could grip her Bible, turn the fragile pages and read until she grew calm. But, nothing about Mrs. Cartwright was as it used to be—except her mind. Her mind was still painfully alert and aware, aware of the fact she was most likely stuck in this bed to the end of her days. Oh, how she longed for that end to come, to just float out of this tired body, leaving it behind like a useless cocoon.

With her eyes shut tight, she recalled the joy of running, a fresh spring breeze in her hair. She was running toward her favorite tree, the one up on the hill, facing the fields of grazing cattle while a bright orange sun sent streaks of pink and gold across the sky. At the foot of that tree, her favorite person waited for her, arms open wide for her to snuggle into his chest, the warm, fresh white linen, soft against her cheek as her forehead nestled into his dark, coarse beard.

She could see the page so clearly, teardrop stains blurring the ink of underlined and highlighted words:

"Oh God, thou art my God.
Early will I seek thee.
My soul thirsts for thee,
my flesh longs for thee
in a dry and weary land where there is no water…" (Psalm 63: 1)

With tears running from her eyes to the white curls at her temples, Mrs. Cartwright fell into a fitful sleep. No one was there to see the bony hands relax their grip on the sheets or the pain-free expression that stole across her features.

Kate lifted her head and looked around the room with sleep-heavy eyes. How did she come to be in the master bedroom of the old house? A thick curtain draped from the tall posts of the bed, drawn back with braided and tassled silken cords. In the middle of the floor sat a child. Dim light glimmered on the shining curls and sparkling tracks of wetness on the child's cheeks. With a mother's compassion, Kate was by her side in an instant.

"Honey, what's wrong?"

The confused eyes turned toward her and a soft smile of recognition lit the innocent features. In an instant, the eyes welled with fresh tears and the child threw herself, sobbing, into Kate's arms, the soft, round, fragile little body shook with grief as Kate felt hot tears on her neck. Soon, her own tears flowed as the child's grief became part of her, her own heart breaking with each wracking sob.

Kate felt something in her hand—a small cloth. Through bleary eyes, she stared at the item, a silky cotton handkerchief with a large "P" embroidered in elaborate script in one corner with smaller letters flanking it on either side.

She used the handkerchief to dry the child's eyes. This time, the girl wasn't inclined to speak, but simply allowed Kate to hold her as she continued to weep. Finally, she stood, brushed the damp blonde curls away from her face and reached a hand to Kate.

Suddenly they were outside under a rumbling, slate gray sky. The air felt thick and breathless as if pushed down with a heavy hand.

Soft, urgent voices were speaking somewhere close by. The child pressed against Kate's side, trembling as if her worst nightmare had climbed from under the bed and lurked in the green dimness. The branches before them parted and they saw the backs of two people walking away, a woman in a long gown with mounds of blonde hair piled on her head, and a tall man in a dapper suit with tuxedo-like tails.

Holding the child's hand, Kate followed the man and woman's progress toward the gleaming pool house in the backyard. When the couple went through the iron gate of the pool enclosure, the child led Kate to where they could look through a window.

The hushed voices were clear.

"But Charles was away so long. He'll know this… baby… can't be his!" The woman's tear-choked voice was desperate, pleading.

"Then tell him. We'll go far away, start a new life…"

"But I can't leave Belle…"

"She can come with us."

"It would crush Charles. I could never…" Fresh sobs erupted from the woman. "He's done nothing to deserve this." Her voice was a ragged whisper.

The man's ingratiating posture straightened. "You still love him."

The woman's wide, brimming eyes met his. "He's… a good man," she whispered.

The man took a step back, his face registering the pain of a knife cutting him to the heart. For a startled moment he studied her as his wide, shocked eyes narrowed and his handsome features hardened. "Then he deserves better than you." He spat the words as if to bite off a sob in his throat. "Goodbye, Katherine." He shoved a tall hat on his head and exited the pool house. The iron gate clanged shut behind him.

The young woman gasped and fell to her knees with her wide skirts forming a puddle around her.

Suddenly, Kate was no longer looking through the window. She *was* the woman kneeling on the ground, gasping for air around tight corsets, sobbing as she realized her entire world was destroyed. Kate was the woman who was alone, cold and afraid. Vague memories of stolen kisses, furtive glances, and secret meetings, all exciting and discreet, paraded through her mind. Every memory was a link in a chain trapping her to the ground, pulling her deeper and deeper into the soft earth.

But wait! Her husband need never know. She'd heard rumors of a solution. She would be the best, most devoted of wives—after. She would erase this horrible mistake once and for all, quickly, before her corsets got any tighter and her husband discovered how she had betrayed him.

Still trapped in the mind of the guilty young woman, Kate opened her eyes to dirty, dingy light and the smell of blood and death. Fear, like choking smoke, engulfed her and welled up in her throat, cutting off her screams with its horror. This was a mistake even worse than the affair! "No! Please, no!" she screamed. She thrashed against strong arms that held her down as a sickly sweet smell filled her nostrils. She screamed again as a sharp pain pulled her heart from her body and she felt warmth ooze from between her legs as strength and hope gushed out.

The scene changed. Kate was in a bed, the same bed where she had woken before but this time she was still trapped in the body of the other woman. She was so hot and thirsty as if flames ate at her from the inside. There were faces coming and going before her, precious faces of the sweet blonde child with tear-streaked cheeks and a handsome, mustached man who patted her hand and kissed her brow. But Kate's arms were too heavy to reach for them and she could not say anything to ease their pain. They whispered their love as tears fell, tears she had caused.

Hell was inside her, the flames growing hotter by the second, burning her alive…

Kate was screaming. She opened her eyes but darkness still surrounded her while horror gripped her mind and panic filled her lungs.

"Shhh." Warm, small arms wrapped around her. "It's okay Mommy. I'm here."

Phoenix stroked her hair, kissed her wet cheek, wrapped the comforter around Kate's shoulders against the chill and drew her back down to the pillow. "You're alright, Mommy. It's a nightmare."

"Jesus loves me, this I know…" Phoenix's sweet, off-pitch voice was little more than a whisper as her singing battled with the demons in Kate's mind.

CHAPTER 16

ADVENTURES & HYPOTHESES

Lilly was bored… and hungry, and angry, and if one more person told her, "Don't touch that!" she was going to hit them, or throw one of those special things. Even Mrs. Hayney, who was usually so nice, had snapped at her. She just wanted to taste the pieces of colored flowers in the pretty bowl. It smelled like cinnamon and apples. Why couldn't they put useful pretty things in that bowl, like candy? And what was so bad about digging for worms in the houseplants? The dirt outside was too cold and hard to dig in and she wanted to go fishing. Why couldn't Daddy take her fishing? He kept saying, "Not today."

Well then, she would just go by herself.

It was pretty outside. The grass and leaves sparkled like they were coated in sugar. Lilly stuck her tongue to a sparkly leaf. Blah! Just ice. So she picked up a long stick—and started hitting every sparkly thing in sight.

Winston, who had been tagging along hoping for some attention of his own, slunk away. He had experience with human pups and long sticks.

Lilly spun in circles in the pretty, trimmed bushes and watched the glitter shake off the leaves like pixie dust. She jumped to hit the lowest branches on the trees. What fun! She was making snow! She lifted up her face as the sparkles of coldness landed on her cheeks and on her tongue. At least it felt nice. Soon she grew tired of this too. It wasn't fun without a playmate.

A loud, gurgling swoosh from the direction of the pool house caught her attention. That sounded interesting. Yes, Mommy and Daddy had told everyone not to go near it, but she could look at it couldn't she?

Careful to avoid the spying windows of the house, Lilly peeked in. Darn. The water was still too low to see from the fence. The loud swooshing, sucking noise made Lilly jump. Now she just had to know what was going on in there.

Lilly could climb like a monkey so the metal bars in the opening of the wall around the pool was no problem, especially with the vines to give little boots and hands something to grab. The points at the top were tricky, tugging at her jeans and ripping her jacket, but soon Lilly was up, over, and proudly in one piece.

This was the first time in weeks workers weren't in the pool house, carting off wheelbarrow loads of broken cement, digging deep in the dirt or, as Lilly peeked in just a few days ago, placing bright tiles. That had looked like so much fun, but she hadn't even been allowed inside the gate. Now she looked down at the clean, bright blue tile with golden flecks catching the dim winter light. The whole place was bright and shiny like a new penny. She liked that.

She also liked that nobody was around to tell her what to do.

Lilly plopped down at the edge of the pool and dangled her boots. The water was still too low to touch. It was dirty too. She was disappointed not to be able to see the bottom. She went back to the locked gate and reached through the bars to grab a rock and returned with it to the edge of the pool. She reached toward the water and let the stone drop from her fingers, watching it sink into the milky depths. After a couple seconds, Lilly felt a light "plink" through her hands as it found the bottom. She giggled with delight and trotted back to the gate, reaching for more rocks, big and small. She didn't even know the word "science" but that didn't stop Lilly's joy of discovery.

Liam wasn't "big enough" to do anything. No one was painting anymore. They were moving around furniture and hanging pictures and hanging drapes and being picky and telling him over and over, "Out of the way, Liam!"

Fine. He'd get out of the way. He wandered up to the third floor. No one was working up here because no pictures would be taken for the magazine on the top floor. Good. He'd liked the house better before it was full of stuff he couldn't touch. The two small rooms up here and the attic were the only places left where a kid could play war or cops-and-robbers or even hide-and-seek without hurting a "nanteek," whatever that meant. Just looked like old furniture to him.

He didn't even pause in the small purple room with the window that looked out the front of the house. That was a girl's room. He could feel it. Nope, the attic was the place for a spy hiding from "Notsees". Luckily, mom hadn't found out he could open the attic door. As usual, he lifted up on the handle and slipped in the old credit card. Man, he was a genius.

Phoenix hid in her bedroom. She couldn't wait until this whole magazine thing was over and all the people went away. Until then, she'd keep her nose safely under the green gables of Avonlea.

"Hi, Phoenix!" The familiar voice made her smile. She turned to see her favorite friend in the world, the one who made her feel safe and pretty and special. "Let's play in the garden!" With that, the beautiful, blonde girl faded away, as usual leaving nothing behind but a light scent of purple.

Phoenix had stopped being surprised by her friend's sudden entrances and exits. She'd also stopped trying to convince anyone her pretty visitor in the lacy dress was real. Maybe the other kids were right. Maybe she was crazy. Somehow that didn't scare her anymore. Her crazy world was nicer than their real world any day.

Rollins struggled with the curtain rod in the master bedroom. He'd hung several this morning but now he'd hit something hard in the wall and the drill bit was getting nowhere. What was that? Something in the garden caught his eye. Lilly was sneaking around the pool house. Aw, he'd better go get her before the little stink got herself clogged in the filter.

It wasn't much fun spying on and hiding from nobody. Soon Liam slumped on the attic window seat feeling forgotten along with all the dusty boxes and discarded furnishings. Hey! Where was Rollins going? Wait a minute. There was Phoenix, too. Maybe they were having a secret meeting. Now that was worth spying on.

Cal was avoiding her. Kate struggled with acres of draperies and tried to focus on the task at hand rather than the quiet cowboy who hadn't even said "good morning," but she was unable to concentrate and, for the third time, heavy rings started sliding off the rod. Kate swore in frustration and pulled up sharply on the rod, trying to keep the drapes in place and avoid another trip back down the monstrous ladder. The yank left the remaining fabric and rings behind and, with a yelp of fright, Kate toppled. She grabbed for the window casing with one hand while retaining her grip on the rod with the other but continued to fall, scrabbling for a foothold or handle as gravity took over. With a pinging "thud" the end of the rod fell against the window and Kate found herself suspended with one foot on a leaning ladder and one hand slipping down the window like a three-dimensional game of Twister gone tragically awry.

The situation would have been comical in a far-fetched "I Love Lucy" sort of way if she hadn't thought she was about to die.

"Good God! Kate!" Jansen rushed in just in time to see the ladder tip from her toes toward an antique end table and lamp. With a frantic dive, he threw himself beneath Kate's floundering form, receiving a hard thud to the chest that knocked the wind out of him. They landed in a lump and watched the disaster before them. The lamp crashed to the floor while the ladder cut a large scar down the table with a heart wrenching "SCREE!" as the rod bounced from Kate's hand for another thump against the window. This time it was more of a hollow slap followed by what sounded like the crackle of thin ice giving way underfoot as spider web cracks snaked their way across the window.

Finally, just the sound of their labored breathing, a second's gratitude as Kate realized she hadn't broken her neck and a quick, "You alright?" to

Jansen who dislodged her shoulder from his ribs with a grunt.

It was a moment Kate would never forget. In all the years she'd known him, Jansen had always been the responsible one. He rarely raised his voice, preferring to work through issues without outbursts or accusations. This time, though, something snapped.

 When Lilly put her mind to a task, she worked fast. Already, several sticks and flowers floated on the water's milky surface. She was searching for the perfect thing that would not float or sink, but would go down slowly. And how did a big ship stay up on the water, but a little rock went straight down? Unfortunately, no one thought to explain displacement to a four-year-old, so Lilly was forced to theorize for herself.

Further scrounging unearthed some brick slivers. Hmmm. Quick hunting and gathering produced a small deck of assorted sizes and shapes. Perfect. Lilly flopped to her belly at the pool's edge and began dropping them, first one-by-one, then by twos and threes, eyes darting, senses absorbed in the activity. She didn't even notice the other young face suddenly reflected next to her own.

"Whatcha doin?"

"Look." Lilly took two brick slivers of similar size and dropped them at the same moment. "See?"

Excited, the two little girls with blonde curls discussed rate of descent, buoyancy, density and displacement without ever using words with more than one syllable.

"People can do it too," her companion enthused. "If you lay out flat in the water, you stay up. That's how daddy taught me to swim."

Through the hedge, Phoenix watched and marveled. Of course she could see Lilly's friend. She knew the blonde curls and blue eyes well. Joy flooded her heart. She wasn't crazy. Lilly could see her too!

With a happy smile, Belle turned toward her. "Come 'ere, Phoenix!"

Lilly chimed in. "Look at this!"

Phoenix clambered over the fence, joyful in the discovery she wasn't insane.

Rollins' pace slowed as he heard their voices. Good. No one was drowning. He crept closer. Belle? Who the heck was Belle? Oh no. Now Lilly was talking to Phoenix's imaginary friend too. Great! It was contagious. Anyone could see it was his civic duty to snap them back to reality.

"What're you doin?" Rollins' voice was gruff and loud, causing the girls to jump in fright. Unfortunately, the decorative tile was slick and Phoenix was crouching close to the edge. With a shriek, she toppled into the milky water.

Lilly's scream catapulted Rollins into action. In one bound, he was atop the fence, but his baggy jeans hung on the arrows making a valiant leap to the ground impossible. Frantically he yanked at the thick material.

A rush of dirty water squelched Phoenix's yelp of fright. Sure she could swim, but heavy clothing began to drag her down and the frigid water froze her limbs and mind. The fluffy boots were becoming bowling balls on the end of her legs, dragging her under. She thrashed and bobbed up, her face barely popping through the surface, but she might as well have been fighting quicksand as her efforts failed to break the force bent on sucking her to the bottom.

Kate didn't even recognize this angry person with the unshaven face and piercing eyes.

Jansen shook her. "What were you thinking? All you had to do was call for help! You coulda killed yourself!"

She had never seen him like this.

Jansen had never seen himself like this. The sight of his wife plunging headfirst was a final, heavy straw, cracking his careworn, sleep-deprived composure.

"I'm sorry!" Kate felt something dying inside. He'd never laid a hand on her in this way.

Mr. Briggs came into the room, seemingly unaware of the tension between them. He bent to examine the table. "I can touch this up, make it good as new."

Kate was vaguely aware of the others—Mrs. Hayney cleaning up the lamp, a couple of guys lifting the ladder—but mostly she was filled with a desire to escape; away from this old house, away from unending hassles and frustration, away from the constant pressure of bills and children. And far away from this angry stranger who held her shoulders.

Kate's ears zeroed in on a sound. Someone was yelling. Her heart froze with a dreadful premonition as Liam's frantic voice burst from the back of the house. "She fell in! She fell in!"

That could mean only one thing. Kate tore from the room and out the back door with Jansen right on her heels. Panic dogged every step as the shouts from the pool house grew nearer.

"Phoenix!" Phoenix could hear the voice clearly. "Take off your boots!" Belle's voice was right in her ear, calm and commanding. Phoenix focused on the sound, grasped it like a lifeline, and obeyed the order with fingers she couldn't feel, pushing with all her might on the mounds of heavy mush that anchored her down. Finally, she was free! Her foot brushed against something solid. It must be the bottom of the pool. If she could just push against it… But her body wouldn't do what she wanted. A calm thought entered her mind. Maybe this was it. It wasn't so bad. She could just relax… quit fighting.

Rollins pushed free of the pants only to find he was hanging by his ankles. Frantically he tore at the denim and boots that entangled him, finally flopping to the tile. He scrabbled to the pool's edge and dove where Lilly was looking, the icy water clamping tight on his chest. He reached the bottom and groped in all directions. If only he could see through the muck. Where was she? His heart sank as he realized he was at the top of the plunging deep end. His lungs were beginning to scream for air, but he forced his way deeper. He had to find her.

There was a flash to his left and he felt the current of something rushing past him. Blindly he followed the movement and grasped a handful of clothing. His face broke the surface. Phoenix was beside him!

Kate saw the iron enclosure looming before her just as Rollins disappeared into the pool with a splash, but she hardly gave it a thought as she vaulted the bars. She felt a sharp pain as she cleared the pointed tops of the iron fence but it didn't matter as she rushed to throw an arm around Lilly who was straining forward at the pool's edge as Jansen hopped in the water, following Rollins' path. Suddenly, Phoenix and Rollins broke the surface. Jansen was in the water, helping to shove Phoenix up to Kate's waiting arms. Her daughter was dead weight in the waterlogged jacket. Kate pushed back the tangled mass of red hair from the pale, still face. The beautiful eyes fluttered as Phoenix coughed and gasped. Kate sobbed with relief and pulled her daughter close.

"I'm sorry, Mom." Phoenix shivered as Kate carried her toward the house and a hot bath.

"Mom, you can stay."

Kate froze in shock. Phoenix hadn't allowed anyone to be present when she bathed for the past six months therefore Kate had assisted with the outer clothing and then had turned to exit. Her daughter removed the remaining frigid underclothes, slipped into the hot water, and gave Kate a dazzling smile. It was a miraculous smile, a relaxed, content, fully happy smile.

"I'm alright now," Phoenix said through blue lips and chattering teeth. "Can I tell you something?"

CHAPTER 17

STUCK IN THE PAST

Rollins stood under the hot spray and thought as he thawed. Everyone believed he was a hero, but he didn't really do anything besides rip his jeans and hop into icy cold water in his underwear.

So what was that light he saw? And he could swear there had been an extra person when Phoenix was lifted from the pool and he'd been treading water in his briefs. He shut his eyes and tried to recall the scene. Dad was in the pool, Mom was reaching for Phoenix, Liam and Cal were outside the gate, and Mrs. Hayney was trotting up to them. Then there was Lilly, on her knees beside the pool and… another girl in white.

Was he going crazy too?

A half hour later, Kate shut the door to the manufactured home with a bemused expression. She didn't know what to think. She was fading, adrenalin levels were dropping her with a thud, but she wanted to talk to Jansen. Her news wouldn't dig them out of debt or put the old house in photo-perfect condition, but it was very good news.

Her eyes were drawn to a gaping hole where the huge sitting room window had been. Cal was on the porch, wielding a huge push broom. Other than that, the injured house appeared deserted and their drive was free of all vehicles besides Cal's truck.

"What happened?"

"Jance scared 'em off."

"And the window?"

"Scared that off too."

Kate stared at the carnage in disbelief as Cal told of Jansen sloshing back into the house, wet through and through, only to give a swift kick to the already cracked window. Afterwards, he'd grabbed a large crowbar and continued beating the daylights out of that window until every piece was smashed from its frame.

"Everybody just decided to leave and let 'im get it out of 'is system." Cal glanced up from the broom's rhythmic swishing. "How's our mermaid?"

"Sleeping. Rollins too. Glad to be warm no doubt." Kate had no energy to panic again, but inquired about Liam and Lilly nonetheless.

"Ima took 'em to her house when the smashing started. They followed 'er like sheep as soon as she mentioned cocoa and cookies. She even brought some for you."

"Really?" Kate was surprised how that simple thought brought a thrill to her exhausted body and mind. "Lead the way, shepherd."

Jansen drove and drove, the truck's heater losing the battle against the aching chill of his wet clothing. He was grateful for the misery. It felt like some kind of penance for his failure. Dear God. What had he done? Why had he brought his family here? It was just one more in a long line of disastrous decisions. He ran a hand over his face, rubbing at the bloodshot eyes and stubble as he saw once again Phoenix's pale face coming out of the water. He'd thought she was dead.

He swerved into the tall grass of the roadside ditch, slammed the truck into "park" and wept like a baby.

The warm, rich chocolate flowed down Kate's throat like a tonic, bringing memories of Christmas mornings at Grandma's house. Christmas. It was only two weeks away and they were flat broke. She couldn't worry or care. She'd almost lost something she couldn't live without so gifts and tinsel didn't matter. The bite of chewy, buttery cookie turned to sawdust in Kate's mouth as she recalled last Christmas. To think they'd actually invited Rollins' friend, Alex, to Christmas dinner.

The thought of Alex turned Kate's thoughts to that mysterious conversation with Phoenix. She wanted to dismiss it as simply a child's reaction to intense trauma, perhaps an unconscious dream. But the actual change in Phoenix, the glowing, peaceful countenance, was undeniable. A silent tear traced its way down Kate's cheek. She'd thought that dazzling smile was gone forever.

How she wanted to tell Jansen. Another wave of worry swept over her. "Where did Jansen go?"

"Just took off."

"I know the glass was already broken, but…" She sniffed and wiped at her cheek. She could feel herself coming unhinged. Better find a private place for the impending breakdown.

Cal watched Kate out of the corner of his eye. He'd seen the momentary glimpse of childish joy that had turned just as quickly to sadness and a flash of painful anger. He loved the mystery of her emotions. It reminded him of the ever-changing Texas weather, unpredictable and exciting. He enjoyed watching them play across Kate's face, unguarded and passionate, like the unleashed forces of nature in the wide, clashing sky. In fact, he enjoyed watching her do just about anything.

Cal cleared his throat. "He'll be alright, Kate. Just boilin' over a bit. Everybody needs to sometimes."

Kate reached to give Cal's wrist a squeeze. "Thank you. Jansen needs a good friend right now."

Cal's hand caught hers. The contact was warm, protective and comforting. He held her fingers so gently. "You okay?"

She nodded and shrugged even as crocodile tears spilled in tandem to run down her cheeks.

Jansen remained slumped over the wheel as the flood drew to a close. He was absolutely wiped out, no strength left to worry. It was almost a vacation. He drew a numb arm across his nose and leaned his head against the seat. Something deep in his core gave up. Obviously, his best efforts were failing. It was a harsh reality, one with which he'd become acquainted at the age of fourteen.

He could see it so clearly. His dad, the man who'd taught him to hunt, ride a horse, fish, and just about every other cool thing a dad could do, lay in that antiseptic, white hospital bed, shriveled until he weighed less than his son.

Jansen had remained by the bedside, wanting to be there when his dad woke to say something important, those final words to live by and that last "I love you, son." That's the way it was in the movies.

But his father had finally just lost the battle to take his next breath.

Just like that, he was gone.

In the coming days, the well-meaning phrases drummed over and over in Jansen's young mind. "The Lord works in mysterious ways." "He's in a better place now." And, the one that struck fear to his heart. "Guess you're the man of the house now."

Two things he knew for sure. One, he'd never be able to fill his dad's shoes. And two, if God was the one who "took" his dad to a "better place," he hated God.

If he hated God so much, why had he kept saying, "Oh God! Oh God!" when he was sobbing his guts out just now?

Because, when it came down to it, there was nowhere else to go.

"Ya got me," Jansen stated aloud through chattering teeth. He started laughing, a bitter, angry hilarity that bubbled out of his soul like acid. "Big joke, huh. Just wait until I fall on my can and have nowhere else to turn."

Another scene flashed into his mind. The family was camping close to a swift-flowing stream. Four-year-old Jansen, always fiercely independent, wanted to swim there but had been warned of the danger. Late afternoon he had snuck away, determined to wade in the beautiful, flashing water. He'd felt so proud and adventurous. He'd show them he wasn't a little boy anymore.

The thrill was short-lived, however, when his feet swept out from under him and he plunged headfirst into the rushing, frigid water. Instantly, strong arms had grasped him, drawing him, sputtering and gasping, out of the churning current. No lectures had been needed or given.

In years to come, Jansen's father had delighted in telling and re-telling the tale of shadowing his headstrong son through the trees knowing that, "Shore 'nuff, that little cuss was gonna do what he blamed-well wanted to do. Had ta give him just enough rope to hang himself or he'd never learn."

The memory of his dad's slap on the shoulder and hearty laugh brought another wave of grief. It had taken thirty years, but Jansen Walden's tears for his deceased father finally saw the light of day.

CHAPTER 18

ON A CLIFF'S EDGE

Mrs. Cartwright thrashed and mumbled in her sleep. Amy dabbed at the hot, dry brow and tried to force another sip of water from the straw, but the old woman's mouth was clenched tight.

When Amy had arrived for her three-to-eleven shift, she was alarmed to discover Mrs. Cartwright's fever dangerously high. On her chart, it was simply noted that meal trays returned untouched and the old lady had slept all day.

When she checked pulse and blood pressure, Amy's concern mounted. Surely the frail body couldn't take much more. At her insistence, the doctor made a perfunctory visit and shook his head. "Nobody lasts forever. Better contact the family."

Now Amy gazed down with pity on the sleeping woman. She'd never seen a visitor for Mrs. Cartwright. Who could she call?

Among the sparse furnishings, Amy once again perused the small collection of old portraits. Various men and women in bustles and cravats gazed back at her, serious and silent. The most modern photograph showed a much younger Mrs. Cartwright and a dark skinned gentleman with the Eiffel Tower in the background. Amy peered closer at the handsome man in the photograph, recalling the day she'd asked Mrs. Cartwright about the photo. "Is this your husband? Woo, girl. He looks like Denzel Washington. No wonder he swept you off your feet!" Mrs. Cartwright had grinned and swatted a hand toward Amy as if shooing away a fly.

Amy wondered how people had responded to the marriage of black and white back in what looked to be the 1940s. Amy and her husband had been through their own share of grief on that issue. Even their kids were often teased for not being black enough or white enough. Personally, Amy thought her children were just perfect

Now, feeling like a snoop, Amy rifled through the small drawer of the writing desk, discovering a stack of ribbon-entwined letters and cards. Most were postmarked twenty years ago and mailed to an address in New York. That wasn't much help.

A small newspaper clipping that was wedged among the cards fell to the floor. The picture of an old house and a smiling man accompanied a caption involving an historic homestead opening to the public as a county museum. Hmmm. It wasn't much of a lead and the story was old, but at least it was local.

Rollins woke with a start and stared around his bedroom, cast in deep heather shadows of the fading winter afternoon. He was ravenously

hungry, as usual, but that wasn't what woke him. He'd been dreaming. What was it? Vaguely he tossed through his thoughts, attempting to bring the retreating subconscious back to the surface, but the harder he tried the more elusive it became. Finally, he skulked to the kitchen for a sandwich. The refrigerator and cabinets yielded slim pickins'. With all the focus on Pedigo Manor, most of the family's meals had been frozen dinners, cold sandwiches, or cereal. At the moment, even their cereal stash was low. He poured a bowlful of some healthy, grainy, bland stuff. The grocery outlook had to be grim indeed for him to resort to his mom's leaves and twigs breakfast cereal.

"Aw man!" A scant quarter inch of milk remained in the carton. He'd never be able to choke that stuff down without tons of milk. Worse yet, the milk was sour. Disgusted, Rollins dumped the slop in the trash, trading it for the ever-faithful peanut butter jar and a spoon.

He flipped on the television. As usual, there was nothing worth watching. They had been planning on installing cable, but until then, the major networks were downright depressing. The most riveting program was a show about cooking fish… that just made him hungrier.

He peered out the front window toward Pedigo Manor. Only Cal's truck remained in the driveway. Maybe everybody had gone to eat?

He wandered the house, finally peeking into Phoenix's room. That was funny. He crept closer for a better look. Amazing.

Rollins felt like he was studying one of those drawings in a kids' magazine that ask, "What's wrong with this picture?" Well, there were a number of things. For starters, her drapes were wide open. Paranoid Phoenix would never allow that. Second, she lay on her back, arms spread wide, with the covers mussed and twisted around her legs. Of late, his sister had always slept in a tight ball with wrinkle-free sheet and blankets pulled over her eyes. Third, her hair was in wild disarray, spread out on the pillow and flopped across her face, the luminous red curls resembled a woodland sprite napping among mossy trees. He couldn't remember the last time she'd set it free from a thick, tight, ponytail. Weird.

Part of him wanted to stare, to enjoy the sight of his sister looking as carefree as gutsy, fearless Lilly, but instead he backed out of the room. He'd never fancied himself a poet, but the only way to describe his red-haired sibling at the moment was "otherworldly." Kinda gave him the creeps.

Maybe he was just jumpy from the pool incident. That was probably it. He'd thought his sister was drowning, had jumped into freezing water to save her, and had ended up hallucinating. It was enough to put anybody on edge.

How he wished he had a beer to steady his nerves. Fat chance in this house. Rollins pilfered the cabinets. Darn. Even that old bottle of wine mom and dad saved for some unknown special occasion was missing. He reached toward a bottle in the spice cabinet. Red wine vinegar? Guess it would have to do.

To be on the safe side, he stationed himself by the front window to keep a lookout before opening the bottle. Whew! This stuff was stout.

Just as he screwed up his courage to pour some of the noxious liquid down his throat, he yelped and dropped the bottle. The little blonde girl—his hallucination—was right outside the window.

Cal's hand reached to wipe the tears from Kate's cheeks. Once again, the cowboy was surprising her. The gentle touch and concern in his eyes made her feel like the most cherished, precious person on the planet. The unexpected tenderness dissolved her last remaining grain of composure.

When his arms went around her, Kate's flood of tears soaked his shoulder.

The images running through Cal's mind were breathtaking.

He longed to lay her down and love her, body and soul, until every heartache was forgotten. She'd gaze up at him, those expressive hazel eyes reflecting candlelight, the shining mane tousled and free, and smile with contentment as she fell asleep in his arms.

Kate didn't cry often, but when she did, she did a thorough job of it. Rarely had she allowed Jansen to witness a meltdown. If she was upset, he tended to think he, as her husband, had somehow failed her. So they had fallen into a seemingly thoughtful routine to spare each other unnecessary grief. He strove to be infallible. She kept her tears to herself.

In the past six months, this solo suffering had become exhausting.

It was so comforting to feel the strength of a man's arms around her when she was most vulnerable. The firm, muscular shoulder pressed against her cheek was like a poultice drawing poison deep from her soul until trust ran clear and free. The whispered assurance and warm hand stroking her hair brought memories of her father when she was very young and he still had strength to spare for someone else.

Cal was feeling anything but fatherly. The actuality of lovely Kate in his arms was taxing the limits of his self-control. She was his best friend's wife! That fact had been slapping him in the face for months now; months of realizing he'd never really loved before. Sure he'd had girlfriends and even a short term live-in or two, but those experiences had only convinced him bachelorhood wasn't such a bad thing. Not once had his desire for a woman extended beyond pleasing himself. Now it seemed perfectly natural to want nothing more than to make her smile. It struck him what a glorious thing it must be to make love with that goal in mind.

A crash upstairs broke the tender moment. Kate jumped back and wiped at her smeared face. Cal handed her a handkerchief from his pocket and tried to act interested in investigating the noise.

For Kate, the feel of the small, silky square of cotton in her hand triggered the strangest sense of déjà vu. She studied the unadorned piece of fabric as a shudder of dread flowed through her that had nothing to do with mysterious noises in a creepy old house.

Rollins' fists clenched as he watched the scene through the kitchen window. Cal stepped aside and allowed Kate to exit the kitchen ahead of him, his eyes carefully following her movement. No way! The creep was checking out his mom! Wait a minute. Where'd that fancy blonde kid go? Rollins peered around the yard for a glimpse of the fluffy white dress and blonde ringlets that had nearly stopped his heart and had lured him to this very spot. Oh well, he'd deal with weird kids playing hide-and-seek later. For now, Cal was absolutely real, and Rollins was old enough to recognize when a guy was itching to make a move. He'd see about that!

And on the way, he'd nab those cookies the jerk left behind.

Jansen was warm and light, as if a lead suit had just slipped off his shoulders. He saw flashes of himself, coming and going, achieving, failing, joyful and sad, people and places he'd known and left behind; he was free to weave in and out of his memories, released from the constraints of time and space. All of these things weren't lost, they had just been tucked away like props for a stage play, hidden behind the curtain when they were no longer part of the story. But that's the way it all felt now, as if everything that had gone before was just pretend. This moment, this concrete and ethereal moment, was the prelude to the main event. He was free to move forward, to step behind the curtain and have all the answers to mysteries that had plagued him for time out of mind—but something held him back.

The play wasn't over. Act three's climax was just unfolding. But he wasn't ready. Just a short moment's rest in the shadows, a moment to regain his bearings, then he'd step back into the heavy costume and harsh light. But not yet... not yet.

Mrs. Cartwright's fever continued to rise. At Amy's insistence, the doctor made another visit, offering a prescription for painkillers to "make the old woman's last hours more comfortable." Amy wanted to hit him. Did he truly think there was no hope or was he just in a hurry to get home to dinner?

She spent every possible moment at Mrs. Cartwright's side. She didn't know Mrs. C's history, but she was certain this kind woman didn't deserve to die alone.

About five in the evening, the white haired woman became especially agitated, the bony hands clutching at the bedclothes, the muscles of her face straining and grimacing, alternating between pain, anger, and what appeared to be petrifying fear. The closest thing Amy had ever witnessed to Mrs. Cartwright's agitated display was watching her own husband as he lived and breathed professional boxing bouts on television, grimacing and dodging as if his movements were somehow affecting his champ like the joystick on a videogame.

Amy checked Mrs. Cartwright's vital signs once more. Blood pressure and temperature were both climbing. How Amy wished she could surround Mrs. C. with loved ones, with soft, smooth children's hands gripping the old woman's fingers and precious, familiar voices whispering love and comfort.

It was a complete shot in the dark, but Amy reached for the phone and dialed information. "Could I have the number for a Mr. Jefferson Briggs, please?"

Phoenix began to stir, still fuzzy and drowsy, from the best sleep she'd ever had. It was really dark. Wow! It was really dark, and she was okay with that. But she did wonder where everybody was… and she was so hungry. But it was plain old curiosity and real hunger, not absolute panic and wanting to calm herself by hiding in her room and stuffing her face with Oreos. She smiled in awe at the significant difference. Maybe the things she saw and heard when she thought she was dying really happened after all.

She shut her eyes and sighed, recalling the… the… what could she call it? Was it light? Was it warmth? Was it liquid love? All she knew was she had melted into it like a sponge soaking up water until every little hole was filled up. And she had been full of holes. Every rip and tear had burned in that light. Every fear had sizzled in that melting power that made her so sad she had felt as if her heart was going to burst right out of her chest.

And then He had been there. She didn't have to question who He was, she just knew. She had tried to describe him to Mother, but it was impossible. The closest thing she could think to say was that He was "pure love with fiery eyes; kind, gentle eyes that chose to turn down their power so it wouldn't burn my eyeballs."

Even now, when she closed her eyes, Phoenix could see those eyes looking into hers, telling her without words that she was loved and precious—and pure.

She couldn't help herself. There, in the dark that had petrified her for months, nine-year-old Phoenix jumped on her bed and laughed with joy.

The scene changed. Jansen was sitting in the corner of a boxing ring taking a squirt of water from a plastic bottle, mouthpiece shoved back into his swollen, bleeding lips, eyes puffed shut so the swirling images of caretakers and pressing crowd were smudged blurs in a harsh, hard world.

"Okay, champ. This is it. Dig deep and blast him from the basement! This is your moment!" Jansen felt a sharp pressure next to each brow. Warmth flowed and was mopped away. His father's face took shape before him, intense and insistent as a bell sounded and he stumbled straight ahead.

There was the opponent, standing tall and strong, anticipating Jansen's approach. Aah! Blood and sweat burned his eyes, stole his vision. Bam! He took a hard blow to the jaw. Lights swirled as his legs turned to rubber. Blindly he swung back, connecting with nothing but air as his opponent pummeled him, lightning fast combinations coming from all sides.

Who was this guy and why did he want to beat the hell out of Jansen? There wasn't a quadrant of his body that didn't scream in pain, but the odds were too high. Somehow, he had no doubt this was a fight to the death. No, worse than death; this was a fight for his family. Without them, what good was he? There was too much to lose.

With every shred of primal instinct, Jansen threw himself against the blows. Forget rules, forget form. With pure, panicked, brute force, Jansen drove the guy to the ground. So what if his enemy was stronger and hit harder, Jansen would still win. Finally, Jansen pinned the guy. His opponent's arms were trapped under Jansen's knees as he continued to unleash his rage although the face before him already resembled road kill.

Jansen heard a bell but continued throwing blow after blow, ensuring this threat to his family would never resurface. Red and blue lights swirled around his head, strong arms pulled at him but he fought them. He had to make sure the guy was dead. He strained for a good look at the now unmoving form.

The features were familiar despite their swollen, bleeding state. Jansen removed the glove from his hand, finding he was clutching a handkerchief in his fist. Resisting the arms that held him, he strained forward and swiped the cloth across his enemy's face. He only had a split-second's identification, but it was enough.

The bleeding face was his.

CHAPTER 19

STEP INTO THE LIGHT

Ima Hayney stirred the scrambled eggs on the stove and tried to pay attention to the children's excited voices but she was worried. That poor Walden family was set to crack. They were good people but even good people could blow it when life got to be too much.

And there was something else brewing. She was no fool. That Cal was plumb smitten with Kate, his eyes watching her like a love-struck pup when he thought no one was looking. And that Jansen was too distracted to notice.

It all felt too familiar. She'd heard stories about the old place through the years, something about a tragic past and a young man killing himself over his unfaithful wife. But that was almost a century ago. Surely it was just rumor, a good excuse for folks to say the place was haunted.

Regardless, Ima Hayney wasn't gonna stand by and do nothin' when there were kids involved. That fox Cal would just hafta do his chicken stealin' at those dance halls he liked so much and not under Ima's very nose.

"C'mon kids. Eat up quick. We gotta get you home."

Kate clutched the handkerchief in her hand as she hurried up the stairs. The feel of the thin, smooth fabric square was triggering something but the recollection was buried by the emotions of the present. Her husband was missing, her daughter had nearly drowned and had some kind of vision, but Kate couldn't shake the feeling of Cal's arms holding her. She assumed Cal was as embarrassed as she was. What was he supposed to do when a desperate mother of four melted down all over him? And how pathetic that the desperate mother had kinda enjoyed it?

She chattered about what could have made the noise. Was it an animal? A breeze through an open window? But Kate was just trying to break the tension and it wasn't working. Her world was falling apart and, fool that she was, she had loved being held by Cal. In fact, there was a cord wrapped around her middle pulling her back toward his chest as surely as a fish on a hook.

If only he would say something. But he was so quiet, and when their hands brushed on the banister he yanked away. Poor guy. She'd probably pushed him way out of his comfort zone.

In a voice that was overly bright she suggested they go separate ways to cover more ground.

"Kate."

That was all. Just her name. But it was packed to the brim with a statement—and a question—and an apology. She froze and, against better judgment, she looked.

If he had met her eye it would have been easier but Cal was looking at his fist on the banister, therefore she had time to take note of every shred of body language: the clenched jaw, the taut posture as if bracing against a stiff wind.

Then he glanced up. No words—just that look informing her loud and clear if she so much as batted an eyelash to encourage him, all bets were off.

Jefferson Briggs answered the phone. His easy manner changed to shock and then to a sad smile. "I'll be there in fifteen minutes."

His hand shook as he placed the circa 1970s corded phone on its cradle. "Well, well, Jedediah. Looks like the pieces are finally comin' together, eh?"

Rollins swung through the kitchen for the cookies. It was quiet. Too quiet. Should he yell? Nah. He'd rather catch the S.O.B. red-handed.

With a bracing gulp of hot chocolate from Mrs. Hayney's thermos, Rollins headed for the stairs.

"Phoenix!"

Phoenix stopped jumping, her red hair hanging in ringlets across her eyes. "Hi, Annabelle. Boy, do I have somethin' to tell you!"

"Not now. Come with me."

Her friend looked scared. But wait, Annabelle wasn't afraid of anything. "What is it?" Phoenix asked.

But the petite figure with bright curls and white dress was already out on the lawn, racing toward the old house, so Phoenix hopped off the bed and ran toward the front door of the doublewide. Too bad she couldn't slip through walls too.

It was liquid gold flowing through Kate's veins to have a man look at her like that, like he needed to breathe and she was his air. But there were a million reasons why she shouldn't be enjoying it, namely a husband and kids and morality and… she felt herself slipping toward him. Maybe this was how her father had felt when he couldn't resist alcohol. No. This was worse. This was standing at the top of a bottomless pit and falling in—and pulling everyone she loved with her.

But Cal's eyes, so adoring, so gentle, were the very thing she had missed and needed. Her eyes flicked to his mouth. God, no! He knew. She had told him with that one look.

He took that last step that brought him to the landing, that brought him closer, his eyes reading her soul.

THUD!

Kate flinched and looked toward the sound. She walked into the darkened bedroom where she'd heard it. She was groping along the wall—where was that light switch?

A hand rested on her shoulder. It wasn't the boogey man. She would have been less frightened if it was.

Her fingers touched the round, antique switch and a monumental struggle ensued. Cal was so near she could feel his warmth. His hand squeezed just a bit tighter on her shoulder and he came closer, perhaps just an inch, but it made her warmer, made her able to feel his breath on her hair. The light was at her fingertips. With a Herculean effort, she flipped it. The light was sluggish and flickered but came on.

Cal gasped and stared at the light fixture overhead. His head whipped around to view the tall ladder still folded on the landing exactly where he'd left it. His hand dropped from Kate's shoulder.

Amy grasped Mrs. Cartwright's hand, watching carefully for that telltale last gasp of breath. It was so sad, so tragic that this sweet woman should die alone. She should have family surrounding her, little pudgy hands grasping hers, tear-streaked faces smiling and thanking her for a life well-lived, a life that had passed on a heritage of love.

With a swipe at the tears on her cheeks, Amy determined to do what she could to make this moment what Mrs. Cartwright deserved. She reached for the tattered, black book on the bedside table and turned to the passage on a page that was so worn it threatened to fall from the binding.

"The Lord is my Shepherd, I shall not want..."

Mrs. Cartwright gasped, her chest rising with a feeble breath as the grip on Amy's fingers tightened. Amy leaned closer, speaking the words of the Psalm in a trembling voice.

"He restoreth my soul
He leadeth me in paths of righteousness..."

She stopped reading. Mrs. Cartwright's eyes were open, looking past Amy with an expression of astounding joy. From the lips of the withered woman who had never uttered a sound in Amy's presence came a squeal of delight and... a giggle.

Amy turned to follow the old woman's gaze toward the open door but saw nothing besides the greenish fluorescent light spilling from the hallway. But there was a scent... something that reminded her of soft spring days, and raindrops on garden flowers.

Mrs. Cartwright gripped Amy's hand with almost painful strength and moved as if to sit up then collapsed back on the pillows, eyes still fixed on the doorway. A shadow fell across the bed.

Amy jumped and looked. At this point she wouldn't have been surprised to see an angel with feathered wings. Instead, she beheld a tall, angular man with white hair combed back from his forehead.

The man came to the bedside and smiled down. "Hello Miss Annie."

Mrs. Cartwright's eyes opened wide and she reached toward the man who took her outstretched hand.

The man nodded up at Amy. "Thanks for calling me, young lady."

Mrs. Cartwright's face grimaced with effort. She opened and shut her mouth. Finally, a rasping, whispered word came from her lips. "Jeff-rey?"

Amy marveled as Mrs. Cartwright, with a surge of strength and coherence, returned the newcomer's hug with fierce strength.

Kate felt an icy breeze on her shoulder where Cal's hand had been. She wanted to cry out from the loneliness it had left behind. But, what was that? There was a large picture frame lying face down on the floor on the other side of the room. Maybe that was the noise they'd heard?

She crossed the room and lifted the frame to reveal a small, dingy something beneath it. She picked up a tattered, yellowed piece of cloth, frayed around the edges, with embroidered initials in one corner.

It was Kate's turn to gasp as the dream came back to her with blinding clarity. She had been in this very room and had held this very item—a handkerchief with an ornate P in the corner.

Kate trembled as the dream came back to mind with heart-stabbing clarity. She was seeing that child crying in the floor; little shoulders heaving with sobs, eyes full of despair, blonde curls plastered to tear-stained cheeks. The face changed in her mind. The hair turned from flaxen to copper, the nose to a familiar, freckle-kissed one.

The hazel eyes of Phoenix stared back at her. Oh God! It could be her. It could be Phoenix—and Rollins—and Liam—and little Lilly. She, Kate, could cause that pain four, no, five times over!

Sorrow gripped her heart and she broke, just dissolved in tears right there in the floor with the yellowed handkerchief clutched in her right hand and Cal's handkerchief in the other.

Cal's hand was on Kate's shoulder, but there was no longer any temptation.

Pain had inoculated her.

"Kate. What is it?" Cal was on the floor with her. His arm was around her shoulders.

She shrugged him away, shaking her head but she was unable to speak around the horror in her throat as a new fear grew. The thought of Jansen flooded her mind. He needed her. Where was he? Here she was toying with attraction to his best friend when something was very wrong.

A rueful laugh escaped her lips. Yes, something was very wrong. His wife was set to drive a stake in his heart.

She gasped as fresh sobs tore through her.

Cal looked on in confusion, his libido sounding a hasty retreat as he realized what was going on was much deeper—and, yes, he'd even say more sacred—than he could fathom. He reached to brush back a strand of hair from Kate's cheek. "Please, Kate. It's okay."

She just flinched away from him.

"Hey! Get away from her!"

He'd not heard Rollins enter the room but Cal sure felt the grip on his shoulder that sent him sprawling across the floor.

"Now look, kid…"

But Rollins was on him, fists flying, spitting curses in his face as Cal's entire body focused on deflecting blows. With a gasp, he felt something pop in his side.

"Rollins! No!" Kate was there, pulling at Rollins' arm but Rollins wasn't finished. He came at Cal with murder in his eyes.

Cal didn't know karate, but he knew survival. With all his might he jumped at Rollins, throwing his entire weight behind the blow and sending Rollins flying against the wall. With a "whoosh" he heard the air rush from Rollins's lungs and saw the surprise in the boy's eyes.

There was a sound from the doorway, something between a scream and a strangling noise and both men turned. Phoenix was framed there, tears streaming down her cheeks, horror etched across her features.

Ice-cold water in the face couldn't have cooled Rollins' rage faster. In an instant his hands were at his sides as he and Cal took painful gasps of air.

"It's okay, Honey." Kate ran to her. "It's just a big misunderstanding."

"HALLOO THE HOUSE!" Mrs. Hayney's voice echoed from downstairs as the front door slammed. Four sets of eyes looked around in shock. Blood ran from Cal's lip and he was clutching his side. Rollins was grasping his knees and gasping to breathe while Kate and Phoenix's faces were wet with tears. How could they explain this?

Suddenly, each one in the room heard it. A giggle. It was a child's suppressed laughter as if a hand was pressed to their mouth. The sound flitted around the room, carried on a breeze that brushed each cheek like the phantom touch of a butterfly wing.

The other three looked to Phoenix but she was staring toward the brightest spot of light in the center of the room. Her tragic expression was gone, replaced by joy.

"What is it, Phoenix?" Kate whispered.

But her daughter ignored her and tilted her head as if trying to understand—something.

"It's nine thirty! Thought it was time these kids was in bed!" Mrs. Hayney called as the sound of noisy footsteps echoed on the stairs.

"Up here!" Kate answered. But her eyes were on Phoenix whose lips were moving as if in conversation.

Sadness filled Phoenix's eyes and a large tear ran unchecked down her cheek. "I'll miss you," she whispered.

They all heard it again. A giggle flitted around the room with just the slightest rustle of… what was that… taffeta? And they saw Phoenix, eyes darting around the walls until her hair swirled and lifted, caught in a tiny whirlwind. Her eyes drifted up to the ceiling as if watching a balloon disappear into the sky.

Liam and Lilly burst into the room. Liam stopped and looked around at the stunned faces while Lilly announced, "I smell purple! Belle!"

Lilly squinted and waved toward the light fixture, an expression of rapture on her cherubic face. "Yay, Belle! You're fwying!"

Jansen was cold… so cold. He tried to open his eyes but the flash of light hurt. His teeth chattered so hard it felt they would rattle clean out of his head. He felt a touch on his hand and small fingers curled around his with a surge of warmth that emanated to the tips of his numb toes. "Ow!" He gasped as the numbness sounded a painful retreat.

"You've been busy, haven't you," Mr. Briggs stated.

Mrs. Cartwright's only answer was a sad shake of her head.

"Sweet Miss Annie," Mr. Briggs caressed Mrs. Cartwright's wrinkled cheek and wiped at the wetness trickling from the corners of her eyes. "I had an interesting conversation with a little girl today. Seems she has a friend who plays with her when she's lonely. Most people tell this child it's just her imagination but it kinda makes me wonder. Do you know anything about a little girl named Lilly?"

Mrs. Cartwright's eyes grew wide and she made a sort of choking noise that made Amy jump to assist her. But such a look of pleading joy was on the old woman's face, Amy froze.

"Have you been praying, Miss Annie? You always were quite the prayer warrior. Sounds like, even from this bed, you've been making a tremendous difference."

Mrs. Cartwright's eyes welled with new tears. Again, she opened and closed her mouth in an effort to speak. Finally, one word. "Really?" The blue eyes welled with fresh tears as Mrs. Cartwright leaned forward and squeezed Mr. Briggs hand with white-knuckled intensity.

"My sweet Miss Annie," Mr. Briggs whispered, "I do believe, even here, you're still blessing the little ones, aren't you?"

Mrs. Cartwright let her head fall back onto the pillow as her face lit with joy.

"You are positively glowing, Miss Annie," Mr Briggs brushed Mrs. Cartwright's hair back and planted a kiss on her hand that still clutched his. "You have never been more beautiful, or more loved than you are right now."

And Amy had never seen such a glorious smile.

CHAPTER 20

MATTERS OF LIFE
& DEATH & LIFE

Five sets of eyes stared around the room, blinking, amazed, unbelieving, frightened. Only Phoenix and Lilly appeared at ease, still gazing toward the light, expressions of rapture on their upturned faces.

"Belle has a new dwess," Lilly stated.

"Belle? Who's Belle?" asked Liam.

Kate was afraid to speak, afraid to disturb the breathless magic in the air. But to a child, any moment is fair game.

"Why does it smell like flowers? Hey, Cal, you're bleedin'. What's the matter with Rollins? Mom, why're you cryin'?" Liam's questions rolled on, forcing Kate's feet back onto responsible ground.

"Just an accident. Let's get you guys to bed."

"But ya gotta fix ol' Jedediah's picture." Liam pointed to the frame that remained face down on the floor. "Mr. Briggs told me he's the guy who built this place."

"I'll get that," Cal offered.

"No. You get lost." Rollins glared at him.

Kate rolled her eyes and reached for the picture frame. She could have the thing re-hung and the kids in bed before Rollins was finished with his macho act.

In fact, feminine efficiency was already in full swing with Mrs. Hayney shooing the younger three toward the stairs, when Kate gasped and dropped the portrait back on its face.

"What is it, Mom? A spider?" Liam rushed toward her.

Kate braced herself and peeked again, half expecting the mutton-chop, side-burned face to wink at her. "Hello," she murmured. "We meet again."

Suddenly, red and blue swirling lights flashed around the room. All rushed to the window and peered down into the front yard where a police car sat, its revolving dome striking a deep note of terror in Kate's heart.

"We picked up your husband, ma'am," Sheriff Holt announced when Kate opened the door. "Don't worry, he didn't break a law. We sent him on in the ambulance. Been tryin' ta call but…"

"What?" Kate wanted to shake the slow-talking officer. "An ambulance!"

Moments later, Kate and Rollins were en route to the hospital with Cal, bouncing along the country roads at breakneck speed behind the wailing police car. Kate had gotten the distinct impression Officer Holt was thrilled to have an excuse to drive like a scene from "The Fast and The Furious". For her part, Kate had come close to breaking one of his laws by throttling the maddening, grinning man when he wouldn't give her any more information than the fact that Jansen had been found unconscious.

"Now ya wouldn't expect a doctor ta issue a speeding ticket so it's not my place ta give a medical opinion," he had stated with his permanent toothy grin.

"I'll drive her over, George." Cal stepped in when he saw the sparks flare in Kate's eyes.

Rollins hadn't asked and he hadn't been invited but he planted himself in the center of the pick up seat even though his long legs were crammed against the dash. After about five miles of testosterone-laced silence, Kate issued a quiet, "Thank you for driving us."

But before Cal's perfunctory "No problem" was out Rollins interjected a mumbled "asshole."

Kate slapped Rollins' arm as Cal drawled, "Ya got somethin' ta say, boy?"

"Lots."

"Then say it."

"If I said everything on my mind, I'd be grounded for the rest of my life."

"Then I guess you'll have to save it 'til you're man enough."

Kate couldn't believe her ears. "Just stop it, you two."

"Liam's more man than you," Rollins replied through gritted teeth.

"Should be easy for you ta teach me a lesson then," Cal drawled as he pulled to the side of the one-lane road.

"Hey! What're you doing?" Kate watched as the sheriff's lights disappeared around a bend.

But they ignored her. Cal opened his door and Rollins followed him into the frigid night air. "You've gotta be kiddin' me! We have to get to the hospital!" Kate yelled.

But already they faced each other, Rollins in his best combat-ready stance while Cal taunted him. "C'mon Karate Kid. Now's your chance."

Kate felt no remorse whatsoever when she pealed out in Cal's pickup, grinding the gears and scattering gravel on the two opponents as she raced to catch up with Sheriff Holt's lights. She'd be back for them as soon as she checked on Jansen.

"Move on, dear heart," Mr. Briggs whispered. "Be young and free again."

Jefferson Briggs remained holding Mrs. Cartwright's hand even as her fingers relaxed and grew cold. "She was there for me when no one else was, takin' me under her wing, fixin' meals, mendin' clothing, makin' sure I had a ride to church every Sunday. All the things my mother woulda done if she had lived. I hate to think what I woulda become without Miss Annie. Probably been dead or in prison long ago."

Tears ran down his cheeks and dripped onto the bed even as he chuckled. "Oh my! That day she heard I'd been caught stealin' from the five-and-dime she came to the sheriff's station, signed a bunch of forms, paid a fee and sprung me. The rest of that summer, she kept me haulin' rocks outa that field where she wanted a pond. Thought my back was gonna break!

"'Ya like this, Jeff?' she said to me. 'Keep goin' the way ya are and you'll get to make little rocks outa big rocks for the rest of your life.'" Mr. Briggs wiped the cuff of his sleeve across his eyes.

"Lost track of Miss Annie durin' the war. Ol' Jedediah told me she joined up as a nurse and ended up marryin' an officer and settlin' in France. Jed didn't approve of the marriage and there was some sorta fallin' out between 'em. Heard her husband died just a few years after the war and they never had children. Too bad. She woulda been a great mother."

"I think there's a picture of her husband here." Amy brought out the photograph of Mrs. Cartwright and the man Amy had said looked like Denzel Washington. "Quite a handsome pair."

Mr. Briggs took the frame from Amy's outstretched hand. "I saw this photo once. Jed showed it to me not long before he died. Kept it tucked away in a drawer. 'Jeff,' he said, 'this here represents a time I gave way to cowardice. Told my Annie not to marry the man she loved 'cause I wanted to protect her from this world's ugliness. As if she couldn't understand how ugly this world can get after dealing with the Nazis.'"

Mr. Briggs wiped a sleeve across his eyes again. "Said it was his biggest shame and regret. 'We coulda faced it together,' he said. 'At least then we woulda been together.'"

Mr. Briggs looked up at Amy and reached to touch her hand. "Please don't think Ol' Jed was one of the ugly, prejudiced sort. It was just... a different time. Marryin' someone with a different color skin was pretty much unheard of; 'specially 'round here."

Amy's kind expression hardened. "Yes, it was a different time, but some things never change. I married a white man. My kids still get teased because they're 'too white' or 'too black.' I think they're absolutely perfect but it's still tough for them."

"Jed took a very staunch stand against the KKK and their ilk." Mr. Briggs put a hand out to touch Mrs. Cartwright's motionless fingers. "You woulda been so proud of him, Miss Annie, him standin' up in church and calling the actions of those thugs 'the worst sort of cowardice.' Wish you coulda seen him."

"Why didn't Mrs. Cartwright ever come back here?" Amy asked. "She didn't seem the unforgiving sort."

"Never really knew the answer to that. I think part of it was she couldn't afford the passage home and, unfortunately, was probably too stubborn to ask for Ol' Jed's help. Last I heard Miss Annie had become a bit of a Mother Teresa to some war orphans, takin' 'em in, helpin' 'em get back on their feet. There was always more to her than met the eye; so tiny, never dressed flashy, never asked for recognition for charity and such. Just kept on givin'. Kept on prayin'.

"Oh, Miss Annie could pray! There were times I'd come upon her cryin' into the dishwater or singin' a hymn at the top of her lungs when she was feedin' the chickens or sweepin' the porch. There were even times as I got older and lost track of 'er that I would have a dream and there would be Miss Annie, prayin' for me or just sittin' down to talk with me like she did when I was a little tyke missin' my ma.

"Lately, I'd been wonderin' about her, prayin' for her, wantin' to know what'd become of her and... here she is, faithful to her last breath, still helpin' others. Ya don't kill a spirit like that. Ya just set it free."

He reached for the tattered black book still clutched in Amy's hands and placed it on Mrs. Cartwright's chest. "She held on to what counts. Now she and Ol' Jed can reunite. Hope folks can say the same about me someday."

"It's such a shame she wasn't surrounded by loved ones after living a life like that." Amy pulled out a Kleenex to wipe at the remaining wetness at Mrs. Cartwright's temples.

"Oh, you might be surprised," Mr. Briggs whispered.

There was a not-so-quiet mutiny going on in the Walden household. Lilly wanted to see her Daddy and for once Liam was siding with her. Even Phoenix, usually so compliant, was saying she could never sleep wondering if he was okay.

Widow Hayney had had her own misgivings about sending Kate with Cal and Rollins. Something had gone on that had nothing to do with garden-scented ghosts, something that made Rollins look like a raging bull. Pshaw! That blood on Cal's mouth hadn't been any "accident."

Maybe she was curious, but she could justify it by blaming the kids. Besides, she'd have more success wrangling cats than with getting those kids settled for the night.

"Fine. Grab your coats."

Her twenty-year-old Plymouth Bonneville that squeaked as it bounced over rutted roads had never carried more enthusiastic cargo.

Cal allowed Rollins to connect a couple times to further boost the fifteen-year-old's over-confidence. "Look, kid," Cal held his hands open in front of him, "I'm fine takin' licks I've earned fair and square and there's somethin' kinda healthy 'bout a boy wantin' to fight for his ma..."

But in response, Rollins' trash talk reached a deeper level of gutter and his anger built into irrational rage with kicks that aimed for Cal's head. It was time to shut things down. What Cal lacked in youthful angst he more than made up for in experience.

Rollins didn't even see it coming in the midst of an airborne punch/kick combo that Cal sidestepped. Rollins just felt Cal's fist, driven in his gut due to his own forward momentum, and the steel bands of Cal's arms that had him kneeling on the frozen ground with his arms locked behind him and head secured at an awkward angle. Whoa! The old guy could move pretty fast when he wanted to.

"Okay, boy. It's time ta talk."

"There's nothin' to talk about!"

"You're mad 'cause I was ready to enjoy the fact your ma needs a man to hold 'er right now."

"She's got a man!"

"He's gut-kicked. And I don't plan on takin' advantage of that now. But I'd have ta be blind not to notice a woman like your ma. I'm sorry, kid."

"You're a liar! Let me go!" Rollins thrashed and bucked as fiercely as any mustang Cal had ever wrangled. Usually the fight was fiercest right before the horse broke. But after an elbow to the nose and a maneuver by Rollins that thwacked Cal's head onto the frozen ground, the cowboy was beginning to wish he'd brought a rope and a strong horse to incapacitate this kid who appeared to have more venom built up in his whip-thin, muscular body than a riled rattlesnake.

A fresh wave of fury coursed through Rollins. "I trusted you! You're just like him!"

Cal, caught off-guard by the elbow that slammed into his already-painful rib, let go of the vice-grip hold that had been his secret weapon since high school, handed to him by his veteran father—the one thing of worth the old man had taught him.

Next thing he knew, Cal was thrown head over heels and, before he could register his new position of looking up at bright stars in a clear winter sky, pain rained down in the form of Rollins' fists, feet, and knees.

Rollins wasn't seeing a middle-aged cowboy. He was seeing the leering face of Alex and the devastated face of his little sister. With every blow he was fighting back those memories as if he could beat them into nonexistence. But the more he fought, the more it hurt and the more frightened he became that this haunting would drive him insane. "You're insane!" Alex had shouted right before Rollins had shoved Alex's head into a doorframe.

As Cal tasted blood, he thought how fitting it was for him to die with gravel in his mouth, beat to a pulp by the kid of a mom he had the hots for. Justice.

Mercifully, the next blow to Cal's head put out the lights.

CHAPTER 21

MANY MEETINGS

Jansen woke to the searing pain of fire running through his veins and the sound of running water. He would have screamed, but there was a small hand squeezing his fingers. If that was Phoenix or Lilly, he didn't want them to see Daddy scream. He'd endure anything to avoid that.

"I have to go now," a little girl's voice said in his ear as something that smelled like spring brushed his cheek and eased the pain. "Jesus says you'll be all right. I get to see my mommy and daddy now." Those words were followed by a little squeal of delight.

Jansen opened his aching eyes to glimpse wide, blue, dark-lashed orbs and a halo of Shirley Temple curls. But when he blinked, the image had disappeared, replaced by a harsh fluorescent glare. One more blink and Kate was there, her hazel eyes full of fear.

"Oh, thank God, Babe!" She slipped her hand where the child's fingers had been and kissed his forehead.

"Who was that?" Jansen's question came out with a croak.

"Who?"

"That blonde kid holding my hand." He winced at the knifelike pain in his chest.

"Little girl? Curly hair?"

"Yeah." Jansen's eyes were so heavy.

"Sleep, Sweetheart. We'll talk later."

With Kate's warm hand stroking his forehead, Jansen rested.

Rollins stopped.

Everything stopped.

Cal wasn't moving. His hands weren't even covering his face anymore. He just lay there in the dirt with blood running out his mouth and nose.

Oh God.

Rollins didn't even know if he was saying it out loud but those were the only words he could think.

Fear and panic overcame him, just swallowed him whole as he sat there looking at a man he'd pummeled with his bare hands.

Oh God.

Oh God.

Was he dead?

Rollins bent to listen for a heartbeat. He couldn't hear anything but the sound of his own heartbeat and gasping breath along with phrases that pounded in his mind: Murderer! Maniac! Monster! The words hit like a sledgehammer driving shards of fear into his heart.

Cal's face looked so blank and… and… lifeless.

Rollins looked up and down the deserted dirt road. No one. Just him— and the man he had killed.

Oh God. Oh God. Oh God.

Dogs miles away howled as they heard an animal-like scream carried on the winter wind.

Ima Hayney stared ahead into the darkness and tried to concentrate even though she couldn't hear herself think over Liam's chatter and Phoenix's hesitant responses. Liam wanted to know about the blood and the fight—obviously that's what had been going on with Rollins and Cal— but Phoenix kept going back to Annabelle. Both topics were riveting.

Lilly, on the other hand, needed to potty; the downside of too much cocoa.

In the midst of the unceasing chatter, Mrs. Hayney had missed the turn, the one that led to Farm and Market Road 170, the best way to the hospital. But wasn't there a shortcut around here somewhere? Shoot! She'd missed the well-marked road. What chance did she stand to find that little one-lane dirt one that dipped down to the old bridge on a dark night when her night vision stunk?

"Hey! What's that?" Liam's voice piped out.

"Well, Ah swan!" Mrs. Hayney declared as she beheld a deer in the road. Deer? Strange time of year for deer in these parts.

The deer lifted its head and stared into the headlights as Mrs. Hayney slammed her brakes and threw an instinctive arm across the securely buckled Phoenix.

As calm as anything, the deer ambled into the bushes beside the road and melted into the darkness. Bushes! There, on her right, was the one-lane road and the tree that marked it since the road sign was hidden behind those bushes.

Kismet. It was a word not in use in Ima Hayney's pragmatic world, but it came to mind when their lights shone on another lone figure—the shape of a thin young man kneeling in the road.

"Well, Ah swan!" Ima said again. She'd never learned what the phrase meant, it just seemed to fit when there was nothing else to say.

But when she got out of the car and beheld what was on the ground in front of the weeping Rollins, she knew exactly what to say as she knelt beside Cal's unmoving, bleeding form.

"Sweet Jesus!"

"We were fighting... I musta... He won't move... Oh God," Rollins jabbered.

Mrs. Hayney barked out the unignorable command, "Kids! Stay in the car!"

She put a hand to Cal's neck. There was a pulse, faint but steady.

"Is he dead?" Rollins whispered.

Mrs. Hayney shook her head and breathed a sigh of relief.

Rollins didn't even try to hold it back. He just cried.

Amy turned away as the orderlies lifted the sheet-covered body of Mrs. Cartwright onto a gurney. She'd never learned to maintain professional detachment when a life was simply—over. One person was gone and the room would be cleared to make room for another.

She went to stand beside Mr. Briggs who held the newspaper article Amy had used to find him. In a little wooden box that Amy had assumed contained jewelry, he pulled out other newspaper articles with pictures of himself and others that reported various events ranging from the birth of a child to the story of a French marathon runner representing his country in the Olympics. All were well-worn and looked to be at least a couple decades old.

"Did she know all those people?" Amy asked as they perused articles pertaining to pastors, teachers, spelling bee victors, and international heads of state.

"More than that." Mr. Briggs wiped his eyes. "Miss Annie rescued them, got 'em started on the right path, then cheered 'em on from the sidelines… just like she did for me."

At the bottom of the jewelry box was a small photo in an oval frame, one of those early, formal, non-smiling portraits. Amy picked it up, taking note of the distinguished looking man with a handlebar mustache and the tiny-waisted, light haired woman who had a hand on the shoulder of a young girl.

"Was this her family?"

"Yes, but they were long gone before my time. Died pretty soon after that photo was taken, so I heard."

Amy brushed a finger across the face of the little girl. "Such a shame she had no family."

Once again Mr. Briggs used that mysterious phrase. "You might be surprised."

There was no chatter in Mrs. Hayney's car now. Even Liam sat in shocked silence as Rollins rode in the back of Mrs. Hayney's station wagon with Cal's head in his lap, Cal's blood on his hands.

Only the good stuff about Cal came to Rollins's mind now: laughing over sandwiches about the chunk of wood that had flown from the boy's chainsaw to thwack Cal in the butt; the way Rollins had tripped at the five-yard line costing the team a touchdown. Luckily they had won anyway or Rollins wouldn't have laughed about it. They had even talked about girls and Cal had given Rollins friendly warnings about a couple of the local lasses who were cute but wild as March hares. "That's the kind gives women a bad name. Twist ya all up inside, chew ya up and spit ya out. Hard to recover from that kinda poison."

Rollins' poison had come from a friend, a guy who had chewed up his whole family, used and abused them and left them beat up and barely breathing—kinda like what he had done to Cal.

He wanted to throw up. Was he like Alex? Alex had been screwed up by really bad stuff—a dad who messed around with tons of women and had stashes of pornography and sites on his computer that made Rollins, well, want to throw up. Alex had hated his dad, hated the way his mom tried to stay away, consumed with kissing up to rich muckety mucks who could provide funding for her films—maintaining financial security so she and Alex would be okay even if his dad ran out on them—which they had known could happen any day.

But Alex was turning into something even worse than his dad. Was that what happened when you hated someone? Maybe so. At least Alex had never killed anyone.

"Oh God. Please don't let him die," Rollins whispered as they bounced along the dark roads and his hands grew sticky with Cal's blood.

Cal was aware of the car, could feel Rollins' hands on his head, but he was also someplace else, hovering between two worlds, two worlds that had always been interwoven but separate. Now, he had a foot in each and a decision to make.

Someone was talking to him, not in words but in complete thoughts that went directly to his heart. Cal could decide to throw in the towel, step fully into the other existence and give up, or he could stay in the world of pain that was his body and… do what? Was there truly such a thing as redemption? For him? Surely he was too screwed up to be of any use.

And who was this, this, presence? It was so hard to consider climbing back into his world of pain when he would have to leave this cocoon of comfort and peace.

"Who are you?" Cal asked.

Glimpses flew past his mind's eye of brushes with something that felt like this: his grandmother's church with a shaft of sunlight shining through a stained glass window; the wonder of reaching the top of a mountain and crying due to the beauty of hazy valleys and a wheeling eagle far below; the strength that had flooded him when he, at fifteen, had told his philandering dad to go away and had stepped into being the man of the house; the awe and longing that had filled him time and again as he watched Kate, committed to her kids, overwhelmed but not giving up. He'd felt this presence before, interwoven in the fabric of his life like the cotton threads that made up his shirts, unappreciated but essential.

But didn't he have to pray a certain prayer, attend church all the time and give lots of money to have access to this… this… how could a word be big enough to describe it?

So the question wasn't so much "Who?" but "How?" How was he wrapped in this wonderful comfort? He didn't deserve it. He'd run from church and all the trimmings. After all, his dad had been a deacon in the church and what good had it done him?

"You didn't reject Me," the One wrapped around him assured. "You rejected the misuse of Me. I did the same."

He was warm and the pain was gone. Cal opened his eyes to brilliant color, a soft breeze on his cheek and the scent of flowers after rain. There was a child holding his hand, a little girl with shining blonde curls and a brilliant white dress.

"Am I dead?" Cal asked.

"Not yet," the child answered.

"Are you an angel?"

"No silly. They'd scare you to death."

"Then who are you?"

"A friend." She took a deep breath and fixed large blue eyes on him. "I asked to talk to you and He said it's okay."

As she said this she gave a little wave and blew a kiss. When Cal looked in that direction he saw, through hanging boughs and flowering bushes, a figure clothed in a robe of white with the unmistakable dark hair and beard of the One whose name Cal had only spoken as a curse.

"Is He the reason I feel so good?"

"Yes."

"And He's, like, the whole 'walked on water, died on a cross, came back to life' guy… right over there?"

The little girl giggled and nodded.

"Why would He waste his time with me? I've never even prayed."

The little girl rolled her eyes. "Maybe you never said a bunch of thees and thous, but you prayed all the time. Anyway, that's not the point. You've got a job to do and I get to tell you about it."

"Why won't He tell me about it?"

"'Cause you gotta go back and if you talked to Him face-to-face it would tear you up too much to go back."

"I already don't want to go back."

"See?"

"So what's the job?"

"You will help those who need a boost, kinda like you did with Rollins only this time you'll know to point them toward Him." The little girl pointed a dimpled finger toward the dark haired, robed One.

"But I'm no preacher."

"Did you like listening to preachers?"

She had him there. He'd never been able to stand preachers. One bad apple had ruined the whole barrel for him.

"He says you remind him of Peter, a good, honest man who knows he's weak so he'll stay humble."

"He said that?"

"Actually, He said a lot more but I can't tell you or you won't stay humble." She giggled again and her eyes sparkled with such joy Cal had to laugh as well.

"So what about you?" Cal asked. "Who are you and where will you go while I turn into some kinda holy man?"

"Oh! Please don't ever think you're all holy or you'll be no fun at all!"

"Does He let you talk like that?"

"He's so much fun!" the girl declared. "You'll see."

Jesus? Fun? Those two had certainly never been connected in Cal's mind.

The girl leaned forward as if divulging a delicious secret. "I get to go with Him now!"

At those words Cal felt a surge of what could only be described as intense jealousy. "Can I come too?"

She gave a sad shake of her head. "Don't worry. It'll kinda drive you crazy because you'll always want more but you'll find you can stand just about anything as long as He's with you."

"I don't get to go with Him but He's with me?"

"It's hard to explain but, yes. Kinda like a phone call but better because... well, you'll see."

As Cal wrinkled his forehead, trying to understand this concept, the little girl went on.

"You know, He can fill up those holes."

"What holes?" Cal asked even though he knew exactly what she was talking about.

"The holes inside that leak no matter how much you drink or dance or how many women you kiss." She used the words of a child but the understanding in her eyes was ancient. "Sometimes He just fixes the holes and sometimes He will leave cracks so other people can see there's hope for them too."

"How does He do that?"

"Just ask Him."

"But He's way over there."

The girl looked at him with such a "duh!" expression he had to laugh. "Because He can be with me even though He's not with me, right?"

"So...?"

"All right, I'll ask Him to fill up the..."

But that's as far as Cal got because he choked on tears and liquid love rushed through him as if he'd been dunked in something cleansing, painful and joyous. Even as Cal grappled with this logic another thought flooded his being.

"Now that you've met Me, do you still want to run away?"

Cal wanted to laugh aloud. Why would he run from this? He was complete, completely loved, completely fulfilled. There was nothing to compare. The greatest sex, the most fulfilling meal, the most heart-stopping scenery, riding at breakneck speed on a horse or winding through canyons on his motorcycle… none of those things even scratched the surface of this feeling, this state of being. This was what he'd looked for his entire life but had never truly been convinced it existed.

Only one thing kept him from reaching back.

"I don't deserve You."

"Who does?"

Good point.

Even as he thought it the answer came.

"I've done the reaching for both of us."

What did Cal have to lose? He dropped his defenses and let beauty encompass him. It was like flames, painful but enlightening, bringing his life into sharp relief—the one-night stands, the hatred toward his father, the lust for Kate. All of it was swallowed up in this ocean of—grace. There was no other word. Unmerited, unearned favor. The old hymn came to mind.

> *"Amazing Grace how sweet the sound*
> *That saved a wretch like me."*

A wretch? He certainly qualified on that count. But it didn't matter. Not anymore. The good, the bad. It was all swallowed up in that ocean of love.

The garden faded, the little girl faded but the love remained as Cal wept. Slowly the pain of his body returned, but it didn't matter.

CHAPTER 22

FULL CIRCLE

Was she being punished? Kate couldn't believe that both Jansen and Cal teetered close to death. If the situation was supposed to make her allegiance clear, it certainly did. She hurt for Cal and for the pain Rollins had unleashed on him, but she was desperate for Jansen. Although Cal's injuries were more life-threatening, indeed the doctors hadn't held out much hope he'd make it through that first night, soon Jansen was the one who alarmed them. The doctors mumbled phrases like extreme hypothermia, adrenal exhaustion and immune system failure and kept up a steady stream of antibiotics to ward off the infection in his lungs. But still Jansen weakened.

It was Mrs. Hayney who gave Kate the strength to stand up to the doctors. "Don't have no faith in drugs and tests," she declared. "Nothin' wrong with that boy that good home cookin', peace and quiet won't fix and he sure ain't gonna find that in a hospital."

So, after signing reams of papers and agreeing to daily visits from a nurse, Kate took Jansen home—to the old Pedigo place—the place Mr. Briggs, Kate, the kids, and a couple guys from Jansen's work crew had polished into a home.

The first couple days, Kate was concerned she had made a mistake since all Jansen did was sleep. But the nurse assured her his heart was strong and his other vital signs were looking better all the time. Still Kate hovered and prayed and kept him covered against the winter chill as if he was one of the children.

On Christmas Eve, as the afternoon light waned, Kate wandered a quiet house. The kids were at Mrs. Hayney's learning how to pull taffy and the nurse had gone home early to celebrate the holiday with her family. Kate decided to hang Christmas lights in the bedroom where Jansen slept since he wouldn't make it down to the living room to view the monstrous fir Mr. Briggs and Rollins had erected there.

As Kate tussled with the strand that had worked perfectly downstairs but now every other tiny bulb refused to come to life, a weak voice spoke from the bed. "You're not planning on using that ladder are ya?"

In her excitement, Kate stepped on several of the lights and they crunched beneath her shoes. "Ohmigosh! You're awake! How are you?"

"Starving," Jansen whispered. "Need to go to the bathroom."

When Kate brought forth a metal bedpan Jansen added, "And there's no way in hell I'm usin' that."

Kate couldn't remember spending a more tranquil afternoon—at least since the addition of children. She snuggled close to Jansen on the big bed and they talked like they hadn't talked in ten years. It was just a couple hours but it made all the difference in the world as Kate spooned broth into Jansen's mouth and whispered to match his weak tone. He was tired but he insisted on talking, telling her about his failures, his fears, and the strange dreams in which he had wandered.

"You talked a lot in your sleep," Kate commented as she offered him a sip of steaming honey and lemon tea. "Had me worried a few times. Really crazy stuff. The way you twitched and moved looked like you were in a war."

"I think I was," Jansen whispered. "And in every dream I was losing you and the kids. There were floods, masked gunmen, strange beasts, deep canyons you'd fall into and I had to dive in, beat someone up, kill something or someone over and over to save you. Think I finally got the point."

"Yeah?"

"Nothing is worth losing you and the kids. It's usually not so cut-and-dried in real life but the result is the same. Stuff sneaks up and all hell breaks loose and I've gotta fight for my family."

"I had a dream like that once," Kate recalled. "It was back when the tornadoes came after we moved here. I was climbing and everyone was attached to me and I was about to fall until Mrs. Hayney's little ghost blew me a kiss."

"Haven't heard about that ghost," Jansen mumbled and leaned his head into the pillows.

"Well, I never believed in ghosts until we moved here. Had some strange things happen."

"No one would blame ya for goin' a little crazy after the year we've had."

Kate gulped and plunged in. "I'm not so sure Phoenix's friend was imaginary."

Jansen barely opened one eye. "Huh?"

"Lilly saw her too."

"When?"

"Well, right here in this room after Cal and Rollins fought."

"Wait a minute. Cal and Rollins fought?"

Uh oh. Now she'd stepped in it. Kate nodded. "See, Phoenix came into the room and she looked up toward that light…"

"Why were they fighting?"

"Just a misunderstanding. Anyway, then Lilly said…"

"A misunderstanding about what?"

Kate's shoulders slumped. "Rollins thought Cal made a pass."

"Did he?"

"Not really. See, I was the one bawling on his shoulder and … "

"Kate. Did he?" There was no more fatigue in Jansen's voice.

"It was my fault. I probably encouraged him, ya know, talking about Rollins and freaking out about everything."

"No." Jansen shook his head. "It was my fault. I should have been the one you talked to."

"But you were…"

"I wasn't here," he finished. "It's understandable. Not sayin' I won't have to whoop 'im when I see him, but…"

"Rollins already did that. Cal's in the hospital."

Kate brought Jansen up to speed on Cal's condition and he shook his head in amazement. "Never heard of anyone gettin' the upper hand with Cal in a fight."

They were silent a moment until Jansen asked, "How far did it go?"

"Couple of cracked ribs, collapsed lung, broken nose."

"No. Between you and Cal," Jansen asked in a soft voice.

"Nothing happened. Okay, it was close, but then that picture was on the floor when I turned on the light and…"

"Which light?"

"The one up there," she pointed straight up. "I flipped the switch by the door." Kate stopped as Jansen's face grew pale. "What?"

"I'd given up on that fixture. It shorted out every bulb I tried. Cal and I had put the old bulbs back in it just for show."

"But it worked fine." Kate hopped off the bed and trotted across the room to the switch. She flipped it once, twice. Nothing.

"Okay. Carefully get up on the ladder and check those bulbs."

Jansen felt the hairs rise on the back of his neck when the filaments rattled as Kate shook them.

"Jansen," Kate's voice quavered, "if that light hadn't come on—if I hadn't seen the handkerchief…" Kate shuddered. "Things would have been… worse."

"So." Jansen spoke, his eyes still riveted to the bulb in her hand. "Tell me about this ghost."

Christmas Day started out quietly enough. Just a few simple gifts under the tree and the kids peeking in one-by-one to see for themselves that Dad was recovering—the best Christmas gift of all.

Mid-morning, neighbors began dropping by leaving small tokens; jars of homemade preserves from Allie, a big platter of fresh baked cinnamon rolls from Mrs. Hayney, and a few items from neighbors Kate hardly knew. She felt some were motivated more by curiosity than by goodwill but, ah well, the extra cookies and pies were appreciated nonetheless.

About two in the afternoon, Kate opened the front door to reveal Mr. Briggs who carried a strange container in his hands. "Well, hi there!" She greeted him. "What did you bring us?"

But when she started to take the container from him, Mr. Briggs shook his head and held fast. "This is gonna take some explainin'."

An hour later, the family sat around the kitchen table staring at the container as Mr. Briggs finished his story. "Anyway, Mrs. Cartwright requested to be buried on this property alongside her mother and father. Only problem is, I don't know where the graves are."

"So this woman lived here as a little girl and wants to be buried here. Isn't that a bit irregular? I mean, it's not as if she's the family dog or a pet frog." Kate thought the whole thing was a little creepy. "What about her husband and family?"

"He was French aristocracy—in a war hero's tomb outside of Paris—they had no children," Mr. Briggs answered. "I wish you'd known her." He clapped a hand to his forehead. "I'm not thinkin'. Be right back."

In a moment he brought in a small wooden jewelry box and started removing numerous newspaper clippings. "See all these folks? She had a habit of taking children under her wing—war orphans, kids that were abandoned or homeless, even helped me once upon a time."

He continued to sort the articles and personal letters, passing them around the table as his listeners' eyes grew wide with wonder. "Should be more like her in this world." Mr. Briggs pulled a handkerchief from his pocket and wiped at his eyes then blew his nose with such force the kids jumped and laughed, thrilled as always by bodily noises.

They were still laughing and replaying the moment when Kate saw the small oval frame at the bottom of the wooden jewelry box and pulled it from beneath the remaining news clippings.

She was still staring at the young woman in the portrait, wondering why the hairs on her arms were standing at attention, when Phoenix gasped in her ear. Nothing could have drawn the others to gather 'round faster.

"What?" said Liam.

"It's Belle!" said Lilly.

"Who?" said Liam.

"My fwiend," said Lilly.

"That's crazy!" Liam announced.

"Is not!" Lilly whined.

But no one reprimanded their arguing as Kate, Rollins, and Phoenix stared open-mouthed at the small photograph and Mr. Briggs once again made them jump, this time with a loud guffaw of laughter.

"I knew it! I just knew it!" Mr. Briggs slapped his knee and wiped once again at his eyes.

Liam looked from one mute family member to another, his exasperation growing. "WHAT?"

They found the graves where Kate's dream child had indicated—at the edge of the property under an ancient, spreading oak where, when fallen leaves and old branches were pushed aside, they discovered a withered vine that Mr. Briggs said would bear lilacs in the spring. Kate said nothing. She had no exclamations of amazement that had not already been overused.

They were simple, flat markers of granite with the names Katherine Barrows Pedigo and Jefferson Josiah Pedigo and the year, 1912.

CHAPTER 23

IN GOOD HANDS

By the end of the week, news of that "Haunted Pedigo Place" had spread around the county like wildfire along with farfetched stories that made the children laugh. By the time a woman showed up on their doorstep begging to write a chapter about Pedigo Manor to add to her latest book, *Psychic Evidence of Modern Hauntings*, Kate gave up. She threw open the door and invited the woman in regardless of the load of laundry on the couch, dishes stacked in the kitchen sink and the muddy footprints from Rollins' boots that looked like evidence of the existence of Bigfoot.

The woman wandered the house with wide eyes and spoke of "vibrations" and "auras" while even Lilly snickered. The next day, when the same woman showed up with a strange camera and recording equipment, softhearted Phoenix took the time to explain that her friend, Annabelle, wasn't there anymore and had never been a ghost.

For her troubles, Phoenix was patted on the head and told, "Someday, when you're older, you'll understand these things, Sweetheart."

Overhearing this, Rollins set about haunting the woman with booby-trap strings in the garden and loud noises in the attic that seemed to satisfy her notion of what a haunted house should provide. It seemed deceptive, but how could Kate reprimand the kids when they were doing such a good job working as a team—even Lilly became adept at staring intently at nothing in particular until the woman trained her "highly sensitive to otherworldly vibrations" equipment on that spot and spoke in significant whispers, "Ah yes! There is a chill here. These phenomena, no matter how subtle, never get past me."

Kate was enjoying much more laughter in their home these days. And singing. And joking. Phoenix especially was a constant source of sunshine. Kate could have spent entire days simply gazing at their red-haired daughter who was blooming day-by-day, the shine returning to her hair and eyes as she once again became fearless; climbing trees, learning karate with her big brother, and even joining the softball team at school.

Rollins had a debt to pay, not because Cal demanded it but because he insisted on trying to take up the slack of what Cal couldn't do on his ranch while he was mending. Before Kate's eyes, Rollins was becoming a responsible young man, working hard and developing the healthy habit of observing the fruits of his labors.

Allie came around to help at Cal's place when her own ranch duties were light and even took to bringing over home-cooked meals, stating there was no way Cal could mend, as she put it, "on a steady diet of macaroni and cheese and corn flakes."

To Kate, Allie admitted she had long had a crush on Cal. "Why do you think I went to Rustler's so much? For the food?"

Jansen, after putting much of the running of his California business in the hands of two trusted foremen during his recuperation, indulged in his fascination with historic renovation, pouring over pictorials and becoming quite the expert on late nineteenth century architecture. He even served as consultant in the restorations of a hotel in Georgia and a famous mansion in South Carolina.

The book on psychic phenomena, while providing a boost to Jansen's business, also served to bring kooks from around the world to their sleepy town. Almost daily someone would ignore the "no trespassing" signs to snap photos of what was being touted as "the most highly documented case of haunting in an American home."

The local law enforcement relished arresting the trespassers, so when Kate and Jansen decided enough was enough, they installed motion detectors around the property that triggered video monitors at the police station. When word got around that trespassers, even those who parked across the road, would spend a night in jail, the visits all but stopped.

Six months after Mrs. Cartwright's passing, the Walden family stood gazing at Pedigo Manor. Every window of the stately home gleamed and each flowering bush was trimmed to perfection. From where they stood by the brand new iron entrance gate, they could see the top of the white tent erected for that evening's wedding party.

"She looks so pretty," Phoenix mused.

"How do you know it's a 'she?'" Liam asked.

"She's too beautiful to be a 'he,'" Phoenix stated.

As the kids discussed Pedigo Manor's gender, Kate felt her heart flood with gratitude for Mr. Briggs who had suggested they take advantage of the home's fame and allow folks to use Pedigo Manor for special occasions. So far, the ol' girl had played hostess to three weddings, a Bar Mitzvah, and a prom. As long as these festivities remained enclosed in the large white tents and no one harmed the house, Kate was fine with it. She was certainly fine with the fact these special occasions brought in much-needed money that was efficiently eating away at their debt.

"Don't ya think she looks happy?" Phoenix declared. "I think she loves these parties and havin' lots of happy people around."

"That's silly," pragmatic Liam responded. "A house can't have feelings."

"You're siwwee!" Lilly pursed her lips and crossed her still-baby-pudgy arms across her chest. "You're just mad 'cause you didn't meet Belle, right Mama?"

Kate aimed for quick distraction before her youngest offspring could bait Liam into another argument. "You two go clean those hands so we can make cookies."

"Yea!" Liam and Lilly yelled in tandem as they raced for the house.

Jansen put an arm around Kate's shoulders. "I feel kinda bad. We're everyone's getaway spot but we aren't going on vacation this summer. Sure you're okay with that?"

Kate put a hand on either side of Jansen's face and pulled him close for a hearty kiss. "Does it seem like I'm okay with it?"

Phoenix grabbed her parents in a dual hug. "What have I told you two about PDA?" But her wide grin assured them she was just fine with it.

One month later…

"Well Jeff," Jansen dropped the keys into Mr. Briggs outstretched hand. "Take care of the old girl."

"As if she was my own," the white haired gentleman replied as he offered a firm handshake and passed out hugs to each Walden family member.

Except for Phoenix. Where was that girl? Kate had a good idea where to find her.

She walked back up the drive, admiring the clean, manicured lawn and the fresh white pebbles on the circular drive. Pedigo Manor looked— happy. It was well-cared-for and appeared eager to see them off on their adventure. Plus, Mr. Briggs would be on hand to ensure the place wasn't lonely.

Mr. Briggs had a lot to oversee while the Walden family was away for a short end-of-summer camping trip. A crew was coming the next week to film a documentary about historic American homes. Since Pedigo Manor was now on the list of Historic Texas Homesteads and had an exciting reputation, it was perfect. Kate and Jansen were fine with the documentary including their home, but they had no desire for their family to be famous as well. They knew no one could love Pedigo Manor more or watch over it with more care than Mr. Briggs.

Mrs. Cartwright's will had bequeathed her sizeable inheritance to Mr. Briggs for that purpose. How she had known Pedigo Manor would be restored and would be of interest as an Historical Homestead, no one knew. But there was much about Mrs. Cartwright that defied explanation. So Kate quit trying to understand and just remained grateful for an old woman's prayers and for this place God had used to restore her family.

Yes, there was Phoenix, her bright hair shining under the ancient spreading oak at the edge of the yard. She saw her mother approaching but didn't pause in her conversation.

"I thought you'd like lilacs to grow here since they were your favorites. I miss you, Annabelle. I've heard people say 'a friend in need is a friend indeed.' Well, you were the best friend I ever had and I can't wait to get to heaven so we can play again. I'm so glad you're with your mommy and daddy now. I planted some of the lilacs on their graves too even though I know you're all not really here but with Jesus.

"Everybody says 'thank you.' Liam's a little mad that you never appeared to him and Lilly keeps rubbing it in but I told him you only appeared to people who needed friends and he always had friends so he didn't need you.

"I still see you in my dreams sometimes. It's not the same but it will have to do. Mommy's even seen you in her dreams. She said you always blow a kiss. I like that. I'm so glad you're happy now. Thanks again, Annabelle."

Trotting footsteps were coming closer. Of course Lilly, who refused to be left out of anything, was coming to join them.

"Bye, Belle!" Lilly ran pell-mell through the draping chain that had been added to guard the gravesites, tripping over the chain and falling with a thud as the daisies in her arms scattered across the grass. There was no blood, no teeth knocked out so, when Kate realized the child was more concerned about the dropped flowers than her own bodily harm, mom and daughters gathered the scattered blooms, dried Lilly's tears and laid the little bunches of daisies on the gravestones.

After more fond reminiscences, Lilly had the last word. "And thanks for teaching me how to bwaid!" She patted the new granite gravestone with a pudgy hand then hopped up… on to the next adventure.

But Phoenix remained a bit longer, swiping at a tear. "I never had a friend die before," she said. "I mean, I know she's not just dead-dead—that she's happy—but I won't see her all the time like I did. It's sad."

"I never got to ask you," Kate brushed at the moisture on her own cheek, "what did Annabelle say to you that night, you know, when Mrs. Cartwright died."

Phoenix smiled. "She told me to be strong for my family—to pray for all of you like she did because prayer really does change things." Phoenix hesitated and looked up at her mom. "She also said that… that you and Daddy would be okay. I was really glad to hear that."

Phoenix reached out and took her mother's hand. "The last thing she said was that Jesus was my friend who would always be there for me. I wouldn't see Him but I could talk to Him anytime and He would answer me. I just needed to get used to what His voice felt like." Phoenix's brow wrinkled. "Why didn't she say I would get used to what His voice sounded like?"

The "I don't know" died on Kate's lips as she had a sudden surge of inspiration. "Maybe because, as we get older, we get closer to the place where Annabelle has gone, a place where things that can't be seen or heard now are the things that last."

Phoenix wrinkled her nose, obviously not satisfied with what Kate thought was a perfectly respectable answer. "Maybe it's just that Jesus is inside me so I have to learn to listen in here," she pointed toward her own chest, "to hear Him."

"So you've got it all figured out, huh?" Kate teased as the car horn sounded and they hopped to their feet.

Phoenix looked shocked at that statement. "Oh no! Annabelle said life's no fun if you get it all figured out. She didn't even have it all figured out and she had lived, like, forever!"

The happy chatter continued as Phoenix unfolded life's mysteries and mother and daughter made their way toward the idling vehicle.

Overwhelmed by the change in their daughter in the past year, Kate glanced back for one more whispered "Thank you."

Was it a trick of the morning light? Or perhaps the daisies on Annabelle's grave responded to a passing summer breeze—that started fashioning them into a braid?

Kate blew a kiss toward the dancing daisies and continued toward the gate. Some mysteries were beyond her comprehension.

And they should stay that way.

THE END

ANNABELLE
STUDY GUIDE

The following questions can be used over an eight-week period or as one marathon session after all have finished reading *Annabelle*. Feel free to adapt this study to your specific needs. Works well for book clubs, family readings, youth groups or Bible study groups.

CHAPTERS ONE, TWO & THREE

1. We can overhaul our lives with a new home, a new situation, perhaps even a new marriage but past hurts and fears tag along, don't they. Discuss a time when you sought a fresh start but the past still had a grip on you.

2. What truly frightens you? The unknown? Being alone? Death? Failure? Rejection? Ridicule? Have you ever been a fan of scary movies? Discuss this thought: Do we like horror or other terrifying entertainment because it helps us put our own day-to-day fears into perspective?

3. As Kate explores her new home, the town, and her new neighbors, she discovers things to love and things that make her feel like a fish out of water. Have you ever been part of a close-knit community where everyone knew everyone else's business? Discuss: How do you feel our modern trend of social anonymity and the rising disconnectedness in our society affects quality of life?

4. Kate is frustrated and angry after her confrontation with Jansen and

Cal when she discovers the old, vine-covered mystery in Pedigo Mansion's backyard. Has frustration and/or anger ever spurred you into dangerous ground? Did it push you to bravery or stupidity? Please share.

CHAPTERS FOUR, FIVE & SIX

1. Jansen says, "A little neglect and something priceless turns into junk." Discuss how that statement can also be applied to people. Do you know someone who is convinced they're junk due to neglect or mistreatment? Are there experiences in your life that make you feel like trash rather than treasure?

2. Kate is in a pragmatic frame of mind when she witnesses something her eyes don't want to believe but the story Widow Hayney told her underscores the moment. Have you ever experienced something that defies logic or the rules of our physical world? Do you believe there is a spiritual realm that sometimes affects the physical one? Where do you turn to help you understand these mysteries?

3. It's wonderful to have someone capable to take charge like Cal does during the storm. What do you think would have happened if Cal had decided helping Kate and the kids was not his responsibility?

4. Rollins is overflowing with rage. Has there been a time in your life when you wanted to punch and kick and hurt to release toxic emotions? How did you handle it? Are you proud of or embarrassed by how you responded in crisis?

CHAPTERS SEVEN, EIGHT & NINE

1. Kate resists Rollins playing football due to prejudices she didn't

even realize she had. Is there an experience in your past that has caused prejudice towards certain people or situations? Discuss.

2. The reason for the family's pain begins to surface as Kate deals with memories of Rollins' former friend, Alex. Porn and other dangers are way accessible for young people these days. How do you think parents should handle this issue with their teens? Have you or someone you love dealt with a porn addiction?

3. Kate has struggled to keep her emotions in check for months but finally loses control when she's alone next to Pedigo Manor and memories overwhelm her. Do you think the occasional mild breakdown is kind of normal? What is generally the source of overwhelming emotion for you? Why do you think Kate is soothed when she finally gives vent to her emotions. Do you think the rest she receives is a natural result of crying, or is there something bigger at work?

4. Jansen is working so hard to provide for his family and cover expenses on Pedigo Manor that Kate is feeling ignored. This situation is often a breeding ground for dangerous thoughts and attractions. If you could give Kate and Jansen advice, what would you say? Have you ever been in a similar situation?

5. Please close with prayer about issues your group discussed. Something like this: *Dear Father, we live in a fallen world. We speak the freedom of Christ over everything that holds us captive. May we understand the authority Christ won for us on the cross. Help us to renew our minds with scripture and time with You so old weaknesses no longer have such a strong hold on us. We pray for grace and strength and wisdom to know You and live a truly transformed life. In Jesus' name, Amen.*

CHAPTERS TEN, ELEVEN & TWELVE

1. Life, which had already been hard, becomes more out-of-control for Kate as issues with her children escalate. Friends arrange a little break for her. What do you do to recover when life is devastating? Do your go-to activities actually help or add a layer of guilt to your stress, such as excessive junk food or alcohol ? Discuss healthy reactions to stress: a long walk, talk with a friend, a good book, time in nature, etc. Jot down a healthier plan of action for your next recovery time. Share with the group.

2. Kate feels guilty to dance with a man other than her husband. Do you think her guilt is justified?

3. Kate ends up having a deep conversation with Cal during a very vulnerable time. What advice would you give to both Cal and Kate if you could?

4. Kate has a vivid dream of Pedigo Manor in its heyday. Have you ever had a dream that seemed to be some sort of message or divine guidance? Please share.

CHAPTERS THIRTEEN, FOURTEEN & FIFTEEN

1. While we struggle with busy lives and wish for vacations, we tend to fear growing old and not being a vital part of people's lives. Do you fear growing old? Is there an elderly someone who has been a positive influence in your life? What did they do or say that was helpful?

2. Kate and Jansen share a tender moment that reminds them of the reasons they got together in the first place but life soon steamrolls the moment with more drama. What can couples do to protect their relationship when life is so demanding? Regular date nights? Daily

prayer? Long hugs? Daily compliments and saying "I love you?" What are some ways you think couples can keep their love vibrant?

3. While there are great therapists in the world, a bad one, in the midst of trauma, can cause even more pain. Especially these days when insurance policies may prevent us from choosing our care providers, do you ever feel frustrated and helpless? Are you in a situation now where you are not able to attain beneficial health care?

4. How do you handle frustrations that make you feel helpless? Prayer? Rant & Rave? Get depressed? Let's pray together about life's frustrations and those issues that seem hopeless. *Dear Father, though I try so hard to stay sane when life is difficult, I realize I am not the one who needs to be in control anyway. I give you the crazy situations in my life that seem like impenetrable obstacles. I stand my ground and look to You, the author and finisher of my faith and the One in whose hands I've placed my life. I proclaim Your authority and command these mountains to move in Jesus' name! Amen.*

CHAPTERS SIXTEEN, SEVENTEEN & EIGHTEEN

1. With the adults occupied with the finishing touches on Pedigo Manor, the Walden children create their own adventures. What was your favorite pretend game when you were a young child? Do you sometimes wish you could be a child once again, or was your childhood something you'd rather not repeat?

2. Well, it's taken a bit longer than it did for Kate, but Jansen finally hits his own emotional wall. He has exhibited such superhuman stamina, his breakdown is pretty superhuman as well. Do you ever feel that, like Jansen, you are your own worst enemy? Why do we tend to be so hard on ourselves?

3. Kate continues to struggle with her growing affection for Cal, not realizing he struggles in the same way. Have your emotions ever led you into ultra-dangerous waters? What are some guidelines that might have helped Kate and Cal avoid this unhealthy attachment?

4. As Mrs. Cartwright's condition worsens, Amy fears the sweet old woman will be alone when she dies. Do you fear death? What would you feel is the best-case-scenario to exit the land of the living?

CHAPTERS NINETEEN, TWENTY & TWENTY-ONE

1. Kate and Cal are in a dangerous predicament. Why do you think scripture tells us to "Flee sexual temptation"? Discuss the statement, "How could something that feels so right, be wrong?" What would be some of the results if Kate and Cal were to give in to their feelings?

2. Several issues are hitting critical mass in these chapters, including Jansen's struggle. Though Jansen is a very good man who is trying to do his best for his family, what do you feel he is doing wrong? Why is he caught in a battle he cannot win?

3. It becomes evident at Mrs. Cartwright's bedside, that her prayers have had unusual and powerful effects on many lives. Instances of visions in prayer or someone appearing in another person's dreams or even a person appearing in a waking vision are peppered throughout the Bible, even in the New Testament. Does it seem too much of a stretch that God would grant an old woman's dying wish to do His will even when she couldn't leave her bed? Discuss.

4. Rollins is so full of rage that, when he starts giving vent to it, he loses control. Have you ever given in to powerful emotions and then labeled yourself as hopeless, a pervert, a freak, a loser, etc. What is God's view of us when we hate ourselves? Spend some time praying over your own sins.

Ask God's forgiveness. Tell Him you truly repent. But don't stop there. Ask Him to help you forgive yourself.

CHAPTERS TWENTY-TWO & TWENTY-THREE

1. As Kate faces the possibility of Jansen's death, the choice between Cal and Jansen is an easy one for her. Discuss the importance of sacred vows and how such an old-fashioned practice as marriage is still vital to the stability of homes and even our society. How does being married to someone differ from an exclusive dating relationship? What do you think scripture means by the phrase: "And the two shall become one flesh"? Genesis 2:24 Matthew 19:6

2. Pedigo Manor's history has people convinced it's haunted. Do you find tales of ghosts and such fascinating or frightening? How do seances and consulting with psychics and ouija boards differ from what was going on with Mrs. Cartwright?

3. There are spirits in this world who seek to frighten and even control us. The Bible refers to them as demons, disembodied spirits who crave a host. We can make ourselves vulnerable to them by toying with things that separate us from God and make us feel shame: sexual sin, study of witchcraft, or taking mind-altering drugs or even alcohol abuse are a few of those ways we can lower our defenses and become unwitting hosts to evil that longs to suck the life and joy from us. But these beings are not to be feared and certainly not worshipped. Jesus gave us a clear model of how to take authority over evil by invoking the name of Jesus and the power of Jesus' blood, shed to cleanse us of sin, including demonic oppression. Unlike horror movies, this process does not have to glorify evil. Simply pray on your own, or with someone you trust, to be freed from every evil presence. Something like this: *Heavenly Father, I come before you now through the authority and blood of Jesus Christ. I submit*

myself to you and repent of everything I've done to cause division between You and me. I give you my life and choose to know You and serve You with all my heart, soul, mind and strength. Through the power of Jesus' blood that cleanses and saves me, I command every force of evil to be gone from my body and from my life. I forgive those who have sinned against me and release them into Your hand. Night terrors, addictions, feelings of worthlessness, suicide, depression or any other evil, the Lord rebuke you. I command you to go where the holy angels take you. Now, Holy Father, please teach me how to live for You, to spend time with You, and please give me faith to trust You especially when life is hard. I vow to serve You with all that is in me. Thank You for continuing the process of cleansing me and renovating my life to be a fitting home for Your Holy Spirit. Please fill me to overflowing with Your presence. In Jesus' holy and precious name I pray. Amen.

4. As stated in the prayer, when we give our lives to God, He comes to "abide" in us. WE become His home. How would you describe the state of your spiritual house right now? A broken-down shack with a "condemned" sign in the yard? An abandoned building where hoodlums hide and urinate in the corners? A peaceful cabin in the woods? Take a moment to write down how you would describe your spiritual house. Share the description. Now take some time to pray for God to renovate the areas of neglect or even abuse in your heart.

ABOUT THE AUTHOR:

Chana Keefer is wife to the most patient man alive (who happens to be a sexy drummer) and mom to four way-unique kids who are turning into adults at lightning speed. She and her family live in sunny southern California with a gorgeous, spoiled Siberian Husky.

When she needs a break from writing and marketing books, Chana plays with beautiful charms, beads, and glimmering things to craft Bible Jewelry.

If you've enjoyed *Annabelle: A Ghostly Texas Tale* be sure to check out Chana's other #1 Best Selling titles:

THE FALL

Part suspense, part love story, this epic retelling of the fall of Lucifer — through the eyes of an angel who was once his best friend — examines powerful themes of redemption, good, and evil.

Follow faithful angel Rapha as he witnesses the beginnings—of the world, mankind, and a sweeping warfare that continues to this day.

If Stephen King, C.S. Lewis & J.R.R. Tolkien collaborated on a story about our origins and the spiritual realm at war around us, this might be the result.

READER REVIEWS

"I sobbed through about half of this book, laughed in joy, and stretched out the ending so it wasn't over so soon. I look forward to the next installment."

"This novel is a profound and thought-provoking character study, with each turn of page revealing more about the eternally excellent and holy Adonai and the seductive, horrifically evil Lucifer."

"This isn't a Bible study or a statement of orthodox theology—this is a lavish, epic, often violent work of fantasy that is saturated with biblical insight... *Harry Potter* meets *The Book of Common Prayer*."

"I can say that this book has something for everyone: Love, redemption, angels, demons, war, monsters, and more all woven into a story that will enthrall. Absolutely enjoyable, and a thought-provoking experience!"

"First off, I'd like to start this by saying that I am a 17 year old non-believer. Please, keep this in mind. *The Fall* is a wonderful story that has all the potential to bring Christianity to readers of all religions and backgrounds. Even I was moved by Rapha's story, and his story creates a more palatable way for people who don't believe in God to understand him a little better."

"*The Fall* created imagery that made me crave to know the Father's love in the way that Adam and Eve did. It lit a fire in my faith. Great book."

"I was enthralled with this novel. Though fiction, the character of God in this book is spot on. I had chills multiple time while reading and I have recommended it to many people. It is definitely worth the read. Don't miss out!"

"Please, please continue Rapha's story and thank you for the entertainment and the ability to connect my hurting soul to the Healer of ALL"

"I loved *The Fall*! It is much more than words on a page. You can see, hear, and feel the hopes, dreams, struggles and fears of the characters… The passion, insight and love that flow as an undercurrent throughout the text will be a balm to any soul."

"What a gifted writer Chana Keefer is! I am renewed in my faith and am reminded of God's love for mankind."

"When reading the biblical story of creation, it's real easy to dismiss the characters as old-fashioned, not-as-smart-as-I, and to file their story away with the irrelevant myths of ancient folklore. After *The Fall*, I can no longer do that… I saw how angels guard and protect, and how choices have eternal consequence—theirs and mine."

"(*The Fall*) has helped me fall deeper into my Father's arms during a time I've been wrestling with a sense of separation and distance… I can relate to so many of the hurts and heartbreaks that Adam, Eve and Rapha experienced and yet I understand more fully how God's plan is always at work bringing restoration and regeneration."

"The story of Adam and Eve is so powerful and life-changing, yet we are given very few details in the Bible. We take their fall from glory so casually, we joke about fig leaves, apples and snakes. But what must have it been like from their perspective…or from Satan's…or even God's? Chana Keefer expands this possibility with rich, atmospheric, lyrical detail."

"This is one of the most powerful books I have ever read. I found myself on my knees worshiping God in a way I had never experienced before. There were tears of pure joy just being in His presence."

At first I was a little uncomfortable with how much detail there is and how it challenged me to think about what I knew from the Bible. The thing that won me over and over again was the clear expression of Gods love and man's need to know Him.."

"As I read *The Fall*, I marveled at the descriptive narrative; I cried, I laughed, and when it came to a close, it left me hungry for more but forever changed by what I had taken into my life by reading it."

"I've studied some really old literature like *The Forgotten Books of Eden* and have always been fascinated with the story of Adam and Eve. I believe there is way more to it than what we know and believe now and *The Fall* delves into some of those possibilities. Chana Keefer is brilliant in her writing and she has done her research. It's a great read and one of my recent favorite books to get lost in."

"Allow this book to break your heart and open you up to God's boundless love! You will not regret it."

"Very few books have captured my attention like *The Fall*. Very few indeed, such as *This Present Darkness, Piercing the Darkness, House*, and few others by Ted Dekker, Stephen King and others. Before I knew it, I was 20+ chapters into this book on the first day and my wife was wondering if she would ever see my face anytime soon."

"I can easily see this becoming a movie on the scale of *Lord of the Rings*. If the author hasn't received any offers yet, I would venture to say they are in her near future..."

"I loved the 'inside glimpse' into the angelic realm and particularly loved the slant on Eve's temptation. Some have argued it's heresy, but I didn't see anything out of line with God's Word."

"I want to mention also that you don't have to be religious or spiritual to appreciate this book. In fact, keep reading even if it makes you mad. If nothing else, Keefer will engage you. Great writers will always piss off someone."

"I can't wait for the next installment and the movie. This is definitely a keeper and is the beginning of a new era in Christian fantasy."

"The layers of rhythm were my favorite that I'd read since *The Count of Monte Cristo*. Every portion of the book was told with beauty and skill, even when going back and forth between the physical and spiritual planes."

The print copy of *THE FALL: RAPHA CHRONICLES* #1 includes an in-depth study guide; perfect for individual or group study.

THE RAPHA CHRONICLES: BOOK 1
THE FALL

CHAPTER ONE
END OF AN AGE

There was a time they were best friends… a distant memory almost forgotten. Almost.

It would be so much easier if he could forget.

Peace, peace, but there is no peace. Rapha clutches his head in his hands oblivious to the rare trace of fresh air and woodland noises around him, too lost in fractured, tortured memories.

A child's eyes, wide with fear; a woman's ripe belly, torn; screams and cries of anguish splitting the darkness of night; innocence lost; purity destroyed; life swallowed in death. And weaving through every image, the sound of cruel laughter—feasting on mankind's pain.

That face. Rapha squeezes his head but the image burns clearer—*a face bathed in shadows as fumes of death cast waves of beauty and horror, eyes of leeching evil. Those eyes suck him into darkness, willing him to join the nightmare.*

With all the force of his formidable will Rapha wrenches his thoughts from that realm, forcing his eyes open to light and life. A flower—tiny, bright, thriving no more than a few brave hours—faces the sun's feeble light.

With a need for comfort, Rapha stretches face down, breathing in soil and weakly pulsing life. Although fires burn, smokes of destruction rise, and death reigns, here is a patch of green. His fingers grip deep into soft earth as fresh pain rips through him.

Flashing, intelligent eyes; a carefree smile; beautiful hands gesturing with enthusiasm; boyish laughter filtering through a forest glade—ancient memories that bring unbearable torture.

Sobs rumble from the depths of the earth itself, erupting through Rapha's muscular frame.

"I cannot," he gasps, wrestling in his mind with an unseen companion. "It's impossible. He's gone too far for too long. There's nothing, nothing pure—he's made it so...." Rapha's body writhes like a tortured serpent, with agony greater than he's ever experienced, threatening to rip his immortal soul from his impervious body.

But wait. There was a time he tasted deeper anguish.

No. Please. That is locked away—eternal sanity demanded it. But the horrific images descend once again.

The loved one weeps in agony, precious flesh is torn over and over as Rapha's heart feels every rip of the whip, every trickle of spittle, every curse thrown like a poisoned spear. And there, in the crazed mob, everywhere he looks, the twisted, beautiful, triumphant, mocking face of one who was once a brother.

Rapha's earth-crusted hands clutch at his ears but the laughter grows, filling every recess of his soul, stealing every hope and joyful memory.

A joyful memory?

In a flash Rapha is there; catapulted through eons of space and time, before the purity of the garden, back through countless ages to a fresh hilltop lit by a younger, more optimistic sun. He and Luc preferred the plunging cliffs dropping to unseen depths below. Somehow, a spiral dive carried more of a thrill when performed in a temporal world.

"There's something about this place," Luc's eyes flitted from tree to mountain and stream as he stretched golden arms wide as if to embrace the early morning's glow filtering through droplets of mist. "It's not as grand as our flawless, hallowed domain but the appeal is undeniable."

Rapha had ignored the note of restlessness in that melodic voice, choosing to enjoy fresh air laced with flowered perfume and the spiced musk of fertile soil. In the countless years of their friendship, he had learned Luc's passions could flash with the slightest provocation, but usually, if Rapha allowed Luc to give vent to his emotions, the darker frame of mind would pass. And, a visit to this, their favorite retreat, was usually the perfect remedy, a change of pace and a different rhythm that put celestial matters into perspective. With a sigh Rapha settled back into thick green with one arm behind his head to contemplate the crisp blue above. Yes. This was just what Luc needed, a deep breath of contentment.

"Listen!" Luc crouched down as a bipedal creature struggled into view on the steep slope below. It was bent forward as if sniffing the wind, its hair-covered body tense, heavy brow shading deep set eyes that scanned its surroundings. "What do you suppose it's thinking?" Luc said. "Does that puny mind delve beyond putting one pathetic foot in front of the other or is it merely contemplating which part of its putrid body to scratch next?"

This new creature, standing somewhat upright and possessing intelligence beyond Earth's other inhabitants, had stirred Luc's ire. Rapha could not understand why these beings, known as "man," so inferior to angelic structure, should irritate his friend so.

Rapha studied the perfect planes of the face beside him as Luc observed the creature with disdain and declared, "Do you realize it can't live without water? A stiff wind could blow it off this cliff and that's it. The young are even more vulnerable—tiny, squirming things one breath away from oblivion!" A mournful expression shadowed the handsome face. "I'd be doing a favor to end such a pathetic existence…." He raised an arm as if to summon a whirlwind.

"No!" Rapha was accustomed to Luc's teasing but something in his friend's expression warned him the humor had taken on a malicious tone.

Luc resisted Rapha's restraining arm," Just a small puff… oh please… it will know the thrill of flight as it plummets to the ground!"

"We are not to influence them," Rapha was alarmed at Luc's narrowed eyes and the hard lines of repulsion that marred the beautiful face. "You know the command…."

Luc burst into laughter, eyes glittering with the triumph of disrupting his stoic friend's calm demeanor. "As if I would dare defy Adonai!" Relief flooded Rapha as the shadow disappeared from Luc's face. Ah… this was his beloved, teasing Lucifer.

"However…." Luc observed the squat creature, now scratching and snuffling under a bush, "He must have something to record on his cave wall."

Without further discourse, Luc drew himself up to a height rivaling the tall evergreens, revealing himself in all his celestial glory. His body flared like lightning and a whirlwind of smoke rushed up from the ground, causing the bright hair cascading about his shoulders to flow up and out creating both a crown and mantle. With eyes of fire he flung a lightning bolt across the valley as the man creature screamed in fright and threw himself beneath the bush. When Luc turned his smoking gaze toward the trembling being, Rapha moved quickly. Expanding to equal Luc's stature, his own muscular body rising thirty feet into the air, he took one step that resounded across the valley like a clap of thunder and placed himself between Luc and the frightened man creature who howled in terror then ran, fell, and rolled back down the rocky slope.

End of Excerpt.

To download *The Fall* in its entirety, go to:
www.amazon.com/author/chanakeefer

#1 BEST SELLING, TOP-RATED, #1 HOT NEW RELEASE SERIES!

Follow the adventures of country girl Esther & Sky, the international music icon who stole her heart and turned her world upside down.

It's *Anne of Green Gables* meets Rattle & Hum as Esther's love and faith are stretched to the limit. From the sprawling fields of Texas to Scotland's Isle of Skye, & Paris in springtime, Chana Keefer takes the reader on an unforgettable journey of first love one reader calls "what a relationship with God looks like in the midst of sexual temptation."

Contains the complete *One Night With a Rock Star Study Guide* for delving into the many life-impacting topics of this generation-bonding series. Great for groups and Family study!

RAVES FOR THE BEST SELLING
ONE NIGHT WITH A ROCK STAR SERIES.

"This fabulous read is among my top five favorites of all time. I read more than 300 books a year so that is a huge compliment."

"Don't get me wrong, a smutty book is fun to read but this one had me hooked and had zero smut. I really need this sequel!!!!"

"Best read ever in my 50+ years of avid reading! Enjoyed this novel so much I've not started another story and actually have started to reread—first time ever!"

"This is a fabulous book for all ages, but a must read for young girls. It is a life story about choosing to love wisely."

"… everything it should be; real, gritty, honest and beautiful."

"I couldn't help but smile ear to ear and giggle like a little girl the entire book! Chana Keefer captures every daydream every girl has ever had and tells a beautiful love story that stands the test of time."

"I read this in one sitting, a long afternoon/evening of enjoyment."

"There were so many moments that stirred wonderful responses in me —laughter, tears, goose bumps, butterflies, and more. I would highly recommend this to anyone who is open to what a relationship with God looks like in the midst of sexual temptation."

"I can't recommend this book enough. It was an outstanding, phenomenal read."

"Keefer has written a page-turner with every element to make you read the book in one sitting! In a world of trash, this one is a treasure!!!"

"This is so well written that it has something for every young girl, father, rock star want-to-be, model want-to-be, castle-lover, and everyone else to enjoy."

"This is the best book I've ever read. It brings out faith, hope and charity while being breathtakingly patient."

"As I was reading I was filled with a peace that only comes from God…"

"Finally a book with a love scene I didn't have to skim over and feel dirty for having read it!"

"Fun, edgy, emotional and romantic. I couldn't put it down! Thanks to a brave author who wrote a book of quality."

"To put this in the category of chic lit seems to do it a disservice. It is, to borrow from Narnia, bigger on the inside than it seems on the outside. It is a romance—and the word delightful continued to come to mind as I read—one made up of the stuff of daydreams."

"LOVED this book! It's one of my favorites that I keep going back to over and over again! A great romantic and spiritual read!"

"Simple pleasures, family, faith, fun times, romance, disappointment, fear, love—all captured in this beautiful story!"

"Esther was faced with her first true test of keeping true to her beliefs and Sky is faced with wanting something he knows he doesn't deserve. Love it! So stop reading reviews and buy this book! Just be prepared to not put it down until you finish and even then you'll want to reread it."

"I have already recommended this book to my teenage daughter so she can find solace in her personal convictions."

"Excellent storyline from beginning to end. Believable characters and interesting twists and plots. Fun and mystery added for a hard to put down book."

"The book is well written, the characters believable and the ending perfect. Cheers!"

"It is wonderful to see the main character make decisions based on what God wants for her life instead of what is so prevalent in the world—a world where sex and hooking up is the norm and waiting for the right person is not."

"I absolutely loved this book! … I couldn't stop reading it the first time through. I just reread it and had the same problem!"

"I find myself comparing new things I've read to this and nothing seems to compare. Well done. I will read this again and again."

"I wish I didn't have to read 50 mediocre novels to find ONE fantastic novel like this one—if only they could all be this good!"

"This was a combination of (non-magical) fairytale and adolescent fantasy that made me feel young again."

"A Gem. Unpredictable and provokes much thought about how faith works in the real world. Now one of my favorite books."

"Music and hot men? What's not to love? As a person who has a playlist for every little thing that I do, this read like one of my dreams."

"Thank you, Chana, for one of the best books I have read in a long time (a close 2nd to "Nubby" by Nancy Paul)."

"Get ready to feel every emotion and miss some sleep. You will not want to put this book down!"

"I LOVED the romance and edge of your seat excitement."

"It was so real to me, I hated when this book came to an end. Having major book hangover right now!!!! AWESOME read, Mrs. Keefer! This one is now one of my all-time favorites!!"

"This book is in my top five of my all-time favorites. I read it the other day for the second time and enjoyed it even more."

"Chana Keefer paints such a lyrical picture of time and place—from the barns of Texas, to the misty Scottish Highlands—that we are transported there and never want to leave. I read *One Night with a Rock Star* in one day and didn't want it to end!"

"It's one of my favorites that I keep going back to over and over again! A great romantic and spiritual read!"

"I was late for work today because I was reading this book. One of the sweetest, loveliest books that I have read in a long time."

"What a treasure to find a story in this day and time that portrays an awakening of love, an honorable man, and family values."

"Yet again, Ms. Keefer has penned a classic. And yet another of her books kept me up far too late!"

"Wow!!! This is now in my top 10 favorites of all time! Have a box of tissues handy but settle in and enjoy every morsel!

"As captivating as 'Twilight' with the added bonus of God. I read it in one day and started rereading it again the next!"

ONE NIGHT WITH A ROCK STAR

PROLOGUE

As I walk toward the elaborate, new-brick home, a sense of gloom descends. Throughout my childhood this property was abandoned and ignored, but I had reveled in that fact since it meant no one took notice of the frequent visits of a certain freckled tomboy with big dreams.

The wholesome, earthy scent of a southern breeze over dry grass recalls laughter and carefree joy when time moved at a crawl and life was viewed through the rosy haze of endless possibilities.

I have permission from the new owners to look around, but the bright, sparkling windows seem like unblinking eyes. Petra and I round one last corner of the model home, past another ornamental rose bush, and there it is… my old friend. How could life have marched by leaving it untouched? It was ancient when I first stumbled beneath its eaves so many years ago and ancient it remains.

Petra's long, ebony limbs glow in the red-gold light of dawn. The silence is broken only by the crunch of our feet on dry grass and the tinkle of her beaded earrings. I'm grateful for the presence of my fourteen-year-old companion, though she's been warned I might not be the best company today.

"Whaddaya think?" I ask.

"It's beautiful."

I peek at her face to discover real admiration. There was a time this was my private haven, the place I came to rest, to think, to lick my wounds.

That's something I could use right now.

A mourning dove's call, like a voice from the past, breaks the silence, drawing me deeper into youthful memories.

As we enter the wide opening of the sun-bleached wooden beams, the musty aroma takes me through a portal where the past twenty years no longer exist. The little door at the bottom of the stairs is still askew, squeaking its familiar protest at being disturbed. Petra climbs the stairs ahead of me with her customary grace. Her sense of self-assurance is rare for her tender years. I didn't possess it at her age. In fact, I don't possess it now.

As we climb, ever mindful to sweep a hand over our heads in case of webs, a growing sense of sadness consumes me. Why is it that happy memories bring pain?

I look to the right as I reach the top of the stairs, to the spot where the upper level drops off to the ground below and opens to the sky above, the place I'd spent so many hours dreaming on my own. Memories wash over me of the day it became our spot; echoes of a dog's excited bark mix with the teasing laughter of my favorite voice in the world, as eyes look into mine, sparking feelings I've never imagined.

"Hey look! It's still there!" Petra breaks my reverie as she moves toward the pile of hay in the center of the floor. I've told her bits and pieces of my story through the years so, for her, this is a visit to an historic site.

I was twenty that spring, a child masquerading in the body of an adult. The world was simple then. Little did I know how complicated it would soon become.

For years I'd wanted to leave this place. My upbringing had been ordinary, just a small Texas town with Friday night football, rodeos in the summer, and no secrets any time. It took me years to realize just how extraordinary that was. Most of my friends were content to stay and build their lives here. Not me. Big things happened elsewhere. I would see the world, do something important and earth shaking. My horizons were unlimited.

What would I have told the younger me who, twenty years ago, sat on this very spot gazing at these fields, unaware of the gathering storm?

Today, my body reminds me time doesn't stand still. I wince as I shift on the hard floor where I was once able to relax for hours while Petra's lithe form reclines with ease. Even in these humble surroundings she moves with the grace of an African princess. [1]Small wonder her father and I have been approached several times to allow her to model. For now, she's more interested in sports than glamour so that decision can be postponed. How far she's come from the underfed, determined waif we met twelve years ago.

"So tell me everything." Petra's melodic voice interrupts my reminiscence.

"Ya sure I won't bore you?"

"It can't be that boring. It led ya to me."

"True." I return the dazzling smile, then pause to collect my thoughts.

I used to wonder what stories these bleached wooden beams could tell. Today they resound with my memories, the story of a young life perched on the edge of a precipice, wings outstretched for that first breathtaking leap to either fall or fly.

"The day I met him, I had just had the worst week of my life… so far.

CHAPTER ONE

I strolled into the dorm that spring afternoon, wind-tossed and refreshed from an impromptu visit to my parents' ranch. The week had been a nightmare. Monday—failing grade on a feature story. Tuesday—fired from a modeling job because I refused to wear the strings they called a "swimsuit." Wednesday—met with my agent to explain why I had ticked off a client, then forgot an important story assignment scheduled for the same afternoon. Thursday—endured a royal chewing out from my favorite journalism instructor due to aforementioned missed assignment.

The lecture from Dr. Morgan, my disgruntled professor, still pounded in my ears. "It's just plain sloppy! I never would've expected this kind of negligence from you, Esther!"

That made two of us. I was juggling a lot in my life. Sometimes it was insane trying to blend the worlds of journalism student and mediocre print model but, since the occasional paycheck paid my way through school, the juggling was essential. Now, due to modesty (I honestly hadn't been able to tell which string went where) I'd lost two full days of modeling fees.

Friday started with a bang as I flunked a pop quiz in Biology from the lecture I'd been too distracted to listen to on Wednesday.

Ugh! Maybe it would've been better if I'd just stayed in bed… all week.

I haven't mentioned the worst part, the thing that had cast the dark cloud over my life. That very night, Sky, my favorite music icon and, admittedly, big crush since junior high, was in concert downtown and all my efforts to acquire tickets had been thwarted. I tried to be mature, to assure myself it wasn't the end of the world, that someday when I was a famous news anchor they'd beg me to attend, perhaps grant an exclusive interview, but still my dark mood persisted, the perfect ending to the perfect week.

As soon as classes were over that day I had skipped town to indulge in my favorite fix—barn therapy—as effective as chocolate minus the guilt. After a couple hours, I was resigned to my concert-less weekend and drove back to campus, determined to get my crazy life back under control.

Alas, it was not meant to be.

As soon as I entered the hallway to the dorm room I shared with my best friend Marti, she flew toward me, her cornflower blue eyes wild with excitement, her hair a futuristic array of hot rollers as she pulled me into the room shouting, "Where've you been? I've been tryin' to find you fer hours!"

I started to answer, but she cut me off, "Shoo! You smell like a cow. You better get cleaned up quick or you're gonna blow it!" Her Texas drawl became more pronounced when she was excited. At the moment, she was channeling Daisy Duke. This must be big.

"What're you talkin' about?"

She strode to my closet door, yanked it open and pointed at the poster inside. Sky's two-dimensional image stared at me with piercing, gray-blue eyes. My mouth became the Sahara desert and the world stopped turning when she said, "Of course, if ya don't wanna go… "

I think I screamed, fainted for a split-second, then set a new record for showering and drying hair. Marti filled me in on details from our friend and former dorm mate, Andrea, who had secured a spot as a dancer on the North American leg of Sky's tour. Just that morning she had stopped by and she and Marti had hatched a plan for how we could get past backstage security. To help us pass as dancers, she'd provided a couple dresses that had been retired due to wear and tear. Marti's finesse with needle and thread had mended any noticeable flaws.

I asked her about Andrea as I dug for a pair of panty hose without runs.

"If ya mean was she glowin' 'cause she'd been rubbin' shoulders with a god—no." Marti tossed an egg-shaped stocking container at me. "She didn't have a lot of time to chat."

But I wanted details! What was Sky really like? Did she ever talk to him? I smiled to myself as I recalled the rapture of watching him on a recent HBO special. Tall, with the lean-muscled body of a dancer, dark blond hair tousled as if he had just applied hair gel in a speeding convertible, and eyes—ah!—the eyes of a lion imprisoned in the body of a housecat.

"Could Andrea get in trouble for this?" I tried to apply make-up with shaking hands as Marti worked to tame my thick curls.

"I don't plan to get caught, but if anyone gets curious we'll bring out our student press passes and play amateur journalists."

"And if that doesn't work?"

"Look, you know any chance of gettin' to be backstage is worth the risk, right?"

"But this is crazy!"

"So be crazy! Stop thinkin' and hurry up!"

Yes, our dancer friend Andrea was taking a risk but the article about dance auditions for Sky's tour had been my discovery and she had been looking for a way to repay the favor.

The black velvet dress on my bed looked tiny. I prayed it would fit as I shimmied and tugged it into place, grateful not to hear any rips. As Marti zipped the back, she gave a low whistle. The clinging velvet was snug at the waist and hips and flowed to a full skirt that draped lower in the back following the lines of the V at my shoulders. I couldn't resist the urge to spin like a little girl and watch the skirt flare. Marti's dress of peacock blue emphasized her tiny waist and blue eyes. We stood, side-by-side, facing our own reflection.

"We clean up pretty good, huh?" Marti struck a dramatic pose.

"Actually, I still feel like a kid playing dress-up in your attic," I said.

"You're a knockout in that dress."

"I'm a big fat liar in someone else's dress."

Marti took me by the shoulders. "Look Esther, ya don't drink, ya hardly date, ya study while the rest of us are partyin'. Your one weakness is him. So, I'm hereby commandin' you to stoop to some harmless deception to have some fun."

"And I'm supposed to be grateful, right?"

"Indebted for life." She glanced at the clock. "We gotta git!"

I grabbed my backpack off the bed wishing I had something a bit more attractive to go with the dress. "Wait! Shouldn't we take along something to write on? We're journalists, remember?"

"Oh! Right!" She grabbed a writing pad and I snatched up the small notebook serving as my journal. "Now come on!"

We took my car since Marti's sat stubbornly on "E." I felt a bit calmer behind the wheel. At least I could feel in control of something. Besides, I knew the Dallas area since my forays into the modeling world had forced me to learn my way around. Many a nerve-wracking hour had been spent navigating warehouse districts armed with a city map and a messy scrawl of directions. If the police had any idea how many illegal u-turns I had executed in my short career they would put me away for life.

"Let's set the mood," Marti said as we pulled out of the dorm parking lot. She put a cassette tape labeled, "Best of Sky" in the deck and the familiar strains of Sky's "Soulfull" filled the little car.

"Over the hills to new horizons
I fly free.
Leave behind everything that binds me… "

I took a deep breath, relaxing with the flow of Sky's music, though the velvet cinching my waist was very binding.

"Probably drugs." Marti stated, blowing my reverie. "I'm sure he can fly very free with a little pharmaceutical intervention."

"Do ya mind? I'm havin' a moment here."

"Really, Hon." She was serious. "What about that Wade guy in Political Science? He's really cute and you turned him down."

"I told you," I said with a hint of exasperation. "I'd rather not date at all than go out with someone I'm not absolutely crazy about."

She tossed her shoulder-length chestnut curls and rolled her eyes as I continued. "I see the other girls tryin' on guys like they're shoppin' for a new pair of shoes. I'm just not any good at that."

"And," she countered, "you always go for what ya can't have."

"Oh come on."

"You had a crush on Elvis and a guy who was a senior when we were ten. I rest my case."

I started to protest but she was too quick.

"But then you bought Sky's first album." She feigned a swoon, "and I haven't heard about anyone else since."

Ah, the moment I'd first heard Sky had turned my twelve-year-old world upside down. I'd gotten off the school bus that afternoon devastated by remarks from boys ridiculing my chicken legs and frizzy hair. How could I blame them? Arms, legs and feet were sprouting at an alarming rate and the new braces had only added insult to injury. I'd retreated to my bedroom to cry and try to lose myself in a book while my AM radio piped out the week's top forty.

Suddenly, a lovely guitar and piano melody drew me from the depths of Middle Earth, as a soothing male voice began to read my thoughts.

> *Young heart*
> *Don't cry*
> *The pain will pass*
> *Take heart*
> *You'll fly*
> *As far as you dare…*

I held my breath and I drank in every word, hot tears running down my cheeks. The music had pulled out feelings I couldn't express and lifted my mood with its beauty. I purchased Sky's debut album, Idlewise, with my carefully hoarded allowance, memorized every word of every song, and proudly watched it climb in sales to become the debut album of the year.

The first time I saw Sky on television had been equally momentous. Marti and I were in the middle of a sleepover, discussing boys and eating popcorn while The Tonight Show played on TV. When Johnny Carson listed Sky in the evening's line-up, I screamed and dumped my popcorn all over Marti. That night, when he answered Johnny's questions with his gorgeous British accent as fans screamed marriage proposals from the balcony, I knew Sky had ruined me for mere mortals.

"It's safe, right?" Marti's strange statement broke my reminiscence.

"Huh?"

"Ya know, the thrill of love without the pain. That's what you're doing."

"No more psyche classes for you… "

"Really, Esther. Mr. Perfect doesn't exist. Someday you gotta quit playin' it safe."

"What? Like you? Cry my eyes out over some jerk?"

I bit my tongue, but it was too late. When I was still in training bras, Marti, with her big blue eyes and teasing smile, had been a boy magnet. Oh how I envied her—until the tears. And college had been more of the same. Fly high on love, then crash. She folded her arms and stared out the window.

But I hated when she lectured and made me feel like an inexperienced kid. What aggravated me more was that Dad had said basically the same thing.

I could hear him ruining my favorite breakfast of biscuits and gravy as he critiqued my non-existent social life. "Give the poor boys a chance. There's only been one perfect man, Esther, and HE never married."

So I wanted perfection. I could dream, couldn't I?

Luckily, Marti never held a grudge for long and besides, the sight of Sky's name in huge letters on the convention center marquis along with "Tonight!" made the blood pound in my ears. Somewhere, close by, was Sky. THE Sky. This was really happening.

Marti and I squealed in unison.

But the moment of truth—the backstage entrance—loomed. Suddenly the butterflies in my stomach became pterodactyls. "So do ya think they'll slap on the handcuffs before or after the concert?"

"Look," said Marti as she saw me beginning to waver, "I'll do the talkin'. You just work on keepin' those 'deer caught in the headlights' eyes of yours outa sight or we'll be dead, got it?"

I gulped and nodded.

We followed Andrea's directions to a lanky, graceful group in comfortable, sloppy clothes just entering the arena.

"Look at them! We don't fit in a bit." I hissed as we drew close to the dancers.

Marti dug a warning nail into my arm.

Andrea, her shiny black hair pulled into a ponytail, moved back to intercept us. Shoving a parcel into Marti's hands she spoke in a low voice. "This should help. It's backstage passes from two days ago but if you wear them backwards no one should notice." She grinned as she moved back in line. "By the way, I never saw you before in my life."

Soon, we faced the burly security guard. Marti, always good under fire, asked if he could PLEASE tell us how to get to the nearest ladies' room. He grinned, gave the information, she batted her eyelashes and—we were in! I blinked in the sudden dimness, senses accosted by the sound of clangs and shouts, the smell of sweat, machine oil and dust, and the tension of traffic during rush hour.

"What now?" Marti chewed a nail, her large eyes wider than ever. "Andrea said once we're inside we're on our own."

"Well, we're journalists, right? There's our answer if someone asks. If we stay out of the way, we should be okay."

"Do ya always talk like Dr. Seuss when you're nervous?" Marti giggled.

"Like I'm the only one who's nervous." I swatted at the hand in her mouth.

"Okay." She lowered her voice as we dodged a muscular worker pushing a huge black crate on wheels. "The more we can blend in the better, so let's hang around the people backstage, ask a few questions, look like we belong… "

"That's nuts," I said as I tried to keep a calm smile plastered on my face. "The last thing I wanna do is draw attention." Already, I felt like a criminal caught in a searchlight, striped suit and all.

I wanted to hide and she wanted to mingle so, rather than a public disagreement, we decided to part ways to test our theories of remaining inconspicuous.

The women's restroom was a safe haven, but 30 minutes was all I could take of that.

I glanced in the mirror. Yep, there they were, my "deer caught in the headlights" eyes. My hair looked good, coaxed into obedience and tousled as if it just happened to fall that way. The dress accented curves I tended to cover with sweatshirts and jeans while the wide V-neckline exposed an unfamiliar feature: cleavage. My eyebrows were arched and my nose turned up on the end giving me a look Mom said always made me appear I was ready to ask a question. The braces had been off for a couple years; that helped. But in spite of the pretty dress, I still felt like the tomboy whose body had forgotten to look female until I was sixteen.

"God," I whispered, "What am I doing here?" I considered running back to the safety of the dorm, but if I lost my nerve now, I would regret it for the rest of my life.

So, with a deep breath I plunged out of the ladies' room and into the fray.

I made my way through the efficient chaos, dodging several long poles as I navigated an ongoing maze of cords and tried to keep a calm expression plastered on my face. Mom had always taught me, if there's ever a question of etiquette, wait a moment and observe the actions of someone who seems to be in the know. Although the present course of action was much more important than the choice of a salad fork, I paused to get my bearings and observe.

One man in particular caught my eye. He radiated importance as he bustled through the groups of stage managers, technicians, musicians and countless others who had a vital function in this crazy dance. He was dressed in jeans, running shoes, and a "Sky" crew t-shirt but, with clipboard in hand and headset attached to his ear. I doubted anyone would dare question his authority.

He stopped for a quick word with a technician, then flipped back a curtain and entered the darkened hallway beyond. Curious, I made my way toward the curtain. Perhaps if my approach was convincing, I could find a hidden alcove to pass the hours until show time.

I brought the journal out of my backpack and did my best impersonation of the busy man as I made my way toward the curtain. I nearly froze as a voice said, "Hey, dancers aren't allowed back there." But I flipped back the curtain with fake confidence then scurried to a shadowy corner behind a tall, potted plant, fully expecting to be pursued.

It seemed an eternity had passed before my pounding heart slowed and I found the courage to venture from my hiding place.

End of excerpt.
To download or purchase the complete
One Night with a Rock Star series, go to:
www.amazon.com/author/chanakeefer

11 MILLION SALVATIONS.
1,800 CHURCHES.
400 ORPHANAGES.
17 RESURRECTIONS.
3-TIME NOBEL PEACE PRIZE NOMINEE.

From the palaces of kings, to the slums of India, and to the belly of dungeon-like prisons, Kemper Crabb spreads salvation, love, and alleviation of suffering. It started with one suffering child. Armed Gurkhas would not let Kemper near the child for fear he would "alter Karma." The child died—frightened, alone, and unloved. Kemper cried out to God, "Why do You allow such suffering?" God answered Kemper with a vision of the child sitting on Jesus' knee. But He also gave the heartbroken missionary much more: a vision of how to relieve the spiritual and physical suffering of millions.

Included: Kemper's Spiritual Warfare Training Handbook

ENDORSEMENTS:

"Kemper is very, very unique. He set out to help children and has to deal with far darker things of the black market and kids dying. Some have waited a lifetime to hear what Kemper Crabb is saying. His spiritual perspective of what s going on worldwide challenges us to believe in the power of Christ." | Brett Rogers, University of Texas College Director for Young Life Ministries.

"I've known Kemper Crabb for more than 70 years. Mother Teresa nominated him for the Nobel Peace Prize and he's received the Distinguished Alumni Achievement Award from Delta Tau Delta. Kemper is doing a ton of good for others for eternity." | Charles Mallery, Retired Exxon/Mobile Independent Consultant & lifelong witness of Kemper Crabb s life

"This is a must read if you are looking for something to stretch your faith to realize nothing is impossible for God." | Bill Rieser, Celebrate Recovery Pastor at Real Life Church, Evangelist, & Author of VERTICAL LEAP

READER REVIEWS:

"As a Christian wife, mother, and seminary student, I have come to appreciate a good book when one crosses my path. This book is certainly at the top of that list."

"Reading Kemper's story is like reading a chapter out of the bible. Miracles, Angel encounters, healing and God's sovereign power in action!"

"I love to read but I read slowly so the book really has to keep my attention for me to take the time to read it! The story of Kemper Crabb is riveting!"

"Living in the modern world, two foundational truths often escape us:

Evil is real, and God is bigger. *Servant of the King* illustrates, from a first-hand perspective, both of these truths."

"A must read for the believer and the nonbeliever as well. What happens on the mission trips that Kemper takes, and those of us who are honored enough to accompany, is truly miraculous. We are honored to have such a man who believes that 'we can do what Jesus did because it says so right in the Bible.' (John 14:12) A well-written, fascinating story!"

"Not only is it an easy read, but the stories of this Man's life are absolutely incredible. The words in this book have changed me and challenged me to take my life to a new level. It's an EXCELLENT read!"

"Extremely well written book. Kemper is a modern day Paul. Constantly probing the mysteries of Christ! A must read."

"*Servant of the King* is a must read for every believer, especially if you think maybe that the Age of Miracles may have come to an end."

EXCERPT FROM

SERVANT OF THE KING:
MEMOIR OF MODERN APOSTLE KEMPER CRABB

The man drew no attention to himself in the crowd filing toward the waiting airplane.

Clothed in blue jeans and collared shirt, no one would think he had been imprisoned multiple times, held hundreds of dying children in his arms, or worked side-by-side with Mother Teresa.

He was simply an aging man with a kind smile and alert expression. He was overlooked by all—except the one who stood at the door of the terminal, another who was ignored by the crowd—because no one else could see him.

The messenger's words were concise:

"Heavenly servant, it is time to tell your story.

To read more, download, or order a print copy of
Servant of the King, go to:
www.amazon.com/author/chanakeefer

www.ingramcontent.com/pod-product-compliance
Lightning Source LLC
Chambersburg PA
CBHW060309260626
47160CB00007B/2548